THE BEST OF TREK #11

FEATURING A COMPLETE GUIDE TO THE ORIGINAL EPISODES

FROM THE MAGAZINE FOR STAR TREK FANS

EDITED BY WALTER IRWIN & G.B. LOVE

A SIGNET BOOK

NEW AMERICAN LIBRARY

NAL BOOKS ARE AVAILABLE AT QUANTITY DISCOUNTS WHEN USED TO PROMOTE PRODUCTS OR SERVICES. FOR INFORMATION PLEASE WRITE TO PREMIUM MARKETING DIVISION, NEW AMERICAN LIBRARY, 1633 BROADWAY, NEW YORK, NEW YORK 10019.

Copyright © 1986 by TREK®
Copyright © 1986 by Walter Irwin and G. B. Love

All rights reserved

TREK® is a registered trademark of G. B. Love and Walter Irwin

SIGNET TRADEMARK REG. U.S. PAT. OFF. AND FOREIGN COUNTRIES
REGISTERED TRADEMARK—MARCA REGISTRADA
HECHO EN CHICAGO, U.S.A.

SIGNET, SIGNET CLASSIC, MENTOR, ONYX, PLUME, MERIDIAN and NAL BOOKS are published by New American Library,
1633 Broadway, New York, New York 10019

First Printing, November, 1986

1 2 3 4 5 6 7 8 9

PRINTED IN THE UNITED STATES OF AMERICA

WHICH EPISODE FEATURED JOAN COLLINS AS A WOMAN FROM THE PAST?

IS *STAR TREK* A WAY OF THOUGHT?

HOW OLD IS THE *ENTERPRISE*?

WHAT REALLY MAKES *STAR TREK* A CLASSIC?

The answers to these and other puzzling questions can be found in this fascinating collection of *Star Trek* articles. You'll learn about the lives of the "other" characters like Chekov and Sulu. And you will take a walk down memory lane with a complete guide to the original, all-time favorite episodes of *Star Trek*.

THE BEST OF TREK® #11

TREK

The Magazine For Star Trek Fans

Did you enjoy reading this collection selected from the *Best of TREK*, The Magazine for Star Trek Fans? If so, then you will want to read our other publications, as well. Each issue features the same kind of articles and features you enjoyed in this collection, with the addition of beautiful art work and photographs. Best of all, each and every publication features insights and comments by fans just like you, discussing the aspects of Star Trek you want to know about, answering the questions you want answered, going where no fan has ever gone before! In addition, our issues include up-to-date information, reviews, and commentary on the latest developments in Star Trek, films and television, and fandom. Best of all, none of the material in our special TREK issues has or will appear in a *Best of Trek* collection . . . it's all new! In short, TREK issues are the finest, most exciting Star Trek magazines available at any price. Remember, if you aren't reading our publications, you're missing half the fun of being a Star Trek fan! So order a copy of our latest issue today—or better yet, get four issues at a special price!

Current issue .... $3.50, plus 50¢ postage
4 issues $13.00
4 issues (Canada and foreign) $14.00

TREK PUBLICATIONS
1120 Omar .... Houston, Texas 77009

ACKNOWLEDGMENTS

Thanks are due to all of the many fine folks who have helped make our publications a success and this eleventh collection possible: Jim Houston, Leslie Thompson, Joyce Tullock, Herman "Burglar Bars" Taylor, and especially to all the writers who have contributed their time, efforts, and love.

Special appreciation goes to Karen Haas, our former editor at NAL, for her unfailing courtesy and consideration to us during her all-too-brief stay. Thanks and best wishes, Karen!

Thanks again, folks! We couldn't have done it without you.

CONTENTS

INTRODUCTION	9
SHORT TREKS	11
WILL THE REAL LIEUTENANT SAAVIK PLEASE STAND UP? *by Nancy Buchhorn*	12
THE SEARCH FOR VULCAN *by D. Jarvis Smith*	16
INSERTING IMAGINATION *by Bobby Bryant*	20
A STAR FOR VULCAN *by Anne B. Collins*	24
A PROBLEM OF IDENTITY: WAS HOLMES A VULCAN? *by Patricia Dunn*	28
THE TWENTY-THIRD-CENTURY WOMAN *by Patricia Lee Johnson*	31
STAR TREK: THE NEW ARTHURIAD? *by Lynette Muir*	34
WHY DID DAVID HAVE TO DIE? *by Gail Eppers*	38
THE SERVING OF REVENGE *by Janeen S. DeBoard*	40
A CHAIN IS ONLY AS STRONG *by Rowena Warner*	45
THE BLIND SPOT—A REBUTTAL *by Jody A. Morse*	51

WILL THE REAL CAPTAIN KIRK STAND UP!   57
by Shirley R. Gibbons

STAR TREK EPISODE GUIDE   63
Compiled by The Editors

THE NEGLECTED WHOLE—OR, "Never Heard   109
Of You"—Part Two
by Elizabeth Rigel

SPECULATION: ON RELATIONSHIPS,   128
RESPONSIBILITIES, AND RISK
by Sharron Crowson

THE CLASSIC STAR TREK   135
by Linda M. Johnston

THE JOURNEY TO—AND BEYOND—THE SEARCH   149
FOR SPOCK
by Hazel Ann Williams

THREE   166
by Debbie Gilbert
Galactic Terpsichore?
The Minerals of Star Trek
The Great Bird Has Impeccable Taste

ROAD TO THE *ENTERPRISE* (AND BEYOND)   173
by David Gardner

MIND TREK   180
by M. H. Lewis

STAR TREK: ODYSSEY OF SALVATION   190
by Sister Mary William David, S.N.D.

IN DEFENSE OF *PON FARR*   197
by Katherine D. Wolterink

INTRODUCTION

Thank you for purchasing this eleventh edition of articles and features from our magazine, *Trek*. We are sure that you will enjoy this collection just as much as you did the previous ten.

As always, the articles included in this volume express many of the myriad aspects and interests of Star Trek fans and Star Trek Fandom—philosophy, theology, sex (Vulcan), love (Human), astronomy, history, film editing, gossip, shipbuilding, sex (Human), love (Vulcan), and the always burning question of just who the heck is Saavik, anyway?

We're also pleased to include a complete guide to all of the original televised episodes, something that many of you have requested.

As always, we think you'll find all of the articles included to be entertaining, educational, and just plain fun to read.

If you enjoy the articles in this collection and would like to see more, we invite you to turn to the ad at the back of this book for more information on how you can order individual issues of *Trek*. (And, please, if you have borrowed a copy of this volume from a library, copy the information in the ad and leave the ad intact for others to use. Thanks!) If the ad has been removed, you may write us direct: *Trek*, 2405 Dewberry, Pasadena, TX 77502.

If you've been inspired to write an article yourself, please send it along to us. We'd be very happy to consider it for publication, because we're always looking for talented new writers. (Please, don't send us Star Trek stories or novels. *We do not* and cannot publish Star Trek fiction.) Each and every one of the writers included in this volume started out by sending us an article after buying and reading one of our earlier collections. They made it; perhaps you can, too. Our present needs require that articles be a minimum of 2500 words long (about 10—12 double-spaced, typewritten pages), typewritten on white paper, and accompanied by return postage. If you can't meet these requirements or have something special in mind, please write us first.

We want to hear from you in any event. We read each and every letter you send to us, even though we unfortunately don't have time to respond to all of them, and we listen to what you have to say. Please remember that we cannot give you the addresses of Star Trek actors or forward mail to them, nor can we help you get a professional or amateur Star Trek novel published. We *do* want your comments on *The Best of Trek* and Star Trek in general; your comments are the only way we have of knowing if we, and our contributors, are doing a good job.

Again, many thanks, and we hope you will enjoy *The Best of Trek #11*!

Walter Irwin

G.B. Love

SHORT TREKS

We often receive articles that are simply too short for our needs. In many cases, we ask the author to expand the article if we feel there's more to say. Other articles, like those featured below, are fine just as they are, and well deserving of publication. So we keep them on hand until we have enough to put together one of these "Short Treks" features. Many readers have told us that some of the articles in our first "Short Treks" are among their favorites. We think similar feelings will result from this selection.

WILL THE REAL LIEUTENANT SAAVIK PLEASE STAND UP?

By Nancy Buchhorn Cotton

I have been a Star Trek fan since 'way back (haven't we all?), and I never thought I could accept a new character into the Star Trek family, especially after the dismal failure of the characterizations of Ilia and Decker in *Star Trek: The Motion Picture*. But in the summer of 1982, when *Star Trek II: The Wrath of Khan* rolled into theaters, I found a new but welcome addition to the Star Trek family—Lieutenant Saavik.

Kirstie Alley was perfect as the half Vulcan, half Romulan Starfleet cadet. Her naturally eerie good looks and graceful movements add immediate dimension to the fascinating character of Saavik. "Such potential," I thought, especially after reading Vonda McIntyre's excellent novelization of the film.

Alley played Saavik to the hilt, allowing her cool confidence to shine, but never letting it obscure or deny Saavik's naivete and youth. From the very first breathy, "Damn," it was obvious that Alley had found the perfect balance between Vulcan rationality and Romulan emotionality. Although Saavik's Romulan heritage was never directly mentioned in the film, it was apparent from her actions and her words that she was not wholly logical Vulcan. Instead, we saw a young woman who was still struggling with her heritage and the expectations of her mentor and savior, Mr. Spock.

But in *Star Trek III: The Search for Spock*, things changed. Articles appearing before the film's premiere stated that Alley was not returning to play Saavik. I was disappointed. Several months later, an interview with Robin Curtis, the actress slated to take over Alley's role, was published.

Curtis appeared eager and amiable enough, but when I read that she was not particularly a fan of Star Trek, and in fact has never seen *Wrath of Khan*, my hopes dimmed. What would become of the new addition I was so fond of?

My questions were answered in *The Search for Spock*. Although I rated Curtis's performance as "good," and her portrayal of Saavik as "adequate," I still found myself muttering, "Saavik would have *really* reacted this way...," and, "Alley would have played it this way...."

But after several viewings and much thought, I have decided that I did not do Robin Curtis justice.

It was easy, initially, to blame the changes in Saavik from *Wrath of Khan* to *The Search for Spock* on the change in actresses. I don't think anyone would have denied that, to some extent, it must have had an effect. The shift in the content of the dialogue from film to film was also important. Curtis's moments onscreen did not lend themselves as readily to an analysis of Saavik's character as did Alley's. *Star Trek III* was not "The Search for Saavik," after all. Much of her nature has yet to be explored.

But the most confusing and irritating change in Saavik was the disappearance of half of her nature—her Romulan ancestry. In *The Search for Spock*, we saw Saavik not as a half Vulcan, half Romulan struggling to overcome the circumstance of her birth, but, instead, Saavik appeared totally Vulcan. Logical. Rational. Perplexing to those fans who witnessed a different Saavik in *Wrath of Khan*.

I do not refer here to any physical change in appearance (i.e., the highly arched eyebrows). That was added, no doubt, for the simple reason that Curtis's features did not lend themselves as naturally to an "alien look" as did Alley's. I refer instead to the change in Saavik's character. Simply put, Saavik was far more logical, restrained, and downright cold in *The Search for Spock*. The edgy quality in her voice was lost, as were her periodic displays of emotion. Why the change?

The solution is obvious. The same event that had altered the lives of Admiral Kirk and crew—Spock's death—had similarly altered Saavik.

For the first ten years of her life, Saavik was little more than a half-starved animal. Spock found her, guided her, and turned her into a highly civilized and competent Starfleet officer. Saavik owed him no less than her life. In *The Search for Spock*, we saw her attempt somehow to repay that debt by becoming and maintaining all that Spock had stood for. In sum, Saavik was no longer the "daughter" of Spock that we saw in *Wrath of Khan*, but in many ways had become Spock himself. Yet, why should Saavik choose to follow a life, a path, which she must have known, due to her very nature, she could not duplicate? As Spock clearly pointed out to her in McIntyre's novelization of *Wrath of Khan:* "But you are not Vulcan."

The answer seemed to be in the notion of the *katra*; Spock's eternal soul, if you will.

If anyone aboard the *Enterprise* would have known of the Vulcan way of mind melding just before death, it would have been Saavik. Yet, why did she not mention it or object to Spock's burial on Genesis? Perhaps it was simply because Saavik never accepted the concept of the *katra* herself. Another answer could have been that Saavik, like Sarek, believed that Spock's *katra* had been lost; that there had been no time to mind-meld with another. If that were the case, then what was Saavik to do? How could she preserve all that Spock was, all that he had taught and meant to her? The only possible solution for Saavik was to reject momentarily her own unique path that we had begun to see in *Wrath of Khan*, and continue on a path that Spock would have approved and had chosen for his own life—the Vulcan path. When Saavik made this choice, she became the almost total Vulcan we saw in *Star Trek III: The Search for Spock*.

It must be recognized, however, that Saavik was not, and could never entirely be like, her mentor. To continue in that manner would have meant a complete denial of her heritage and her past. Surely Saavik must have recognized this, but at the time she was left with no alternative. She was alone in a world she still did not fully understand. Her guide, her teacher, was gone.

But with the discovery of Spock still alive on Genesis, and the success of the refusion on Mt. Seleya, Saavik no longer needed to preserve and protect Spock's nature by incorporating it into herself. She was free once again to explore and choose her own path.

By the end of *The Search for Spock*, Saavik had become once again the same Saavik we first saw in *Wrath of Khan*. When Spock stopped, turned, and looked first at Saavik, she seemed embarrassed and uneasy. Perhaps, in part, it was due to the intimacy of *pon farr* and the admittance of deeper feelings for Spock; feelings that went beyond any father-daughter relationship. I believe, however, that her uneasiness reflected something more. It was as though she were saying, "I have tried, Spock, but I am not you. Your path is not my own."

In the film's final scene, Kirk, McCoy, Scott, Sulu, Uhura, and Chekov have gathered around their Vulcan friend with tears and smiles and hope for the future. Saavik too was there, smiling. She has grown, yes. Spock's death caused them all to grow. Yet she has become more than a shadowy reflection of Spock. She has reestablished that trait which made her so interesting to those who grew fond of her in *Wrath of Khan*: her uniqueness.

Whatever path Saavik finally chooses, in whatever direction her Vulcan/Romulan heritage takes her, it will be fascinating to watch, and I hope all Star Trek fans will give Robin Curtis the opportunity to guide her.

THE SEARCH FOR VULCAN

By D. Jarvis Smith

Toward the end of the nineteenth century and into the twentieth, there was considerable scientific controversy over the existence of a planet named "Vulcan." This hypothetical world, closest to the Sun, was invented to explain an irregularity in the orbit of Mercury. It "vanished" when Einstein explained this discrepancy using his General Theory of Relativity. Now let the debate begin anew! Only this time, let it be over *our* Vulcan, the home world of Spock and the philosophies of Surak and IDIC. It is not the existence of the planet that is being called into question, but rather its location.

Combing through the mass of Star Trek literature, I have found Vulcan reportedly orbiting two different stars! In some references, Vulcan is the first planet of star 40 Eridani A; in others it is the third planet of Epsilon Eridani. Which is correct? Both stars are located reasonably near Earth in the constellation of Eridanus, "The River." Epsilon Eridani is the closest, a scant 10.8 light-years away, and 40 Eridani is a tad further, 16.3 light-years. Also, both are red-orange spectral class "K" stars and lie fairly close to each other, only about six light-years apart.

Could this proximity have caused a case of mistaken identity? No, for Epsilon Eridani is a solitary star and 40 Eridani is a complex triple star system. 40 Eridani A is accompanied by "B," a white dwarf star, and "C," a cool, red class "M" star.

The earliest reference to Vulcan's location in Star Trek literature is in James Blish's adaptation of "Tomorrow Is Yesterday," where twenty-third-century Starfleet Captain Kirk holds a conversation with twentieth-century Air Force Captain Christopher:

CHRISTOPHER: Mr. Spock here tells me he is half Vulcan. Surely you can reach Vulcan from here. That's supposed to be just inside the orbit of Mercury.

KIRK: There is no such solar planet as Vulcan. Mr. Spock's father was a native of The Vulcan, which is a planet of 40 Eridani. Of course we could reach that, too.

Author Diane Duane also refers to 40 Eridani as the parent star for Vulcan in her novel, *My Enemy, My Ally*, but the most complete description of the planet itself and its orbital characteristics around 40 Eridani is given in Geoffrey Mandel's *USS Enterprise Officers Manual*.

Epsilon Eridani is named as the primary star for Vulcan in Greg Bear's *Corona* and by Vonda McIntyre in her novelization of *Star Trek III: The Search for Spock*. Specific information on the planet and some orbital statistics are supplied by Stan and Fred Goldstein's *Star Trek Spaceflight Chronology*, but although there is no question that they were specifying Epsilon Eridani as the Vulcan sun, they erroneously identify it as a "binary star," which it is not.

Indirectly, Gene Roddenberry gives some clues to Vulcan's location in the novelization of *Star Trek: The Motion Picture*. He has Spock preparing for the *Kolinahr* ceremony one hour before ". . . the rising of the Vulcan suns . . ." Suns—plural. Does this refer to the trinary system of 40 Eridani, or is it another mistaken allusion to Epsilon Eridani? For that matter, could Mr. Roddenberry have had a completely diffferent star system in mind? Also, in the novel and the movie, Scotty tells Spock, "We can have you back on Vulcan in four days . . ." Because, at that time, the *Enterprise* was near Earth, I thought it might be instructive to calculate the speed necessary to reach either of the two stars in question, using the most conservative warp speed formula (the classic warp-factor-cubed-times-the-speed-of-light). Apparently, Scotty was bragging about his uprated "bairns" being capable of warp twelve, because in four days he could reach Epsilon Eridani at just a hair over warp factor ten or the farther-out 40 Eridani at a smidgen over warp factor eleven. No clues there.

Franz Joseph's *Star Fleet Technical Manual* shed only a little light on this subject. This book displays the banner and signet of the "Planetary Confederation of 40 Eridani," indicating that this star system is a Federation member, but does not make any connection with Vulcans. It also presents a chart of the "United Federation of Planets—Principal Stellar Systems." Unfortunately this was of no help, because I checked the stars within five parsecs of Earth (16.3 light years) and it depicts virtually *every* star within that radius. It is a difficult chart with which to work, for Mr. Joseph has renamed most of the stars. "Alam'ak," "Behr'ak," and "Czar'ak" are the names he has given to 40 Eridani A, B, and C, whereas "Pelione" is Epsilon Eridani. He does, however, introduce an interesting device. He displays our own solar system as a "binary" system (Sol/Jupiter), the idea being that Jupiter is an object almost massive enough to become a star, but didn't quite make it. Could Epsilon Eridani have an unseen companion—an "almost" star? I have doubts about this, as such companion masses have been detected circling stars much further away than Epsilon Eridani and no current astronomical references show any for that star. The *Technical Manual* corroborates this by listing "Pelione" as a single star.

If I were just dealing with the feasibility of finding a Vulcan-like planet orbiting either of these two stars, then Epsilon Eridani would win hands down. It has already been considered suitable enough to be targeted for the first serious effort aimed at detecting intelligent life in our galaxy. In 1960, Project Ozma scientists aimed their radio telescopes at Epsilon Eridani, hoping to receive signals indicative of an advanced civilization. Stephen H. Dole, in his noteworthy book, *Habitable Planets for Man*, describes the conditions having the greatest likelihood of producing a "class M" planet. He specifically includes Epsilon Eridani as one of the stars within twenty-two light-years of Earth capable of nurturing such a world and excludes 40 Eridani because of the radiation emitted by the white dwarf star in this system.

Which is it to be? Epsilon Eridani or 40 Eridani? With all the attention paid to this important Federation member, some serious consideration should be given to its location in space. Which is the home star of Vulcan? Waffling will not resolve this issue. Della Van Hise, in *Killing Time*, positions Vulcan in "the Eridani system," a clear evasion.

I choose 40 Eridani as the Vulcan star system and admit I'm swayed by human emotion and not logic. James Blish gave this star primacy in the Star Trek canon and I am moved to certify it as "authentic" in memory of a man whose stories have entertained me all my life. Also, Gene Roddenberry placed "suns" in the Vulcan heaven (no invisible companion of Epsilon Eridani can qualify for that word) and who would dare contradict the Great Bird of the Galaxy? Then there is the perverse satisfaction I get from knowing that, despite torturous scientific calculations of probability, the unlikely *does* occur in this universe. Perhaps Vulcan could have evolved in the exotic trinary system of 40 Eridani, against all odds. Mandel's *Officers Manual* does describe a layer of charged particles around the planet that thwarts the radiation of the nearby white dwarf star, and Spock, no less, in his conversation with Sargon about Vulcan evolution in "Return to Tomorrow," admits that there are ". . . many enigmas in Vulcan pre-history." Is this one of them?

Are Star Trek fans divided into "Epsilonists" and "40-ists" on this issue? Are there other references to Vulcan's location I have missed? I would be grateful to hear from anyone on this subject. I have a feeling that the "Vulcan Debate" is just beginning.

INSERTING IMAGINATION

By Bobby Bryant

Star Trek? Never mind the acting, the sets, the scripts, the philosophy. What made the show special was its *inserts*.

When I think of "Where No Man Has Gone Before," the thing that first comes to mind is the shot of Elizabeth Dehner's ESP rating chart being flashed onto Spock's science station screen. A throwaway shot, onscreen for a second or less—but it was a closeup of a realistic medical report, fully detailed right down to somebody's having circled and underlined parts of it.

In "Mudd's Women," the thing I remember best is the record of Harcourt Fenton Mudd that the *Enterprise* computer displayed on the briefing room screen. Much of the same information was being given out verbally by the machine, but we got to see shots of the twenty-third-century equivalent of Mudd's driver's license.

In "City On the Edge of Forever," I recall the brief cuts of the tricorder displaying newspaper headlines (and quite detailed ones, at that), the footage of Nazi goosesteppers, etc. Because this all had to be optically matted into the static tricorder footage, it was just one more expense for an already expensive episode—but they did it anyway.

What are inserts? Very quick, usually one-time shots that seldom last more than a second or two on the screen and are generally filmed separately from the main-unit work. They are later *inserted* into the main footage in editing, hence the name. Examples in Star Trek include the magazine ads in "Bread and Circuses," Kirk's finger pushing the button to fire the *Constellation's* engines in "The Doomsday Machine," the flashing red alert lights on the walls and helm/navigation panel, and countless full-screen shots of the main viewer on the Bridge.

On Star Trek, inserts were sometimes special optical effects, but the kind we're talking about here generally were not. The classic Star Trek inserts don't serve to establish plot points. They're freebies, thrown in to enhance a scene, to liven it up, to make it seem more realistic. These kinds of inserts add detail, or the impression of detail, without necessarily advancing the plot. Often, they aren't even specifically called for in the script.

In "Where No Man...," the shot of Dehner's ESP report was superfluous to the action; Spock was telling us the same information. The same thing applies for the previously mentioned inserts used in "Mudd's Women," "City," and "Bread and Circuses." In "The Doomsday Machine," Kirk's flipping of the switch was indeed a plot element, but there was no reason why the director couldn't have used the master shot. The extra setup to film the closeup insert of Kirk's hand required more time and money, but obviously was deemed important to the dramatic development of the scene. (The producers were able to get a little more mileage out of the shot by letting the switch and Kirk's hand double for others in one or two later episodes.)

So if these inserts aren't really necessary, why bother? They're a form of layering, adding details that give the impression— sometimes only subconsciously—that the scene is actually more complex than it is, as well as adding visual punctuation marks to the action.

Some good ones: Sulu's chronometer running backward ("The Naked Time"), the shuttle's control panel with the soon-to-be-hit "Fuel Jettison" switch ("The Galileo Seven"), the diagram of the *Enterprise* called up by Kang and his cronies ("Day of the Dove"), and McCoy's medical scanners displaying various information.

(Sometimes inserts went a little overboard on detail. In Star Trek's first pilot episode, "The Cage," an insert was used when Pike used the communicator in his quarters. The insert was a closeup of the communicator, a bulky, mostly transparent thing full of wiring, all-too-obviously a prop. The camera holds on it just a second too long, almost yelling, "Look at this!")

I suspect that the number of inserts per show dropped steadily during the second half of the first season (just as the more obvious marks of physical quality of the program did).

Still, inserts are the kind of footnotes that a show needs to be convincing, and that's a lesson Great Bird Gene Roddenberry largely forgot when he lavished forty-odd million dollars of Paramount's money on *Star Trek: The Motion Picture*. Not only were the sets and staging on the bland side, but there were very few inserts of the kind we're discussing here.

Considering that Roddenberry is the same person who ordered—or at least permitted—somebody to go to the trouble of making up the super-detailed medical report on Dr. Dehner in "Where No Man . . ." for just a one-second shot, it's surprising that he let the first Star Trek film go out looking particularly unadorned. Except for the relatively static "tactical" computer displays, Uhura's "photic-sonar" scope, and some nicely done blinking lights on Spock's thruster suit as it counts down, there are few inserts to complement the plot.

However, when Nicholas Meyer directed *Star Trek II: The Wrath of Khan* in 1982, he more than made up for Roddenberry's omissions. *Wrath of Khan* is a virtual catalog of inserts, most of them in the best Star Trek tradition. Meyer used them as they should be used, as salt-and-pepper for his visual stew. To name just a few:

The wild pan across the *Reliant's* command console as Khan looks for the shields override.

Spock's fingers punching in *Reliant's* code prefix.

The flashing "Radiation" sign when Spock enters the reactor chamber.

The "Commit" readout when Khan arms the Genesis Device.

The protective cover, complete with "Caution" label, that Chekov flips up to fire the photon torpedoes.

The "Nominal" indicator when Spock gets the mains back on line.

In all these instances, we would have had the same scene, plot-wise, if the inserts were not included. We know Spock is going into radiation because McCoy loudly tells us so, and Scotty has just collapsed, muttering the word. We know Khan can't find the override to raise the shields, because he says so. We know Khan has armed the Genesis Device, because David Marcus tells us, and because it begins emitting a lot of light and smoke. And we know the mains are "nominal" because one of the trainees says so a split-second after the insert does.

INSERTING IMAGINATION

All these are *asides* to the main action. Take them away, and you have the same scene. Only it's not quite as good.

If Meyer did nothing else, he probably made better use of inserts in a Star Trek story than anyone else, and that fact may go a long way toward explaining *Wrath of Khan's* feeling of complexity and detail. Not coincidentally, virtually all of his inserts are of things, not people. So were the most memorable inserts in the series.

When Leonard Nimoy directed *Star Trek III: The Search for Spock* in 1984, he, from all reports, decided to play down the technology in favor of the people. He also used relatively few inserts, especially in the sense Meyer did, and I think that fact helps account for why the film seems somehow unfinished and clunky, like a filmed stage play. Except for some generic computer graphics, the "life form" readout aboard the *Grissom*, and the "Good morning, captain" computer greeting on the *Excelsior*, the movie had little of this punctuation. It needed more.

A suggestion for the producers and director of *Star Trek IV*: spend some of the cash on inserts. Maybe some detailed documentation of the criminal charges pending against Kirk and Company would be nice.

A STAR FOR VULCAN

By Anne B. Collins

"Oh, come now," I can hear you saying out there. "We all know that Vulcan's star is 40 Eridani." Yes, I've seen stories and poems with Eridani in the title, intended to be synonymous with Vulcan. But, as a Vulcanophile, I must object. If I am to follow the Vulcan way, I must point out that the choice of 40 Eridani is illogical.

First, where did the notion of 40 Eridani come from? Is it canonical? Did the Great Bird of the Galaxy hatch it? Not to the best of my knowledge. No star is mentioned in association with Vulcan in either the live action or animated TV series. It's not in Bjo Trimble's *Star Trek Concordance*, either. Even in Gene Roddenberry's novelization of *Star Trek: The Motion Picture*, no specific star is mentioned. Nor is it in the chapter on Spock in *The Making of Star Trek*.

The earliest mention I can find is in James Blish's adaptation of "Balance of Terror." Mr. Blish gave no reason for his choice of 40 Eridani as Vulcan's star.

What do we know about Vulcan's star? Out of the myriad stars in the galaxy, how can we narrow the field and consider a few? There are two facts, both firmly based in the live-action episodes, which can guide our search.

1. Vulcan's star is fairly close to Sol, Earth's star. In "Metamorphosis," Zefrem Cochrane, the discoverer of warp drive who vanished into space, instantly and without prompting, recognized Spock as Vulcan. Thus, Vulcan must have been one of the first civilizations contacted by early warp-drive explorers, perhaps Cochrane among them.

2. Vulcan's star, or one much like it, caused the evolution of an inner eyelid as protection against very bright light. We learn this in, of course, "Operation: Annihilate." I've always suspected that Spock believed he was blinded because he assumed the eyelid reflex did not work (it never had before) because he was a hybrid.

What conditions would lead to the evolution of an inner shield? This is *not* a nictating membrane, which is primarily a dust screen. Its internal position will not protect the cornea from injury; its only benefit is to block out dangerously intense light.

But not all light is dangerous. The more energetic light is, the more destructive it can be. The energy of a given photon of light is determined entirely by its wavelength, which we perceive as color. Red light is much less energetic than violet light; the other colors lie in between these two ends of the visible spectrum. Infrared light is even less energetic than red light, and does not have the strength to stimulate the retina's nerve endings.

Ultraviolet light, on the other hand, is more energetic than violet light, and is not perceived because it does not simply move electrons about, but rather strips them away. Ultraviolet light is dangerous! The electrically charged molecules caused by the ripping loose of electrons clump together in abnormal ways that are destructive to cells. The small amount of ultraviolet that reaches the surface of the Earth is known to cause skin cancer in humans with repeated exposure. Greater amounts are very damaging. In arc-welding, the welder must always wear a helmet that permits vision only through a filter, because of ultraviolet light emitted by the arc.

This is the major flaw in "Operation: Annihilate": Kirk bathes the whole planet in ultraviolet light, thinking it harmless. The only way I can square this with the facts of physics is to assume that the parasites were *very* sensitive to one particular wavelength, so that the total amount of ultraviolet light needed was not great.

So how does this apply to stars? All stars are not created equal. Small stars burn their hydrogen fuel at a slow rate, becoming only "mildly" hot and emitting light mostly in the red part of the spectrum. Large stars burn with much more intensity, producing far more energy, and putting out a lot of light in the violet and ultraviolet wavelengths. 40 Eridani is a cool, red star. In fact, it is a cluster of two cool stars and a white dwarf. Any hot planet orbiting even the warmest of these would have to be in a very close orbit. The star would loom gigantic in the sky, glowing with a color much like hot coal. And, just as with a glowing coal, you can look at it all day long and get nothing but a crick in your neck.

"Now I've got you," someone out there is saying. "You're talking about human eyes. How do we know that Vulcan eyes don't have another range of sensitivity?" I have two answers for that. First, and most obvious, is that Spock works easily with instruments designed for humans. He has all sorts of color-coded lights on his console. If his perception were much different from ours, this would cause difficulty. Second, and on a more basic level, is the fact that Vulcan has a nitrogen-oxygen atmosphere much like Earth's, though a little thinner. Eyes are adapted to the "visible" spectrum because those wavelengths are easily transmitted through our atmosphere—the air is transparent to visible light, but murky or downright opaque to wavelengths very far on either side of the visible.

The red Vulcan sky we see in "Amok Time" is probably due to red dust in the air, not to the color of the sun. This is true of Sol IV, also known as Mars.

Now that I've presented the evidence against 40 Eridani, what alternatives do I have to suggest? A hot star fairly close to Earth would have to be very visible to us. From the list of the twenty brightest stars in Earth's sky, I find four candidates: Sirius, Vega, Altair, and Fomalhaut. They are the only stars within a fifty-light-year radius that are very much hotter than Sol. Procyon, although hotter than Sol, is not hot enough to produce the large amounts of ultraviolet light we're looking for.

Sirius is very tempting, for it is very close—8.8 light-years from Earth. In the animated series, however, it is revealed that Harry Mudd sold a love potion to the inhabitants of Sirius IX. Also, if Sirius were Vulcan's star, the human discoverers would probably just have called the inhabitants "Sirians," rather than make up a new name.

Vega, at twenty-six light-years distant, is also a possibility. It is mentioned twice in the series: the Vegan Choriomeningitis Kirk gives Odona in "The Mark of Gideon," and the "colony" Vega IX referred to in "The Menagerie." The colony can be explained if Vulcan is, say, Vega III, but why rename the original Vegans and call them Vulcans?

Altair, although only 16.6 light-years away, is obviously impossible. The only reason the *Enterprise* couldn't go to Vulcan in "Amok Time" is because it was supposed to go to Altair VI! However, diverting to Vulcan on the way to Altair was termed a short side trip.

So we're left with my favorite choice, Fomalhaut (foam-'l-hoat). It's only seven parsecs away from Sol, about twenty-three light-years. It is a Type A star, not the most energetic type, but much hotter than Sol. It is even about the same distance away as Altair, in the same portion of space (as seen from Earth's sky), making possible the short diversion to reach Vulcan en route to Altair mentioned in "Amok Time." And can you imagine the earliest explorers trying to call the natives "Fomalhautians"? No wonder they named the hot, red planet after the Greek god of the forge instead. For that matter, no wonder it was never mentioned in the series . . . I wouldn't dare ask an actor or actress to say the word! I wonder what the Vulcan word for Vulcan is. Probably harder to pronounce than Fomalhautians.

The inhabitable zone for Fomalhaut would be a considerable distance from the star. Therefore, from Vulcan, the star would be a blazing point of light, too bright to look at directly, lest it cause retinal burns. Such a distant orbit could make more likely the existence of a seven-year rut cycle, as seven Earth-years could be the length of one Vulcan year.

If Vulcans, Romulans, probably Rigellians, and possibly others are descendants of colonies established by the Arretians (Sargon's people), it is possible that Vulcan's star might not resemble the star that caused the evolution of the inner eyelid and the seven-year cycle. However, I cling optimistically to the assumption that the colonies would be established in systems as similar to "home" as possible.

A PROBLEM OF IDENTITY: WAS HOLMES A VULCAN?

By Patricia Dunn

Paul Schwartz, in his article "A Theory of Relativity" ("Short Treks," *The Best of Trek #4*), suggested a link between the great detective Sherlock Holmes and the former First Officer of the Starship *Enterprise*, Mr. Spock. Although Schwartz does not claim that they are the same person, he does speculate that Sherlock Holmes was a Vulcan, and possibly "a relative or an ancestor" of Spock's.

Although this is an amusing theory, I am afraid that it is easily disproved. To examine the evidence presented by Schwartz:

1. Both the names "Sherlock" and "Spock" begin and end with the same letters.

This pattern, as we know, is characteristic of the Vulcan family through which Spock is descended in the paternal line. However, even though Sherlock may be an unusual name, it is English, not Vulcan.

2. Both Holmes and Spock are similar in physical appearance and features.

Watson never describes his celebrated friend as possessing pointed ears or a rather greenish complexion. Notwithstanding the fact that Holmes was reputed to be a fine actor and a talented makeup expert, I seriously doubt that he could have masqueraded as a human well enough to escape detection by the eminent Doctor Watson . . . who, although he lacked Holmes's powers of observation, was no fool and was also, after all, a physician. Surely, at some point in their association, perhaps while looking after Holmes during one of his nervous breakdowns (e.g., "The Naval Treaty"), Watson would have noticed that the man's heart was rather oddly located.

3. Both Holmes and Spock are stronger than most humans.

Holmes never displayed the terrific power possessed by most Vulcans. In "A Study in Scarlet," Holmes needs the aid of two police inspectors to subdue the American murderer Jefferson Hope, and in "The Adventure of the Devil's Foot," it was Watson who dragged his half-unconscious friend outside a room filled with poisonous fumes.

4. Both Holmes and Spock revere logic and are adept at solving logical problems.

True. But what of the Vulcan suppression of all emotion? Watson has often described Holmes laughing ("A Study in Scarlet," "The Sign of Four," "A Scandal in Bohemia," and others). Holmes also exhibits at various times depression, anger, chagrin, and other strong emotions.

5. Schwartz asserts that neither Holmes nor Spock (apparently) had close personal relationships with their parents. However, Spock's experiences can hardly be considered common to all Vulcans.

6. Holmes's talent with the violin is well known, as is Spock's use of the Vulcan lyre. But, again, we cannot assume that *all* Vulcans are musically inclined.

Schwartz' evidence is, at best, circumstantial. He also failed to explain how and why a Vulcan came to be living in London in the late nineteenth century. Evidence, as every detective knows, is worthless without motive or opportunity.

Schwartz does suggest that a Vulcan child, perhaps orphaned in a spaceship crash, was adopted and raised by the Holmes family of England. This is possible, and would explain certain inconsistencies in his theory. After all, Kal-El of Krypton was rescued in a similar fashion—although the young Clark Kent resembled a human much more closely than a Vulcan child would have.

It is speculated that Sherlock Holmes may have sired offspring, but no conclusive proof has yet been offered to support this contention. If Holmes were a lone Vulcan stranded on an alien world, with whom would he have mated? The genetic techniques that allowed Spock to be born a hybrid Vulcan-human child would not have existed in that primitive time and place. And if Holmes had no children, how could he be one of Spock's ancestors?

Although meat is not often mentioned in accounts of Holmes's adventures, fowl often is. And on one occasion when Sherlock specifically requests food, it is "cold beef and beer" ("A Scandal in Bohemia"). Spock, as are all Vulcans, is a vegetarian.

Schwartz incorrectly states that Sherlock Holmes had two brothers. He had only one: Mycroft Holmes, seven years his senior and—according to Sherlock himself—his equal in mental agility, if somewhat lacking in energy.

I don't know why Schwartz ascribed a second brother to Holmes, unless he has confused Watson's deceased brother ("The Sign of Four") with this nonexistent second sibling. He is also mistaken about John Watson's middle initial—it is "H," not "A."

In conclusion, I must reject this theory of relativity in favor of the one proposed by Jaclyn J. Murphy in her article, "The Star Trek Family Tree" ("Short Treks," *The Best of Trek #4*). She suggests that if Holmes is an ancestor of Spock's, it is through the human line, as represented by his mother, Amanda Grayson.

This is a much simpler solution to the problem of Holmes's identity. And, as Sherlock Holmes himself would assert, the simplest solution is generally the correct one.

THE TWENTY-THIRD-CENTURY WOMAN

By Patricia Lee Johnson

As Jim Kirk once said, "Worlds may change, galaxies disintegrate, but a woman always remains a woman." But does she really? Has she not effected some change in herself as a result of expanding right, expanding worlds?

The women we see daily, going about their duties on the *Enterprise*, are women that we can relate to. These women—Lieutenant Uhura, Nurse Chapel, Yeoman Rand—are very much the same as we are now. But they emanate a certain assurance, a definite self-confidence. Here they are in what may be considered a man's world, doing men's jobs, and interacting with men. And yet, they seem not at all threatened by their situation. Indeed, when the opportunity for hand-to-hand combat arises, Uhura jumps in with both feet and more than holds her own.

Through all of this, however, these gracious ladies have managed to hold onto that which makes a woman totally unique in the universe—grace, beauty, and an alluring, delicate countenance. Out of uniform and away from their duties, these women are every bit as feminine as any we'll ever meet.

Deep down, where it counts, they haven't changed a bit. Marriage and children are still things to be desired but that life-style is no longer the only avenue open to them. Angela Martine was more than eager to marry her beloved Robert, but when their nuptials were interrupted, she returned to her job with no misgivings. If this says anything at all, it says that she knows precisely where her priorities lie. She is not the scatterbrained, overly emotional thing that men today would have us believe women are.

Marla McGivers, on the other hand, seemed to be just a little unsure of where her loyalties should lie. She was a woman, first and foremost, so her actions, if not admirable, were at least understandable. For all her education and sophistication, she still succumbed to the forceful, disarming charms of a man from out of the past. Who among us would not? Even under Khan's spell, however, she managed to retain her dignity and sense of fair play and rescue her captain. And it was nothing short of raw courage that made her brave a savage new world with the man she loved. The pioneer spirit burned brightly in her. Above all else, the new woman is committed.

Courage was not lacking in Mira Romaine, either. When faced with the unknown, and the horror of possession by alien life forms, she fought to hold onto her own life with every ounce of strength she had. But, as with many brave women throughout history, it was love that helped make her strong.

Dr. Miranda Jones, although certainly a beautiful woman, was nothing short of miraculous. Not only had she taken on the Herculean task of working with a Medusan, she did so without the aid of sight. She accomplished things that most sighted people would have found impossible, and did it all while concealing her blindness. There was no need for pity, no giving up for her . . . She had an inner strength that not many of us are fortunate enough to find within ourselves.

Both Yeoman Rand and Christine Chapel show us a side of the coin that is more familiar to us. Rand, although generally all business—at least on the surface—was a totally different person on the inside. She treated Charlie X with all the gentleness and tenderness a boy his age needed, knowing that the way in which she handled his infatuation with her could make all the difference in his success or failure in adapting to human culture. And the fact that she had tried to get Captain Kirk to notice her legs shows us that, deep down, she is all woman.

Christine Chapel, a romantic to the core, maintained her faith in and love for Dr. Roger Korby until the bitter end. Even after all those years, she still held strongly to the belief that he was basically a good man. And her love for Spock was certainly no passing fancy. Even though things were pretty much impossible for them, she never lost hope, nor lessened her devotion to him.

Let's take a look at the other side of the coin. Consider, for example, Sylvia. While not a woman as we know woman, she was definitely female and in her human guise managed to be most provocative. Although not many would find her admirable, we can at least empathize with her downfall. She fell under the spell of emotion—greed, lust, and every other temptation that human life presents.

In the same boat was Kelinda, who was as cold and heartlessly obedient as any woman we saw on Star Trek. Without sensation to distract her, she was completely devoted to her duty to her race. But when Kirk presented the "problem" of love and physical excitement, she softened and became distracted. And more human.

In Romulan and Klingon women, we see the same strength and femininity as our own females. Women such as the Romulan commander are indeed few and far between. In her, we see the strength to rule over many, much more powerful men, and do so without casting any doubt on their abilities. And yet, when confronted with Spock's overtures, this soldier is completely transformed into the most alluring of creatures, able to respond to him in what appeared to be a very enticing manner. She successfully blended the duties and life-style of a man with the true nature of her gender.

From time to time, we are confronted with an entirely different manner of woman—the android. Although those we've seen on Star Trek were quite enticing counterfeits—virtually impossible to tell from the real thing; acting, speaking, even thinking as we would expect any real woman to—they still lack that certain *something* that makes a woman a woman.

While women's roles have changed in Star Trek's time, the essence of what they are has not. It is hard to picture the twenty-third-century woman driving car pools or being a den mother. And yet, there are women who are mothers. The simple act of mothering will be given to the women of any culture just as long as they must give birth to the babies of the world. A basic biological function thus ensures that a woman must always remain the same inasmuch as her basic reality and consciousness requires.

STAR TREK: THE NEW ARTHURIAD?

By Lynette Muir

Time magazine referred to Star Trek as "The Cosmic Camelot" and other writers have taken up the same idea, notably Marshak and Culbreath in the Introduction to *New Voyages I*: "Man's most shining legends of heroes always seem to carry the dream that the heroes will return again . . . Camelot will live again, and does, at least in the minds of men. Star Trek was just such a shining legend . . ." But just as the musical *Camelot* presented only one unimportant facet of the Arthurian world depicted by T. H. White in *The Once and Future King*, so the term *Cosmic Camelot* totally fails to express what I believe to be the very real and profound parallels between Star Trek and the Arthurian legends. It is these parallels and their significance that I want to explore in this article.

Star Trek is twenty years old, King Arthur is fifteen centuries old. The earliest references to him as a war leader occur in the Latin chronicles of the sixth century. Nevertheless, it was not until the twelfth century that the Arthurian world was created and the stories of King Arthur and his knights became popular throughout Europe; a popularity that they have retained ever since.

The man responsible for this change in Arthur's fortunes, the Great Bird of the Arthurian world, was Geoffrey of Monmouth, who, in 1136, published his Latin *History of the Kings of Britain*, in which he described how King Arthur, with his knights including Gawain and Kay, conquered most of the known world. The Round Table was added to the legend shortly thereafter, and by the middle of the thirteenth century, the stories of Lancelot and Guinevere, Tristan and Iseult, and all the knights of the Round Table dominated European literature.

These early romances may be compared with the original Star Trek episodes as the authority on which were founded all subsequent developments: stories in prose and verse, plays, operas, films, cartoons, parody and pastiche, painting and sculpture. Every century has produced its own versions of the romances, as every year has produced its Star Trek literature and art.

Why? What have these two ideas in common? Why should these romances and this TV series have such consequences when so many others have little or no lasting impact?

The simple answer, I believe, is that they offer a possible ideal; heroes with their feet on the ground and their heads in the stars; an image of society that is not, but could be. For the medieval audience, Arthur's world was a golden age to look back on. For the modern audience, Star Trek is a golden age to look forward to. But the characters in these golden ages were not (will not be) gods or supermen, but human beings with human failings despite their heroic stature.

A close comparison of the two worlds and their heroes reveals some very interesting parallels. James T. Kirk's role may have been consciously modeled on that of Horatio Hornblower, but his character is very different from the shy, fundamentally insecure sea captain. His spiritual ancestor is Sir Gawain, nephew of Arthur, renowned as a fighter and a lover, quick-tempered and generous, the medieval ideal of the prince and leader. Kirk has, of course, many of the qualities of Arthur himself: the leader and king, dedicated to bringing order and justice to a world torn by cruelty and violence; a world peopled by many races, some warlike such as the Romans and Saxons, who have much in common temperamentally and organizationally with the Romulans and Klingons (the Roman characteristics of the Romulan commander in "Balance of Terror" are self-evident).

There are also aliens in the Arthurian world, pagans of strange appearance and beliefs, and some, like Palamedes, considered heroic and right in all but his religion and accepted as a member of the Round Table. There are half-breeds, too, and if Spock thinks he has problems, what about Parsifal's half-brother Feirefiz, whose mother was a Saracen princess, and whose mixed ancestry makes him piebald. (Lokai and Bele take note: Feirefiz is welcomed as a noble warrior by his half-brother.)

The Spock of Arthurian romance is undoubtedly Lancelot, who shares first place in the legends with Gawain, but is so different in character. Noble, reserved, generous, and invincible, he is courteous to all women, but unlike the magnificent and all-conquering Gawain, he rejects their advances even under the most difficult conditions (although Lancelot's abstention from women is due to his devotion to Guinevere, not alien physiology). It would be interesting to see how Spock would have coped with one of Lancelot's most difficult assignments: A damsel refuses to give him information he needs to rescue Guinevere (Kirk?) unless he gets into bed with her. Lancelot reluctantly does so, and ponders how he should lie in the bed; he cannot turn his back to her, because that would be discourteous, whereas facing her might be dangerous. He compromises by lying on his back, unmoving, and the damsel gives up in despair. Spock might have gone for a neck pinch!

Women in Arthurian legends are very like their Star Trek counterparts. First, there is the heroine who appears in a single story and either marries this week's guest star, has a violent but inevitably brief affair with Gawain/Kirk, or dies of unrequited love for Lancelot/Spock. There are also subsidiary groups of women: the messenger-damsels who travel alone through the vast forests "opening hailing frequencies" between scattered castles or bearing news of strange quests and adventures; other damsels act as confidants for the heroines and help heal the heroes' wounds with strange ointments and herbal potions like so many Nurse Chapels with plomik soup.

The technology of Star Trek also has Arthurian parallels. Arthur Clarke has pointed out that a really advanced technology would be indistinguishable from magic, and it would indeed be difficult, for example, to distinguish between the powers of Merlin and the science of the Melkotians. More important is the use to which these scientific or magical devices are put. Star Trek remains believable on a human level because its characters are, ultimately, not ruled by mechanics. Spock sums this up in "The Ultimate Computer" when he declares that computers are admirable and efficient servants but he has no desire to serve under one. Whether they travel by magic ship or transporter, conceal themselves from an enemy by a cloaking device or a magic ring, the heroes ultimately defeat their enemies by their own efforts, mental or physical. Spock may have superior powers but he is neither invulnerable nor immortal; Vulcans in Star Trek fulfill the role of the Other World characters, the fays of Arthurian romance. The Spock/Lancelot parallel is strengthened here if we remember that although Lancelot is of human parentage, he was carried off as a baby and educated by a fay, the lady of the lake.

Doctor McCoy, too, has his Arthurian ancestors, although not among the doctors in the stories. Doctors generally appear only to probe heroes' wounds and inform them they will be healed in a couple of weeks; occasionally they have a more sinister role, such as those who test the "death" of Fenice by pouring molten lead on her hands. Fortunately for her, the potion that induced her death-trance is very powerful and she survives the ordeal and escapes with her lover, Cliges. The faked death is much older than *Romeo and Juliet* or "Amok Time."

McCoy, however, is more important to Star Trek as a person than as a doctor; a man of great compassion and humor, his caustic tongue deflating heroic attitudes, his real belief in the Federation ethos coupled with down-to-earth realism.

These characteristics are found in a number of Arthurian characters, but especially in Sir Dinadan, who first appears in the thirteenth-century prose romance of *Tristan*. Dinadan is a knight of the Round Table who continually mocks his companions, complaining that they are incapable of meeting another knight without immediately challenging him for no reason at all. His cynicism and mockery are much enjoyed, especially by Arthur, for all know that when the need arises, Dinadan will fight valiantly. Like McCoy, Dinadan is a part of the world he is mocking, not an outsider attacking a community that has excluded him. He is critical of what he sees as inhuman, exaggerated (Vulcan?) behavior, not of the basic standards of his world, which, like Starfleet, is hierarchical and formal in structure, with titles and forms of address, precedent, and protocol, but also having a solid foundation of mutual trust, affection, and unity.

In his preface to Malory's *Morte d'Arthur*, Caxton, the printer, summed up the essence of these stories (which were then already several hundred years old): "This said book treats of the noble acts, feats of arms of chivalry, prowess, hardiness, humanity, love, courtesy and true gentleness, with many wonderful histories and adventures." Not a bad description of the voyages of the Starship *Enterprise*!

WHY DID DAVID HAVE TO DIE?

By Gail Eppers

The first time I saw *Star Trek III: The Search for Spock* I was furious! They killed off David just as he was getting interesting. And, apparently, just because of a Klingon whim. It wasn't fair. But when I got to thinking . . . Given that Kruge gave the order, David's death was simply a process of elimination; there were only the three of them down there to choose from. Killing the Spock child would have made the rest of the movie pointless. Let's face it, David was the victim of underpopulation.

Killing Saavik would have been controversial, because her character had been welcomed by fans and highly publicized since the second movie. Killing David not only added to the emotional tension of the film, but left no large holes, either in the plot or in future Star Treks.

Of course, we all know the real decision to kill David took place on a typewriter keyboard, a keyboard owned by the misunderstood "villain," Harve Bennett. Bennett was quoted in *Starlog* concerning David's death: "The death of David Marcus is a tragedy. But truthfully speaking, we really didn't know what to do with the character; David Marcus was not very well defined." He went to add that David underwent a lot of development in *The Search for Spock*, and "I'm sorry we lost him. But we didn't know that until we did it."

In her novelization, Vonda McIntyre clarifies several things that can only be interpreted from the movie. Remember, Kruge was in a desperate situation. His ship was only a scout and he was facing what he thought was a fully manned Federation cruiser. And he was a Klingon. Killing at the drop of a hat (at

WHY DID DAVID HAVE TO DIE?

strategic moments, of course) is the mark of a good Klingon. Also, recall that Kruge's "dog," pathetic though it was, had been killed by the *Enterprise*'s phaser blast. Vonda McIntyre tells us just how much this wounded Kruge. Despite their outward appearance, Klingons do have feelings, and one of the strongest is a reverence for loyalty. And what could be more loyal than a pet?

It is also mentioned in the novelization that Kruge had no idea that David was Kirk's son until Kirk said so. When the *Enterprise* self-destructed, Kruge thought Kirk had committed suicide out of grief for his son, and regretted having killed him. Perhaps, for Kruge, David's death was to even the score for the loss of his pet. But to Kirk, it did more than simply even the score. It gave him incentive to really massacre the "bastards." The way Shatner portrayed Kirk at that crucial moment when hearing the news was perfect. First there was complete devastation, then grief and a desire for revenge.

There may also be plenty of reasons for David's death other than the storyline of *The Search for Spock*. Like Kirstie Alley, Merritt Butrick may have gotten a better offer elsewhere. He has played many diverse roles elsewhere; that same work rules out any fear of becoming typecast. He has played a paraplegic on *Fame*, and he is well-known for his off-the-wall role as Johnny Slash on *Square Pegs*. Also, beyond the idea of the antimilitaristic scientist, the character of David Marcus wasn't much of a "type." Merritt may also have agreed with Harve Bennett that David's death was an important plot development, a necessary evil.

There may be one other reason underlying David's death. David was Kirk's illegitimate son. Now, we all know that no twentieth-century producer in his or her right mind is going to give the leading man an illegitimate son and then keep that son around. Just finding out Kirk had such a son was a shock; letting him have future affairs with an illegitimate "family" around would really overdo it. And what about Carol? Kirk forgot about her once, but wouldn't again, not with a son around. David had to go, because there was too much cumbersome and potentially embarrassing "baggage" that came with him.

Well, I still have one hope. If we're lucky, they could bring Merritt Butrick back as a Vulcan, or Romulan, or maybe even a Klingon . . .

THE SERVING OF REVENGE

By Janeen S. DeBoard

As is usual—and welcome—following the release of a new Star Trek movie, we have seen a flood of articles that dissect and criticize *Star Trek III: The Search for Spock*. Some were written by pros, some by fans, but virtually all were favorable; especially they praised Admiral Kirk's actions in the film, his "restraint" at "not acting out of a desire to avenge David's death." James Kirk, they said, was never more in character, more in control, than he was in this film, with its emphasis on the sacrifices friends will make for each other.

I submit, however, that Kirk has never been more *out* of character, more *out* of control, than he was in *The Search for Spock*. There is only one motivation for the things he does in this story: revenge.

Revenge on the Klingons, on Starfleet Command, and most of all, on himself.

His willful destruction of the *USS Enterprise* was not a last-ditch effort to save himself and his crew or to prevent a dangerous secret—Genesis—from falling into Klingon hands. It was done from the depths of rage and from a desire for murderous revenge upon his son's executioners.

It was a refusal to submit to Starfleet's orders to abandon both Spock and his ship.

It was also Kirk's supreme way of punishing himself for being unable to prevent the death of David. His son had lost his life as Kirk looked on helplessly, so Kirk must lose the thing most valuable to him—his ship. And if he and his crew must also perish as a result, then so be it.

Kirk has finally had to face death as he never has before, not even with Spock. How ironic that his son, the one who told him he had not done so, should be the one to cause Kirk finally to face death. And in his grief and guilt we see at last the legendary control break and fall away. For the rest of the film, Kirk is no longer the well-disciplined starship captain . . . he is simply a man, a grieving father, driven by despair and desperation.

Consider Kirk as he would be in this same situation—orbiting an unstable planet in a crippled ship with only a skeleton crew aboard, facing a shipload of menacing Klingons, and trying to rescue an endangered landing party—but *without* David's presence and Kirk's rebellion against Starfleet. With the *Enterprise* trapped and unable to move or return fire, escaping to join the stranded party would seem to be the most logical course.

Kirk is bold and brash; he is the master of the bluff. But he has never been self-destructive or suicidal, especially when he would take others down with him. He is survival oriented. He has allowed himself to be pushed to the edge of disaster more than once, but never *over* the edge; he has always left himself an out. Kirk has never intended to die, or to allow anyone else—including his ship—to die, either.

Until now. He destroys the *only* chance he might have of surviving, the only possible place he could retreat to with a disintegrating planet underfoot, a vicious enemy overhead, and *no chance* of immediate rescue.

While the Klingons were preparing to board the *Enterprise*, there were a thousand things Kirk could have done to save her. The computer could have been instructed to forget all vital Federation secrets, including Genesis, and then blow the air locks five minutes after the crew beamed down, repressurizing sixty minutes later. It could have been told to shut down all systems until given a password. And so forth. Surely a clever captain would have a contingency plan filed away in his head for just such an emergency.

The most obvious solution was simply to wait in the transporter room and phaser the Klingons out of existence as they materialized. No matter what Kirk did, it is unlikely that the selfish Kruge would have destroyed the *Enterprise* in retaliation. What's the loss of a few subordinates (he kills them himself) against such a prize? He would have enjoyed the ensuing game of cat-and-mouse, attempting to pick off the crew one by one, before leaving with the Federation starship and the secret of Genesis.

Even the chance that the Klingons might blow up the *Enterprise* is better than the certainty of Kirk doing so himself. Such an action was simply not consistent with Kirk's usual stretch-a-chance-to-the-limit style. Even if Kruge did destroy the ship, Kirk and his crew would ultimately have been no worse off, and Kirk wouldn't have the deliberate destruction of his ship on his conscience. He would instead know that he had truly done everything possible to save her.

But Kirk was nowhere near his normal, risk-taking, coolheaded self. He might have been thinking, "No one will take my ship from me . . . the Klingons must die . . . David is dead and I am to blame . . ." By allowing the Klingons to board his ship, he made it possible to take the ultimate revenge on them, on Starfleet, and on himself. That is why he gave the destruct sequence and stalked off to kill more Klingons without so much as a final thought or a backward glance for the ship he had fought so hard to save in episodes past.

It is chilling to watch the series episodes now and see Kirk's shocked reaction whenever mention is made of a captain destroying his own ship. If he had been in his right mind he never would have done it; and if Spock had been in *his* right mind, so to speak, he never would have allowed it.

It is curious that neither McCoy, Scotty, Chekov, nor Sulu made any move to dissuade Kirk. What could have been going through their minds as those final instructions were spoken? Why such fatalism? And when Kirk finally says, in a voice so devoid of feeling a Vulcan would envy it, ". . . what have I done?", what about McCoy's strange remark, "What you've always done. Turned death into a fighting chance to live." But of whose death does he speak?

Certainly not David's. That was a tragedy, but not one that gave the crew any additional chance of surviving. And hardly the Klingons'; they were the enemy, killed out of self-defense. The death of the *Enterprise*? Her destruction only ensured theirs.

The deaths he speaks of are their own, and the speaker is not McCoy, but Spock.

Kirk may have believed he heard McCoy telling him that by destroying the Klingons aboard the ship, he had bought them an additional bit of time on the planet's surface. In actuality, it was

Spock telling him that with their own destruction, together with that of the planet, the *Enterprise*, and the Klingons, they had bought some time for the rest of the universe. Genesis was not yet a Klingons' weapon; but the "fighting chance for life" was for others, not for them.

The message is not judgmental in any way, but merely a Vulcan's final observation of what Kirk has done. It is a logical, "at least this much has been done" statement. The crew stands in silent agreement.

It would seem that Kirk's crew all along accepted the fact that they would not be returning from this mission. Certainly Spock, present as he is in McCoy's mind, and already knowing death, cannot expect to live again. Perhaps this is why they all show such an uncharacteristic lack of self-preservation, and why not one of them offers any alternative to destroying the *Enterprise*. It is sad to see Star Trek's usual strength and optimism—especially that of Kirk—tossed out the window in this film.

In Kirk's blind rush to destroy his enemies and punish himself, the rescue of Spock—the reason for their being there in the first place—is practically forgotten. How could he rescue anyone when he burned the bridge to home? It is quite inconceivable that Kirk had planned all along to somehow take the Klingon vessel and escape in it. After finally killing Kruge, some of his old sense of command returned, but random factors did indeed operate in his favor. It was pure luck that allowed him to learn the command word, get the communicator, and beam aboard the Klingon vessel. Fortunately, he did remember to gather up Spock and take him along.

Spock laid down his life to save the ship and her crew. "He did not think his sacrifice a vain or empty one." Yet, days later, Kirk has made mutineers of his officers and blown *Enterprise* to bits. He has faltered after a lifetime of discipline and finally, utterly lost control. The remaining officers are shadows of their former selves and have thrown their futures away with both hands.

What is Spock going to think of all this? Is it possible that he will blame himself?

Surely he will question Kirk's shocking actions, his lack of foresight, his fatalism, his thoroughly uncharacteristic handling of the entire affair. He might ask: "Was there no other way, if you wished to save me, than to destroy so much in the process?

Why did you suddenly forget all you learned in your years as a starship captain?"

The Klingons have a proverb, "Revenge is a dish best served cold." And now Kirk has shown us exactly what that proverb means. In the desperate heat of revenge, one is likely to perform only blind, self-destructive acts. One must be cold and clear-thinking—as Kirk has always been before—in order to properly serve up revenge.

Else you may find only a shattered cloud where you once had a magnificent starship.

A CHAIN IS ONLY AS STRONG

By Rowena Warner

We seem to have been receiving more than our share of fine articles lately about the relationship between Kirk, Spock, and McCoy—The Triumvirate, The Three, The Friendship, The Center—whatever name fans choose to give this interweaving of characters, there's no doubt that their interaction is one of the most important aspects of Star Trek. But even while agreeing on that, fans still differ wildly on exactly why and how this relationship works. Below, Best of Trek regular Rowena Warner gives us one view.

The Triad. The Triumvirate. The Big Three. Much has been written, discussed, and argued about them, both as separate individuals and as the union to which we apply the above labels.

Plato once described Man as consisting of three parts—the Body, the Mind, and the Spirit—and it is this trichotomy which has been adopted by Star Trek fen to describe the union of Kirk, Spock, and McCoy. I agree with such assessment on the surface, but in order to obtain a true understanding of the intricate complexities of each subset of that Triad, one needs to turn over some topsoil and get to the root of the matter.

There seems to be a consensus in parts of Star Trek fandom that the Triad is all-powerful, but each individual component alone would be incomplete. This line of thought has become a pet peeve of mine, and after running into the theory again recently, I started to do some thinking (a dangerous pastime—my family takes off for New Zealand every time they hear my "wheels" beginning to whirr).

It seems that we tend to view the Triad as an entity with three separate, distinct parts, but we ignore the smaller, more complex part of which each larger part is composed. That's like describing the human body as being made up of the head, the torso, and appendages. It's obvious one need not be a surgeon or biologist to realize there is far more to it than that.

The idea that Kirk, Spock, or McCoy would be incomplete outside the Triad seems preposterous to me. If this were indeed true, how could they have possibly attained the positions of captain, science officer, and doctor *before* teaming together to form the Big Three? On the contrary, it is the completeness which each individual brings to the Triad that makes the whole a viable, successful "entity." A chain is only as strong as its weakest link. There are no permanently weak links in the Star Trek chain because each link shares the same intricate characteristics and is capable of performing the same functions as the other two links. When momentary weaknesses occur in one, it is immediately compensated for by one or both of the remaining links.

Kirk, for instance, represents the "body" of the Triad, but when called upon, he can also become the "mind" or the "spirit," whichever is required in any particular situation. This occurred in several episodes and was often labeled "character rape," for the act having one member of the Triad entering into the domain of another is taboo among the fen. In some instances, I agree with this assessment, but in others, this occurrence is quite interesting to analyze, and demonstrates the wide range of capabilities possessed by each individual link in the chain.

When I speak of the "body" or the "physical" segment of the Triad, I am doing more than just making reference to the physical act of slugging it out with a villain. This segment also includes all areas such as Spock making use of the nerve pinch, McCoy administering a sedative to render a foe unconscious, or Kirk ordering the firing of phasers or interfering in a race's culture in order to save that race from stagnation and/or extinction. The "physical" also includes the mental thought and decisions that precede the above actions. So, it's obvious that in many instances Kirk, Spock, and McCoy have all been representative of the "body" of the Triad.

The same is true of the "mind" and the "spirit." The "mind" includes not only separate thoughts and bits of data collected to form logical conclusions, but also consists of examining various alternatives, and attempting to arrive at not necessarily the most logical, but rather the *best* decision for all concerned. Although we think of Spock as representing the "mind," Kirk and McCoy are also more than capable of performing the "mind" division of the Triad, for each of them is in a position where they must think and make daily decisions regarding life and death.

The third component, the "spirit," is again well represented by all three. Remember Kirk's passionate speech in "Return to Tomorrow"—"They used to say, if man could fly, he'd have wings . . ." And what about Spock's toneless, but equally passionate criticism of the Vians in "The Empath" —"What purpose can be served by the death of our friend except to bring you pleasure?"

The best demonstration of Spock's display of the "spirit" is at the end of *Wrath of Khan*. The "mind" contemplated the entire situation carefully (and quickly) and Spock realized he was going to die no matter what decision he made, so was it not more logical to repair the warp drive and save the others? Of course, but this is where the "spirit" enters, the force that drove him to take that first step and the subsequent ones which eventually carried him to Engineering. Once there, just think of the "spirit" he possessed that made him actually walk to his death inside that reactor chamber! When a lion attacks, it's much easier to cower against the bars and close your eyes than it is to deliberately stick your head in the animal's mouth.

Kirk displayed "spirit" in *The Search for Spock* when he risked everything to restore one missing and one weakened link to the chain. McCoy displayed "spirit" when he lay down on that slab of stone ready to sacrifice his life in an attempt to return Spock's *katra*. (I'm sure you must realize by now that "spirit" is a word synonymous with "love," whether it be love for one person, an idea, or the entire universe.)

But what happens when one link in this chain becomes momentarily weakened? It is the completeness and diversity of the other two links that prevent the chain from breaking or The Triad from collapsing. An example of this occurred in "The Devil in the Dark." When Spock came upon Kirk with the Horta, there was no "mind" present as he rather spiritedly yelled, "Kill it, Captain!" It was Kirk who realized that there was no need for the "body" or the "spirit," so he strengthened the momentary weakness caused by Spock, and became the "mind" when he counseled the First Officer to wait.

In the scene in "Shore Leave" when Kirk and Spock were attacked by the plane, the "mind" was abandoned entirely because what was needed then was not thought, but action—they had to get the hell out of there, fast! Also, the "spirit" entered into their actions when they attempted to save each other instead of themselves.

In "The Empath" one link of the chain (McCoy) is almost totally broken, so it is up to Kirk and Spock to give added strength to the whole. In doing this, Spock became the "spirit" in the comfort he gave McCoy, and Kirk became the "mind" in his attempts to obtain the Vians' assistance.

"Mirror, Mirror" provides an interesting look at this "chain" and what happens when one of the links is missing completely. Spock is still in his own universe where he, of necessity, becomes all three links in the chain by making the physical move to put the alternate universe Kirk and his compatriots in the brig, and by utilizing the "mind" or thought process in attempting to determine how to reverse the problem caused by ionic interference. The "mind" and "body" actions here are accompanied by an undercurrent of "spirit," that is, the overwhelming desire to bring his captain and the rest of the crew back to their own universe.

In the alternate universe, things are even more interesting. McCoy takes on the "body" as he uses a sedative to knock out a crewmember and proceeds actively to assist Scotty in working on the transporter.

Kirk, on the other hand, realizes the "body" and certainly the "spirit" would be useless in obtaining his desired objective, particularly against the alternate universe Spock. Without his own Spock present to represent the "mind," Kirk assumes the role himself and becomes almost a mirror image of his friend as he presses the logic of sparing the Halkans. The "body" or "spirit," if used against the alternate universe Spock, would have done more harm than good, and quickly realizing this, Kirk chose the third course available to him.

In "The Conscience of the King," Spock and McCoy, more or less, switch roles. It is Spock who presents the strong and somewhat impassioned speech because he is the one who is convinced that Karidian and Kodos are one in the same. The doctor provides the "mind" by standing back and giving mental support as Spock presents his case and by offering verbal support when he states that Spock is only doing his job.

In "The Apple" we again see a role reversal of the "mind" and the "spirit" in the argument between Spock and McCoy with respect to interfering in the Vaalan culture. At first this reversal is unclear, for on the surface we see Spock presenting a calm, logical argument, whereas McCoy comes forth with an emotional counterattack. But it is not the method of argument, but rather what is being said that proves interesting.

Spock wants to leave the Vaalans alone—"These people are healthy and happy." The Vulcan who is always so curious about the next step in the equation or what lies beyond the next cosmic hill, does not want the "wheels of progress" to run over these people. They are innocent and naive, and he wants them to remain a pure and unspoiled society. Spock desires to withhold from them the very curiosity that he takes so much pleasure in satisfying. I found it amusing that he called McCoy's reaction to the system "emotional" when Spock himself seemed quite emotional in his support of that same system.

Just as strange as his empathy toward this culture is McCoy's denouncement of it. The doctor who constantly complains about the complexities of life and wishes for simpler days, wants to give the Vaalans the very progress that he so verbally abuses—". . . they need to advance and grow . . . This isn't life, it's stagnation."

Some may call the role reversal in this argument "characterization rape," but I look upon it as an interesting and heretofore unseen insight into the characters of Spock and McCoy.

I believe the closest this "chain" ever came to breaking completely was in "The Tholian Web." With the "body" removed from the picture for most of the time, Spock, again of necessity, had to become more the "body" than the "mind" in that he was suddenly the commanding officer and was forced into making decisions affecting all on board. He dared not assume the "spirit" at that time, not even when he announced Kirk's presumed demise, because (1) a display of emotion at that point would have been disastrous for the entire crew, and (2) McCoy was displaying more than enough "spirit" for both of them.

It was Kirk, oddly enough, who provided the "mind" in his

tape that Spock and McCoy listened to in his cabin. The speech was calm, quiet, and well-planned as he made logical suggestions and gave them assurances that the chain *could* remain strong even if one of the links became permanently missing.

There are many other scenes in both episodes and movies that I could cite as depicting the diversity of each component of The Triad. In "Journey to Babel," Spock is torn between the "mind" and the "spirit" as duty tells him he is the only logical one to assume command, while love for his father urges him to Sickbay. Kirk understands this struggle taking place within his friend and relieves him of command, thereby freeing Spock of the "mind" and allowing him to give full rein to the "spirit."

In "Arena" Kirk ran the entire gauntlet of components in The Triad, at first being very much the "body" or physical link in the chain, but when it grew evident the use of this segment was futile against the Gorn, he then became the "mind," carefully weighing all factors and arriving at a logical conclusion (i.e., the gunpowder and diamond projectiles). After achieving his victory, he won an even greater one by refusing to kill his opponent, a definite exhibition of the "spirit." Without this ability to utilize all three branches of The Triad, it's extremely doubtful that Kirk could have defeated the Gorn, and if by some lucky coincidence he did succeed in doing so, the death of his "enemy" would have served no purpose other than to give him and his race, of whom he was the representative at the time, the label of "uncivilized."

There are still other scenes that illustrate the wide range of capabilities possessed by each member of The Triad, but hopefully, I've offered sufficient argument to demonstrate my point. Kirk *is* predominantly the "body"; McCoy the "spirit"; and Spock the "mind" of The Triad, but it is their ability to recognize and then assume whichever component that is required for any given situation, which gives strength to each link and, therefore, the entire chain of The Triad. Alone, each is a complete, well-rounded, whole, and functioning individual. Joined together as The Triad, they are totally awesome.

THE BLIND SPOT—A REBUTTAL

By Jody A. Morse

A new subject of debate popped up in Star Trek fandom a few years ago: Should the roles of Kirk, Spock, and so on be eventually taken over by new actors? Naturally enough, as time passes, this debate grows even hotter, for several obvious reasons. In this article, and the one following, two of our readers give their response to an article that said, "yes, let's have new actors." We think that you'll be fascinated by the difference in attitude and approach taken by two writers on the same side of the issue.

In Janeen S. DeBoard's article, "Star Trek Fans—The Blind Spot," (*The Best of Trek #9*), she made some rather interesting comments. Chiefly, she suggested that other actors should portray Kirk, Spock, and the other officers of the late *Enterprise*. She proposed that these new actors should appear in flashbacks, offering us glimpses of the illustrious crew's past, as-yet unreported adventures. This, she believed, was the only way that Star Trek could continue after Shatner and the rest of the original cast were no longer able to reprise their famous alter egos. Taken at face value, each of these suggestions is creative and certainly "logical." Yet it seems that in trying to expose the fans' blind spot, she produced one of her own.

Allow me to explain. Ms. DeBoard obviously cares for the original characters. In fact, she even calls them "friends." It's only natural, then, for her to wish her friends continued prosperity and long life, if not some degree of immortality. Few fans, I think, would find fault with such feelings. In this case, however,

I believe she allowed her emotions to cloud her judgment. She simply could not see the forest for the trees.

All right, then, just where did she go astray? First of all, a casting change of the type she described would simply not be acceptable to a vast majority of fans. Several fan polls taken over the years illustrate this fact. *Trek's* own "Fan On the Street Poll" (*The Best of Trek #8*), reported that, when asked their opinions of a major cast change, forty-one percent of those polled thought Star Trek just "wouldn't be the same." Ms. DeBoard cites James Bond, Sherlock Holmes, and others as examples that audiences will accept different performers playing the same characters. True enough. In mundane society (what nonfans refer to as "the real world"), moviegoers are conditioned— nay, almost programmed—to plunk down five or six dollars, gather an armload of soft drinks and assorted munchies, sit down in a darkened, crowded room, and allow their normally well-guarded perceptions of reality some time off. This is what theatrical critics call "the willing suspension of disbelief." For approximately two hours the audience watches a superhero from another galaxy fly forth to make the world safe for democracy, while not once looking for the telltale wires. They know they're there, and yet from the time of the opening credits until the house lights come back up, they almost believe a man can fly.

So it goes, whether it's a superhero, a Western cowpuncher, or secret agent—or any of a multitude of fictional characters. We're more interested in how Agent 007 will foil the latest threat to global security than we are in who is playing the role. That's because we cease to be aware that we are watching an actor— we're watching Bond, James Bond.

So it is with Captain Kirk, right? Wrong. It must be remembered that for most fans Kirk, Spock, and the others are not just characters in a movie. They're flesh-and-blood people! You won't find thousands of people eating, sleeping, and dreaming James Bond. Their attachment to Bond lasts as long as it takes to reach their cars, at which point the bond is severed. (Sorry, I couldn't resist.) On the other hand, there is a large segment of the population that spends much of its free time probing the final frontier.

When a fan pens a Star Trek story and writes, "Spock arched one eyebrow and said, 'Regrettably, doctor, modern medicine has yet to find a cure for poor humor,' " just what is the image he sees in his mind? He sees Spock, yes. But look closer. He sees *Leonard Nimoy* as Spock. The tone, inflections, features, and timing that the writer imagines are those of one man—Spock, as played by Leonard Nimoy. His face and voice are indelibly engraved in the author's memory. And we too, when we read his story, recognize them and smile warmly, for we are visiting an old friend again. If we gaze up at the silver screen and see another actor portraying Spock, then that is exactly what we'll see—an actor, not Spock.

Imagine waking up one morning and finding a stranger cooking breakfast in your kitchen and claiming to be your mother. She doesn't look like your mother, nor does she sound or act like her. Even the meal, although the ingredients are essentially the same, lacks that "special flavor" of Mom's. Sounds like something out of *Invasion of the Body Snatchers*, doesn't it?

Now onto the question of flashbacks. Even though it might be emotionally satisfying to learn more of what transpired during those "secret years" after the original five-year mission, and between *Star Trek: the Motion Picture* and *Wrath of Khan*, such storytelling would seem to be regressive, not progressive. After all, Star Trek always made it a point to look forward, not backward. As Ms. DeBoard herself said, "Change and growth, innovation and experiment—these are the things which have kept Star Trek alive all this time." Well said. But isn't that exactly what the motion pictures are doing, allowing our old friends to evolve and expand? If you insist on exploring the past . . . Well, that is what fanzines are for, to flesh out the gaps in the Star Trek mythos. Personally, I'd prefer to explore the future—it's infinitely less predictable and thus infinitely more exciting.

So, then, let's allow Kirk and Spock to continue to mature, together with those men who portray them. They certainly appear to be improving with age. They're becoming more wise, less impulsive. Where a younger Kirk might leap into a battle with the Klingons just for the hell of it, the now-Admiral Kirk would stop and consider the consequences of his actions, both to himself and to those close to him. *Then* he'd probably go ahead and take the plunge. But at least he'd have taken the time to think about it, "reason it out." We now see a "new" Kirk, but because he is still portrayed by William Shatner, he is still "our" Kirk.

And so the human adventure continues . . . Or does it? Logically, we cannot expect Kirk, Spock, and the rest of the old entourage to stay bound to space forever. As much as we might like to deny it, they're human beings, not gods—and even for gods there comes a point of no return. They'll go off on their own to forge their separate destinies, pursue their own careers, and yes, eventually die. Now don't get me wrong . . . I like Kirk and the rest as much as the next fan, but I would rather see them pass quietly into the realm of myth than see them eternally recycled into the past.

So in that case, the *Enterprise* crew is gone and Star Trek is dead, right? Wrong! If we insist on character growth, then we must also insist on the continued growth of Star Trek itself. The movies are definitely doing their part. Consider where we now stand: Kirk and Company have violated Starfleet directions by stealing the *Enterprise* and going off to Genesis. They are in hot water with the brass. They have lost the beloved Big E, but they are in possession of a hijacked Klingon Bird of Prey. And Spock is back, although he may not be "as good as new." Now where do we go from here? The possibilities are endless. However, there will come a time when all the loose ends are tied up and they all go their separate ways. But wait . . . Starfleet is still around, isn't it? The United Federation of Planets remains united, doesn't it? The Klingons and Romulans still plot to conquer our galaxy, don't they? There are still strange, new worlds to be explored, aren't there? You betcha!

Starfleet is a big operation, with many ships of many types, both old and new. They need crew persons to man those ships. Perhaps somewhere among them is a budding science officer or a potential starship captain. Now wouldn't it be great if we could get to know these young men and women, watch them develop into first-class officers and join them on their many adventures? Star Trek dead? Not by a long shot!

But there are a few problems, a few obstacles in our path, including Starfleet itself. Sharron Crowson, in "Speculation: On Power, Politics, and Personal Integrity" (*The Best of Trek #9*), saw Starfleet and the Federation becoming "ponderous bureaucracies." Indeed, this seems to be the case. What's worse, the high-ups in the fleet seem to consider officers such as Captain Styles to be prototypes for the future, much like the *Excelsior* herself. Well, as we've seen, "new" doesn't necessarily mean "improved." Sharron's suggestion that Kirk and Company confront the brass and give them a few "pointers" brings up some interesting possibilities. But does it have to be Kirk? Why not someone else?

Suppose there was a young captain, due to take on his first starship command. Throughout his stint at the Academy, he studied the record of Admiral James T. Kirk. He looks up to Kirk as the paragon of what a Starfleet officer ought to be. In fact, to him Kirk has become almost a legend. Suppose that even though the Federation is indeed losing sight of its goal to explore strange new worlds, that spirit is reborn in our new captain, through the inspiration of his idol. Why, he might even defy Starfleet and take his ship on "a little training cruise." Now wouldn't that be an exciting premise for a new television series? A new ship, with a new crew, yet still part of the ever-expanding Star Trek universe.

Still, there are those who would resist such a shift of emphasis, claiming passionately that "there will never be anyone like Spock." No argument there. But that doesn't mean we shouldn't give other characters a chance. If NBC hadn't taken a similar chance, we would never have had Spock in the first place. Sure, a character like Spock is a rare find, but do we really believe that such an inspired creation was only a fluke? Do we believe that it could never happen again? Poppycock, as Dr. McCoy would say. Where there's one fascinating character, there are bound to be others. Take Saavik, for example. Created long after the original series was canceled, she has emerged as one of the most popular regulars, and her popularity continues to grow. Regardless of which portrayal you prefer, Kirstie Alley's or Robin Curtis', I doubt if anyone would deny that Saavik is one interesting lady and a very complex personality. Perhaps as time goes on, we'll get a chance to know her better, for her character is well worth expanding.

As for considering Saavik as an example of one actress successfully replacing another in a role in Star Trek, we must remember that Saavik is a relatively new character and that our image of her is not nearly as concrete as those of the other regulars. Even so, most fans were angry and upset at this change, even if they didn't consider it a serious breach of continuity; many of them still consider Kirstie Alley to be the "real" Saavik.

I look forward with great anticipation to the next "generation'' of Star Trek, and to the new friends I've yet to meet. Of course, this doesn't mean we have to abandon our old friends entirely; they can make frequent guest appearances. Imagine a chance encounter between our young captain and Captain Sulu, or Captain Spock, or a certain female Romulan commander. After all, it's a small universe . . . and as large as the imagination. How will our new crew react to such situations? No doubt just as Spock predicted in *Wrath of Khan*: "Each according to his gifts." And we'll all be richer for those gifts.

In closing, I'd like to remind you that Gene Roddenberry didn't create the Star Trek universe merely as a playground for Kirk and Company. It is a playground for us all. There's plenty of room for other ships and other voyages. The more, the merrier!

WILL THE REAL
CAPTAIN KIRK STAND UP!

By Shirley R. Gibbons

I read the article "Star Trek Fans—The Blind Spot" by Janeen DeBoard (*The Best of Trek #9*) with great interest. I think Ms. DeBoard did a fine job with her presentation of the subject. I disagree with her opinions, however, and hereby request equal time to express my own point of view.

I, too, have been a devoted Star Trek fan since it first aired in September of 1966. I was also one of the "thousands of fans" who wrote a letter pleading for a third season renewal of the series when cancellation was announced at the conclusion of the second season. I have literally devoured everything involving Star Trek I could get my hands on, ever since I discovered what a "fascinating" world it is. Therefore, I cannot let the opportunity escape to stand up and be counted for: "No casting changes for central, ongoing characters in Star Trek!" I hereby cast my vote for the following reasons:

William Shatner, Leonard Nimoy, DeForest Kelley, et al. have literally breathed life into the persons of Captain Kirk, Mr. Spock, Doctor McCoy, and the other essential characters of Star Trek. These special friends would not now be who they are to each of us if not for the individual personalities responsible for their creation.

Ms. DeBoard stated in her excellent article: "actors grow old," "play other parts," "have other concerns." Of course, all of this is true. However, I shall attempt to explore each of these statements individually.

1. "Actors grow old." Unfortunately, true. Like all of us, our heroes must face that reality. However, the makeup available

today, plus the artistic application of same, is superb, thus making it possible, when necessary, to erase traces of age. A man or woman in his/her seventies or eighties can realistically portray a person in his thirties or forties with the aid of said makeup. (We all know the reverse is true.) Case in point: Western actor Roy Rogers. Roy still looks as young today as he did in his western films of the 1950s, thanks to makeup. Roy still has active roles in television episodes and commercials today.

2. "Play other parts." As to the actors and actresses of Star Trek playing other roles—so what's to stop them? Contracts today are structured to allow plenty of leeway for such an occurrence. For instance:

William Shatner portrays *T.J. Hooker* in the weekly television series of the same name, and still finds time for filming made-for-television movies (such as *Secrets of a Married Man*, 1984).

Leonard Nimoy has appeared in many movies in recent years—*A Woman Called Golda*, to name one. He also can be seen on several television commercials. And who can forget his superb series, "In Search Of . . ."?

DeForest Kelley is virtually retired from filmmaking. Although he receives many offers, he continually refuses to accept any roles except the part of our beloved Dr. McCoy.

Nichelle Nichols has been busy starring in a stage production, *Horowitz and Mrs. Washington*, in Kansas City, appeared in *Antony and Cleopatra* for Bard TV, and also appears in the film *The Supernatural*.

James Doohan, Walter Koenig, and George Takei all have had roles in various other movie and television films. (In my area of the country, they all can also be seen in various television commercials.)

3. "They have other concerns." To my knowledge, Star Trek has not prevented any of its actors from doing anything they really wanted to do. In fact, they stay so busy, I find it difficult to keep up with all their activities. For instance:

Bill Shatner owns a horse ranch where he raises thoroughbreds, then travels around the country showing his beautiful animals.

Leonard Nimoy has proven his capabilities as a director by his excellent work on *Star Trek III: The Search for Spock*, not to mention other directorial projects that are too numerous to mention here. He will also once again be in the director's chair when filming begins on *Star Trek IV* in the near future. I have been privileged, as have many of you, I'm sure, to have heard Mr. Nimoy speak at a college lecture. I understand he still includes such appearances in his busy schedule whenever possible.

Walter Koenig is a perfect example of diversified living. In addition to his fine talents as an actor, he also has the distinction of being a writer, producer, and director. He also teaches acting and theater.

George Takei has been quite involved in politics. In 1973, he ran for a seat on the Los Angeles City Council, losing to his opponent by a mere three percent of the vote. When not acting, George stays busy with community and cultural affairs, in addition to serving as Vice-President and Chairman of the Personnel Committee of the Southern California Rapid Transit District.

Nichelle Nichols is a lady to be reckoned with when it comes to the "other concerns" department. Not only is she constantly staying active in motion pictures and stage productions, but her record of accomplishments with NASA's Women in Motion Program speaks for itself. At present, she is working on a one-woman show, and a major film project.

James Doohan spends much of his time making personal appearances at Star Trek conventions and video stores across the country, meeting his loyal fans and promoting Star Trek. He also keeps busy filming commercials for television.

It is my very firm belief that as long as there is evidence that these actors are willing to continue in their roles in Star Trek, they should not be replaced. Why rock the boat with thoughts of replacement, whether it be now or in the future? I'm sure that those in the Star Trek family know, beyond a shadow of a doubt, that they are loved and appreciated by their devoted fans. If you have ever attended a Star Trek convention, a college lecture, or a personal appearance in a video store featuring one of our friends, then you know what I mean. They have endeared themselves to young and old alike. It is sheer pleasure to see a small toddler beam with happiness when lifted up to sit on Mr. Chekov's or Scotty's knee, and pose for a picture with their hero while a proud mom or dad snaps the shot for posterity.

Picture, if you will, Jimmy Doohan seated at a table in a video store while more than 150 people wait more than two hours to get Scotty's autograph, pose for a picture with him, or just say a few words to him. (One devoted fan even presented our redoubtable Scotsman with a bottle of Scotch!) The gleam in Jimmy's eyes matches the grin on his face at the undying love and devotion of his fans.

One really enthusiastic fan showed up dressed to the boots like Captain Kirk, exclaiming to all who would listen that he had come to have his picture taken with his favorite "Engineer"!

Scenes such as those just described tell me in no uncertain terms that there is no sign of discontent or frustration and boredom among our heroes and heroines of Star Trek. When a new film is announced, many of the actors themselves are just as excited as we, the fans, are at the prospect of continuing voyages. And with Mr. Nimoy now directing Star Trek films, there is not the slightest doubt, as far as I'm concerned, that future epics will be *true* Star Trek! After all, he is well aware of what it takes to "grab" the inner soul of us "true-blue, dyed-in-the-wool" Star Trek believers!

We all will forever be indebted to "The Great Bird of the Galaxy," Gene Roddenberry, whose dream 'way back when for a "different" science fiction television show was realized only after much hard work, frustration, disappointment, and even failure. But in the long run, wasn't it worth it, Gene? We, your loyal followers, certainly think so!

Ms. DeBoard raised the question in her article: "What if we, the fans, had refused to accept anyone but Gene Roddenberry as the producer for Star Trek?"

We are fortunate indeed that Gene stuck with his "baby" long enough so that everyone else involved has a firm idea of what his dreams and hopes for Star Trek were—especially the actors who had worked with him from the beginning. By the time Gene relinquished the production end of the business to other capable persons, his permanent stamp was firmly embedded in the work. Also, because Mr. Roddenberry was not an on-camera member of the cast, his face was not known to the viewers. Therefore, he would not fall in the same category as the actors; a change of producers is not nearly as noticeable as a change of actors.

Let me now direct your attention to another category of Star Trek: the novels. I thoroughly enjoy reading each new Star Trek novel, and eagerly haunt the local bookstore in anticipation of its arrival every other month. I derive great pleasure as I read each new adventure by picturing in my mind's eye Mr. Shatner, Mr.

Nimoy, Mr. Kelley, and all the rest in their respective, *familiar* roles. The book comes alive for me, and I literally become lost in the world of the twenty-third century. I have even been known to shed tears while reading a particularly moving scene. If any of the Star Trek cast were replaced, I fear it would affect my acceptance of future novels.

A great factor in Star Trek's continuing popularity is the chemistry that exists among the cast members. Their long association with the roles and with each other, and the projection of themselves into those roles, forms a magic that exists nowhere else in television or movie history. This magic also extends to the novels.

I agree with Ms. DeBoard's statement that history is full of examples of various talented actors portraying the roles of Hamlet, Sherlock Holmes, and James Bond, to name only a few. But picture, if you can, anyone else playing Marshal Matt Dillon, Perry Mason, Gilligan, Starsky and Hutch, the Cartwrights, and so on.

Should something in the future happen to prevent one or more of the original cast from continuing in his or her role, it would not mean that Star Trek and all it stands for would die. As long as there are reruns and videotapes of the original seventy-nine episodes, as long as there are the motion pictures, as long as there are new novels, these special friends *can* and *will* continue to live on for the delight and enjoyment of future generations. After all, our own children have provided a whole new crop of Star Trek fans to carry on the legend as they discover its beauty and fascination.

Who can say what the future will bring? Who can deny that science fiction is forever creating new concepts that excite and stretch our imagination? As Mr. Spock would say, "There are always possibilities."

Who of us could have predicted that Star Trek would still be around (with its original cast intact!) *nineteen years* after its television debut? I submit to you, my friends, that if not for the unique chemistry of those who brought Star Trek to life in the first place, it would not have survived this test of time.

The real heart of Star Trek will continue to survive as long as Captain Kirk, Mr. Spock, Dr. McCoy, and all the rest of the crew of the *Enterprise* remain unchanged. They are each *who* and *what* they are only because of the incomparable talents of the individual personalities who literally projected themselves into their roles. They are the ones who made the characters come alive for us in the first place!

The concept of Star Trek cannot be destroyed because it not only gives us a hopeful, intriguing look into tomorrow, but it emphatically states that Infinite Diversity in Infinite Combinations really *does* work, and *must* be the way of life to come if we are to survive to reach that future!

The one thing that could, and most probably would, destroy the Star Trek world we all know and love, is the replacement of *any one member* of this special cast.

Of course, there is always room for new additions to the Star Trek family, providing such a character is handled correctly. A new permanent member *must* mesh well with the other members (i.e., Lieutenant Saavik).

It is good to know that the Star Trek cast members are all active in Science Fiction Star Trek Conventions around the country. If there were any thoughts in their minds of being typecast in their Star Trek roles, the love and devotion of their fans long ago proved to them that "that ain't so bad after all!" They have carved a permanent niche for themselves in all our hearts until the end of time—and beyond!

So, as we fervently hope for the return (in whatever form) of our beloved *Enterprise*, let us no less fervently hope for the return of the original and familiar crew in *Star Trek IV* and all future adventures.

STAR TREK EPISODE GUIDE

Compiled by The Editors

In the past, we occasionally received letters saying something like, "I think there are Star Trek episodes I've missed. Could you give me a list of them?" We usually referred such pleas to one or more of the excellent Star Trek reference volumes where complete episode synopses and cast listings could be found. It recently occurred to us, however, that all of these references are out of print and quite difficult to find even at cons or in used bookstores. Because all of our Best of Trek books have, happily, remained in print, we decided to include a complete episode guide in this volume to serve readers as a permanent reference.

The date of the original broadcast of each episode follows the title, then primary guest stars, director and writer credits. Then a brief synopsis of the episode. Additionally, we included comments together with many of the synopses: items of historical importance, trivia, fan interpretations, and so on. We decided early on not to rate the episodes; such ratings are totally subjective and usually not informative of anything but the prejudices of the person doing the rating.

We feel that such a combination of facts will be both informative and entertaining for our readers. We only wish that we had space to describe each episode completely, as well as including all of the cast and production credits. But that would take a separate volume twice as large as this book! (Maybe someday . . .) As always, we'll be looking forward to your comments and observations.

"The Cage" (never aired; filmed in November and December 1964) Directed by: Robert Butler Written by: Gene Roddenberry

Cast: Jeffrey Hunter (Capt. Christopher Pike), Leonard Nimoy (Mr. Spock), Peter Duryea (Navigator Jose "Joe" Tyler), Majel Barrett, a.k.a. M. Leigh Hudec (Number One), Adam Roarke (C.P.O. Garrison), John Hoyt (Dr. Philip "Bones" Boyce), Laurel Goodwin (Yeoman J. M. Colt) Guest Stars: Susan Oliver (Vina), Meg Wyllie (The Keeper), Jon Lorimer (Dr. Theodore Haskins)

Returning from a disastrous engagement with the natives on Rigel VII, the *Enterprise* encounters a distress signal from Talos IV. Beaming down with a party, Pike is amazed to discover human survivors. Among them is Vina, a remarkably beautiful young woman. She lures Pike to a cave, where he is captured by fragile-appearing, large-headed aliens. The survivors vanish; they, and the distress call, were an illusion.

Pike awakes to find himself in a glasslike cell. A menagerie of alien creatures, all in similar cells, surround him. The Talosian leader, known as the Keeper, displays their irresistible mental powers to Pike. Vina again appears; she urges Pike to make the best of it, he can't resist for long because they always know what he's thinking. Pike and Vina are mentally placed into a series of entirely convincing situations which, as the Talosians intend, bring them closer together. But still Pike resists.

Having failed to blast their way into the cavern, a landing party from the ship prepares to beam inside. But only the women, Number One and Yeoman Colt are transported down. The Keeper informs Pike that because Vina seemed undesirable, he now has a choice. Pike has discovered that strong emotions, such as hate, block the Talosians' powers, and he is able to grab one of them when he tries to collect the "useless" phasers. With his hostage, Pike and his people make their way to the surface, where Number One sets a phaser to overload. The Talosians finally realize humans are willing to die rather than suffer even benign captivity. They explain that they only wanted to repopulate their barren planet, and of all the races they investigated, only humans showed the necessary ambition and drive to succeed. They are free to leave.

Vina decides to remain, however. The women beam up and Pike is shown her reason: She is actually middle-aged and hopelessly crippled from the crash. At Pike's urging, they restore her illusion of beauty, as well as implanting in her mind a scene of

Pike remaining with her. Pike beams back up and the ship warps out of orbit.

This was the first Star Trek pilot film. Portions of "The Cage" were intercut with new footage to form the two-part episode "The Menagerie" in Star Trek's first season. It is believed that no complete color print of this episode still exists; a complete black-and-white print is owned by Gene Roddenberry and occasionally shown at conventions and lectures where he appears.

Star Trek Series Cast Regulars: William Shatner (Captain James T. Kirk), Leonard Nimoy (Mr. Spock), DeForest Kelley (Doctor Leonard "Bones" McCoy), James Doohan (Lt. Commander Montgomery Scott), George Takei (Lt. Sulu), Nichelle Nichols (Lt. Uhura), Majel Barrett (Nurse Christine Chapel), Grace Lee Whitney (Yeoman Janice Rand), Walter Koenig (Ensign Pavel Chekov), John Winston (Lt. Kyle)

First Season Episodes

"The Man Trap" (September 8, 1966) Directed by: Marc Daniels Written by: George Clayton Johnson Guest Stars: Jeanne Bal (Nancy Crater), Alfred Ryder (Prof. Robert Crater)

Professor Crater and his wife, Nancy (an old flame of McCoy's), are due for annual checkups. Strangely, Nancy seems, to McCoy, not to have aged. It is soon revealed that she is actually a creature with illusory powers; the real Nancy died and the creature took her form in exchange for receiving salt from Crater. Having already killed one crewman, the creature gets on board the *Enterprise*, and kills again (including Crater). It again appears as Nancy to McCoy, causing him to hesitate almost too long to save Kirk's life. McCoy kills it, but all regret that they were forced to destroy the last of an intelligent race.

This was the first Star Trek episode aired on national TV.

"Charlie X" (September 15, 1966) Directed by: Larry Dobkin Written by: D. C. Fontana, story by Gene Roddenberry Guest Stars: Robert Walker, Jr. (Charlie Evans), Patricia McNulty (Yeoman Tina Lawton), Abraham Sofaer (Thasian)

Seventeen-year-old Charlie Evans is rescued from the seemingly-deserted planet Thasus by the USS *Antares*, then transferred to the *Enterprise*. Kirk takes the boy under his wing, hoping to teach him social mores, but Charlie is more interested in Janice Rand, on whom he has a crush. Charlie soon displays mysterious and powerful mental powers, which he uses to impress Janice and revenge himself upon imagined slights. Only Kirk can control him, but Charlie eventually defies him and uses his powers to take over the ship. A Thasian appears, explaining that his race granted Charlie the powers to enable him to survive. To protect the ship and crew, the Thasian returns Charlie to Thasus.

"Where No Man Has Gone Before" (September 22, 1966)
Directed by: James Goldstone Written by: Samuel A. Peeples Guest Stars: Gary Lockwood (Lt. Commander Gary Mitchell), Sally Kellerman (Dr. Elizabeth Dehner), Paul Fix (Dr. Mark Piper), Paul Carr (Lt. Lee Kelso), Andrea Dromm (Yeoman Smith), Lloyd Haynes (Lt. Alden)

The *Enterprise* is assigned to broach the force-field at the edge of the galaxy, and suffers damage from the strange energy in it. Both Mitchell (Kirk's best friend) and Dr. Dehner are affected by the energy, which causes their mental powers to expand exponentially. Mitchell's abilities develop faster, and he soon decides he is a god. Spock advises Kirk to kill Mitchell while it is still possible, but Kirk cannot bring himself to do so, choosing instead to abondon Mitchell at an unmanned mining colony. On the planet, Mitchell escapes. Kirk hunts him down and, with the aid of a still-human Dehner (who dies in the effort), kills him.

This was the second pilot for Star Trek, filmed in July 1965, and the episode that convinced NBC to buy the series. Many of the principal parts were recast, including the doctor, before filming began on the series in May 1966.

Many fans consider events in this episode to mark the beginning of the Kirk/Spock friendship. For the first time, Spock calls Kirk "Jim," and admits that he has emotions, albeit controlled.

"The Naked Time" (September 29, 1966)
Directed by: Marc Daniels Written by: John D. F. Black Guest Cast: Bruce Hyde (Lt. Kevin Riley), John Bellah (Dr. Harrison), Stewart Moss (Joe Tormolen)

On the frozen planet Psi 2000, *Enterprise* crewmen contract a virus that relaxes inhibitions and releases one's basic nature. Soon, many of the crew are infected—Sulu becomes "d'Artagnan,"

Riley reverts to a sentimental Irishman, Spock cries because he never told his mother he loved her, Kirk fears losing the *Enterprise*. Riley capriciously shuts off the engines, and the ship is spiraling in to crash. McCoy discovers an antidote, but Spock and Scotty have to "cold start" the engines. The resulting backlash sends the ship backward through time; the crew now has three days to live over again.

This is the first episode to feature Kevin Riley, a favorite with fans although he appeared only twice. This is also the first episode in which Christine Chapel appears.

"The Enemy Within" (October 6, 1966) Directed by: Leo Penn Written by: Richard Matheson Guest Stars: Jim Goodwin (Lt. John Farrell), Edward Madden (Technician Fisher), Garland Thompson (Tech. Wilson), Don Either (double for Kirk)

Due to a transporter malfunction, Kirk is split into two beings, one mild and rational, the other ruthless and emotional; also, several members of a landing party led by Sulu are stranded in sub-zero temperatures. Kirk's "evil" double cannily escapes detection until he drunkenly tries to rape Yeoman Rand. He is captured, but the "good" side of Kirk finds that he is unable to act decisively—he needs his ruthless side to be a commander. Scotty repairs the transporter as best he can, but is dubious—it could kill both of them to be reunited. The two Kirks join their compassion and courage, and are again united into one man. The landing party is rescued in the nick of time.

"Mudd's Women" (October 13, 1966) Directed by: Harvey Hart Written by: Stephen Kandel, story by Gene Roddenberry Guest Stars: Roger C. Carmel (Harcourt Fenton "Harry" Mudd), Karen Steele (Eve McHuron), Maggie Thrett (Ruth Bonaventure), Susan Denberg (Magda Kovas), Gene Dynarski (Ben Childress)

The *Enterprise* rescues the captain of a small merchant ship, Harry Mudd, and his "cargo": three breathtakingly beautiful women. The women unnaturally affect the men of the *Enterprise*, so much so that Kirk becomes suspicious of Mudd. Mudd turns out to be an intergalactic conman, and the women have been taking the outlawed "Venus drug," a substance that artificially makes humans beautiful and irresistible; they are actually quite plain. The effort of saving Mudd and the women overextended the lithium crystals; Kirk orders the ship to a mining colony on Rigel XII. Mudd secretly contacts the lonely miners, who refuse to give Kirk the crystals until he surrenders the prisoners. Kirk has no choice but to give in, but before he can get the crystals, Eve runs away into a sandstorm, ashamed of the deception. Childress finds her, and they fall in love without the help of the drug. He gives Kirk the crystals and Mudd is again to be sent for rehabilitation.

Harry Mudd is also very popular with fans; he, too, appeared in only two episodes. Mudd appeared a third time in the animated episode "Mudd's Passion"; the voice was that of Roger C. Carmel.

"What Are Little Girls Made Of?" (October 20, 1966) Directed by: James Goldstone Written by: Robert Bloch Guest Stars: Michael Strong (Dr. Roger Korby), Ted Cassidy (Ruk), Sherry Jackson (Andrea), Harry Basch (Dr. Brown)

Kirk is amazed to receive a message from Dr. Roger Korby, long thought lost on Exo III. He beams down with Korby's fiancee, Nurse Chapel. Korby reveals he's been in hiding to develop an amazing discovery—duplication of humans with android doubles. With the aid of his giant android Ruk, Korby makes a duplicate of Kirk and sends it to the *Enterprise*. However, Kirk has managed to instill the double with an irrational bigotry, which alerts Spock that something is wrong. Kirk discovers that Ruk is the last of a race of androids who turned on and destroyed their masters, thereby forcing Korby to destroy Ruk. Korby is revealed as an android himself, explaining his irrational behavior. He pleads with Christine to love him, but when she turns away, he destroys himself. Christine decides to remain on the *Enterprise*.

Most fans feel that it was only after this episode that Christine began to fall in love with Spock, regardless of her behavior in "The Naked Time."

"Miri" (October 27, 1966) Directed by: Vincent McEveety Written by: Adrian Spies Guest Stars: Kim Darby (Miri), Michael J. Pollard (Jahn)

Beaming down to a planet that is almost an exact duplicate of Earth, Kirk and the landing party discover it is populated solely by children, all of whom are hundreds of years old, thanks to a virus that prolongs the life of children. But it kills adults. All except Spock are infected and must remain isolated on the planet until a cure can be found. Miri, a girl nearing adulthood, gets a crush on Kirk. When he offhandedly hurts her feelings, she and her friends steal the communicators, depriving McCoy of the use of the ship's computers. Running out of time, Kirk risks facing the children directly, and manages to convince them that they all will eventually contract the virus and die. In the meantime, McCoy successfully tested a serum on himself. The children will now age normally and will be cared for by Federation experts.

"Dagger of the Mind" (November 3, 1966) Directed by: Vincent McEveety Written by: Shimon Wincelberg (S. Bar-David) Guest Stars: James Gregory (Dr. Simon Adams), Marianna Hill (Dr. Helen Noel), Morgan Woodward (Dr. Simon van Gelder), Suzanne Wasson (Lethe)

A manic escapee from the Tantalus V penal colony is actually Dr. Simon van Gelder. Beaming down to investigate with psychiatrist Helen Noel, Kirk is captured by colony director Simon Adams, and subjected to electronic brainwashing under the "neural neutralizer." Spock learns of the plot through a mind meld with van Gelder. Helen manages to escape and cut off the power, freeing Kirk and allowing Spock to beam down through the security shields. They discover that Dr. Adams has fallen under the spell of his own device and was killed.

This is the first episode to feature a mind meld. When McCoy suggests they try it, Spock says that he could not have done so himself because of cultural inhibitions.

"The Corbomite Maneuver" (November 10, 1966) Directed by: Joe Sargent Written by: Jerry Sohl Guest Stars: Anthony Call (Lt. Dave Bailey), Clint Howard (Balok)

Warned away by an alien space buoy, Kirk decides to forge ahead. Soon an immense alien ship appears. It is commanded by Balok, who appears on the viewscreen as a fearsome monster. He condemns the *Enterprise* to destruction. Kirk bluffs, saying that the "corbomite" in the hull will destroy both ships if they're fired upon. Caught by a tractor beam, the *Enterprise* breaks away, apparently disabling the larger ship. Kirk then decides to answer a distress call. He discovers it is manned by only one person, a childlike being who is the real Balok. Kirk, and consequently his people, have passed the test of compassion and friendship. Kirk decides to leave previously xenophobic Lt. Dave Bailey onboard as an envoy to Balok's race.

"Corbomite" was a bluff Kirk was to use again. In this episode, Spock comments that the fearsome false face of Balok reminded him of his father.

"The Menagerie" (Part 1—November 17, 1966; Part 2—November 24, 1966) Directed by: Marc Daniels and Robert Butler Written by: Gene Roddenberry Guest Stars: Malachi Throne (Commodore Jose I. Mendez), Julie Parrish (Miss Piper), Sean Kenney (injured Pike), Hagan Beggs (Lt. Hansen), George Sawaya (Chief Humboldt)

The *Enterprise*, arriving at Starbase 11, discovers that no one there sent the orders. Spock takes the opportunity to call on Captain Christopher Pike, who has been paralyzed in an accident. He is in an automated wheelchair, unable to move or even speak; his only means of communication is through a small, blinking light. It's soon revealed that Spock has been tampering with the computers; he virtually kidnaps Pike and the *Enterprise* and sets course for forbidden planet Talos IV. Kirk and Mendez give chase in a shuttle, which Spock is forced to take aboard when its engines fail. He surrenders himself, but refuses to unlock the computers; the ship is still heading for Talos. Mendez orders an immediate court martial. At the trial, Spock offers as his defense scenes of his and Pike's first visit to Talos IV. (Footage from "The Cage.") By the time the ship reaches Talos, Kirk understands that the images are coming from the Talosians, and that Spock is offering Pike freedom from his physical body. All charges are dropped in deference to Pike's record, and the Talosians warmly welcome him "home." Kirk allows Spock to see him off, warning him that they'll talk about Spock's recent "tendency toward emotional behavior." The last image Kirk receives shows Pike, his youth and health restored, walking arm-in-arm with Vina.

"The Conscience of the King" (December 8, 1966) Directed by: Gerd Oswald Written by: Barry Travers Guest Stars: Arnold Moss (Anton Karidan), Barbara Anderson (Lenore Karidan), Bruce Hyde (Lt. Kevin Riley)

Dr. Leighton, of Planet Q, tells Kirk of his suspicions that

Shakespearean actor Anton Karidan is actually Kodos the Executioner, who killed millions on Tarsus IV twenty years ago. He's mysteriously killed, leaving only Kirk and Kevin Riley as surviving witnesses to the massacre. Kirk is convinced Karidan is Kodos, but has no evidence. He orders the troupe aboard the *Enterprise*, hoping to confirm or deny the identification. Kevin is poisoned; he recovers, then seeing Karidan and convinced he's Kodos, tries to kill him. Kirk stops him, wanting to bring Karidan to justice. When Karidan's daughter Lenore tries to kill him, Kirk realizes that she has been killing to protect her father. Kodos takes the fatal phaser blast intended for Kirk, and Lenore goes insane.

"Balance of Terror" (December 15, 1966) Directed by: Vincent McEveety Written by: Paul Schneider Guest Stars: Mark Lenard (Romulan commander), Paul Comi (Lt. Andrew Stiles), Lawrence Montaigne (Decius), John Warburton (Centurion), Stephen Mines (Specialist Robert Tomlinson), Barbara Baldavin (Spec. 2/C Angela Martine)

Kirk is officiating at the wedding of Robert Tomlinson and Angela Martine when news of a Romulan attack on Outpost 4 arrives. The *Enterprise* pursues, but the Romulan ship has a new invisibility screen. The ships play cat-and-mouse into the Neutral Zone between the Romulan Empire and the Federation. A view of the Romulan bridge shows them to be Vulcan-like; Lt. Stiles, whose family fought in the Romulan Wars years before, suspects Spock of being in collusion with them. The Romulan Commander is a man tired of battle, disgusted by his "dishonorable" sneak attack, and wanting only to go home, but Kirk's relentless pursuit forces him to turn and fight. A final clash leaves both ships damaged. A poisonous coolant leak causes the phasers to misfire; Spock repairs the damage, fires the phasers, and pulls Stiles and Tomlinson from the room. The Romulan ship is disabled, and the Commander orders it self-destructed. Stiles recovers and begins to rethink his bigotry toward Vulcans. Sadly, Tomlinson dies, leaving Angela heartbroken.

This episode was Mark Lenard's first appearance in Star Trek. Barbara Baldavin appeared in the next episode as "Angela Teller"; fans now assume she used the hyphenated name, Martine-Teller. Lawrence Montaigne appeared next in the first episode of the second season, "Amok Time," as the hapless Stonn. This episode was the only appearance of the original "Bird of Prey" Romulan vessel; when next seen again ("The Deadly Years"), the Romulans are using Klingon-style ships.

"Shore Leave" (December 29, 1966) Directed by: Robert Sparr Written by: Theodore Sturgeon Guest Stars: Emily Banks (Yeoman Tonia Barrows), Bruce Mars (Finnegan), Oliver McGowan (Caretaker), Barbara Baldavin (Spec. 2/C Angela Teller), Perry Lopez (Lt. Esteban Rodriguez), Shirley Bonne (Ruth), Marcia Brown (Alice Liddell)

An unexplored planet seems perfect for shore leave, which the *Enterprise* crew sorely needs. On a landing party to investigate, McCoy sees a white rabbit, followed by Alice (of Wonderland). Kirk encounters Finnegan, the bane of his Academy days, and Ruth, his first love. Sulu encounters an angry Samurai. Yeoman Barrows first dreams up Don Juan, then a Black Knight, who impales McCoy on his lance, killing him. Kirk and Spock soon realize the entire planet is an amusement park, albeit a dangerous one, where even casual wishes become reality. A caretaker appears, confirming their theory. With him is a healthy McCoy, brought back to life by the aliens' advanced science. Beyond confirming the need of all advanced races to play occasionally, the caretaker refuses to answer Kirk's questions, but invites the crew to spend their leave enjoying the wonders of the planet.

"The Galileo Seven" (January 5, 1967) Directed by: Robert Gist Written by: Oliver Crawford and S. Bar-David, story by Oliver Crawford Guest Stars: Don Marshall (Lt. Boma), Peter Marko (Gaetano), Reese Vaughn (Latimer), Phyllis Douglas (Yeoman Mears), John Crawford (Commissioner Ferris)

Spock, McCoy, Scott, and four others are stranded on a barren planet when their shuttlecraft breaks down. On the *Enterprise*, Kirk must contend with Commissioner Ferris, who wants to abandon the search, as well as instrument interference from a nearby star. Two of Spock's crew are killed by giant, hostile humanoids, causing McCoy and Boma to exchange bitter words with him. The shuttle is repaired just as the *Enterprise* is leaving the system, and Spock jettisons and ignites their remaining fuel to serve as a beacon. They are found, and McCoy realizes that even Spock can take a gamble.

This episode is considered by many to be the beginning of Spock and McCoy's friendship, despite the harsh words that pass between them. Stock footage from this episode, as well as the full-sized shuttle mockup, would be used throughout the series, giving the impression that all the shuttles onboard the Enterprise were named Galileo 7.

"The Squire of Gothos" (January 12, 1967) Directed by: Don McDougall Written by: Paul Schneider Guest Stars: William Campbell (Trelane), Venita Wolf (Yeoman Teresa Ross), Michael Barrier (Lt. DeSalle), Richard Carlyle (Lt. Karl Jaeger)

Kirk and several crewmen are captured by Trelane, the self-styled "squire" of Gothos, a planet that exists where none should. Trelane has viewed Earth culture of the eighteenth century, and patterned his life on it. Displaying godlike powers, Trelane forces the crew to participate in indulgent, childlike games. Kirk manages to destroy his power source. Warping out of orbit, the crew is shocked to see Gothos apparently following them. Angrily, Kirk beams back down and faces off with Trelane. They duel with swords, Trelane using his powers to toy with Kirk. As he is about to kill the captain, two glowing spheres appear. They are Trelane's parents; he is, after all, only a willful and spoiled child. They apologize to Kirk (refusing to reveal more about themselves) and return him to the ship. Trelane is to be punished for abusing his "pets."

William Campbell returned in "The Trouble with Tribbles" as the Klingon, Captain Koloth.

"Arena" (January 19, 1967) Directed by: Joseph Pevney Written by: Gene L. Coon (from a story by Fredric Brown) Guest Stars: Carole Shelyne (Metron), Jerry Ayers (Lt. O'Herlihy), Grant Woods (Lt. Commander Kelowitz), Bobby Clark/Gary Coombs (Gorn)

The Gorn attack Federation base Cestus III because they feel it infringes on their territory. Kirk follows their ship, intending to battle, but both ships are intercepted by the Metrons, an advanced race. Kirk and the Gorn captain are transported to the surface of a barren planet, there to battle to the death. The Gorn is a huge lizardlike creature, much stronger than Kirk. Kirk stays out of his way long enough to use minerals to form gunpowder, then fire sharp crystals into the Gorn's hide with a makeshift bamboo cannon. Wounded, the Gorn cannot prevent Kirk from attacking him with a knifelike crystal shard. Kirk refuses to kill the helpless Gorn, however, defying the edict of the Metrons. A Metron appears; he tells Kirk the true test was of mercy, not killing, thereby Kirk has "won." He returns them both to their ships, and the area is declared off-limits.

Fredric Brown's original story involved a battle between a human and a ball-like creature. By killing the creature, the human assured the survival of his race.

"Tomorrow Is Yesterday" (January 26, 1967) Directed by: Michael O'Herlihy Written by: D. C. (Dorothy) Fontana Guest Stars: Roger Perry (Capt. John Christopher), Hal Lynch (Air Policeman), Ed Peck (Col. Fellini)

The "slingshot effect" of a near-collision with a black star sends the *Enterprise* back through time to the 1960s. SAC fighters are scrambled to intercept the "UFO," and one of them is inadvertently destroyed by the *Enterprise*. The pilot, Christopher, is reluctantly beamed aboard. Kirk and Sulu beam down to destroy photos and computer records, encountering military police. Spock frees them with Christopher's help. The only problem now is what to do with Christopher (and an air policeman who was accidentally beamed up, as well). Because his son is destined to be on the first Saturn probe, they can't take him back with them. Spock and Scotty devise a way to return the men back to a time just before they were beamed up, while the ship is in the process of returning to its own time. The men do not remember anything; for them, none of it ever happened.

The time-travel process could be duplicated and was used again in "Assignment: Earth." "Captain Christopher" was one of the names Gene Roddenberry considered giving to his starship commander when first planning Star Trek.

"Courtmartial" (February 2, 1967) Directed by: Marc Daniels Written by Don M. Mankiewicz and Stephen W. Carabatsos, story by Don M. Mankiewicz Guest Stars: Elisha Cook, Jr. (Samuel T. Cogley), Percy Rodriguez (Commodore Stone), Joan Marshall (Lt. Areel Shaw), Richard Webb (Lt. Commander Ben Finney), Alice Rawlings (Jamie Finney)

Computer tapes seem to show that Kirk panicked in a crisis and caused the death of Ben Finney; a court-martial is ordered.

The prosecuting attorney is Areel Shaw, an old flame of Kirk's; the defense attorney is Sam Cogley, an old-style lawyer who disdains and distrusts computers. Testimony weighs heavily against Kirk, particularly the fact that he and Finney were once close friends until Kirk caused him to be reduced in rank. Spock, by playing chess with the computer, finds that it has been tampered with, and the only other person with the skill to do so was Finney himself—therefore, Finney must still be alive. By isolating the sound of the crew's heartbeats, Finney's hiding place is discovered, and he admits to the deception. Kirk is cleared and wins a kiss from Areel. Cogley eagerly takes on Finney's defense.

"The Return of the Archons" (February 9, 1967) Directed by: Joseph Pevney Written by: Boris Sobelman, story by Gene Roddenberry Guest Stars: Harry Townes (Reger), Torin Thatcher (Marplon), Charles McCauley (Landru), Christopher Held (Lindstrom), Brioni Farrell (Tula)

Enterprise crewmen are being brainwashed—"absorbed into the Body"—into the computer-controlled, static society of Beta III. (The natives call them "archons," because of a visit to the planet a century before by the USS *Archon*.) The computer, known as Landru, is also draining the engine's power. Kirk and Spock, working against time, manage to locate and convince the computer to destroy itself, freeing the people of the planet to self-determination.

"Space Seed" (February 16, 1967) Directed by: Marc Daniels Written by: Gene L. Coon and Carey Wilbur Guest Stars: Ricardo Montalban (Khan Noonian Singh), Madelyn Ruhe (Lt. Marla McGivers), Mark Tobin (Joaquin), Blaisdell Makee (Lt. Spinelli)

A "sleeper ship" from the 1990s is found to contain Khan Noonian Singh, a despot who fled the aftermath of the Eugenics Wars, and his followers. Awakened, Khan plots to take over the *Enterprise* with the aid of the ship's historian, Marla, who is totally infatuated by him. He succeeds, but is unable to force any of the crewmen to cooperate with him. He places Kirk in a decompression chamber as an example, but Marla frees the captain, and he and Spock retake the ship with knockout gas. Khan escapes to engineering, where he plans to blow up the ship, but is narrowly defeated in hand-to-hand combat by Kirk.

Unwilling to turn Khan in for rehabilitation, Kirk decides to maroon him and his followers on Ceti Alpha V, a planet that can be "tamed." Marla decides to go with Khan. Spock comments that it would be interesting to return in a hundred years or so to see what grew from the seed Kirk planted.

Of course, we learned of the tragic fate of Khan and his people in Star Trek II: The Wrath of Khan. *Star Trek fans now generally agree that the bias against genetic experiments caused by the "Eugenics Wars" is partly responsible for the fact that people in Star Trek's time still age and become ill or infirm much as we do today, as well as for many other anachronisms seen in the series.*

"A Taste of Armageddon" (February 23, 1967) Directed by: Joseph Pevney Written by: Robert Hamner and Gene L. Coon, story by Robert Hamner Guest Stars: Gene Lyons (Ambassador Robert Fox), David Opatoshu (Anan 7), Barbara Babcock (Mea 3)

Eminiar VII has been waging a centuries-long computer war with its neighbor Vendikar; citizens "killed" report to disintegration centers. Federation Ambassador Fox beams down despite warnings to stay away. The *Enterprise* is declared "hit" by the computers, and Fox, Kirk, Spock, and the rest of the landing party are taken captive. They escape and destroy Eminiar's computer link; now the council will be forced to talk with their counterparts to prevent real war. Fox offers his good offices to make a real peace.

"This Side of Paradise" (March 2, 1967) Directed by: Ralph Senensky Written by: D. C. Fontana, story by Nathan Butler and D. C. Fontana Guest Stars: Jill Ireland (Leila Kalomi), Frank Overton (Elias Sandoval), Eddie Paskey (Lt. Leslie), Grant Woods (Lt. Cmdr. Kelowitz)

Strange alien spores found on Omicron Ceti III have prevented colonists from dying from Berthold radiation; they also induce feelings of harmony and peace, as well as stifling ambition and aggression. Leila Kalomi, who was in love with Spock years ago, exposes him to the spores, which release his emotional side to the point where he becomes a carefree romantic. Very soon the entire crew is affected, and begins beaming down en masse. Kirk is the last to be exposed, but manages to shake off the effect when he realizes he would be giving up the *Enterprise*. Theorizing strong emotions destroy the spores, Kirk beams up Spock and taunts him into anger. The Vulcan almost kills Kirk before coming to his senses, and they use ultrasound to free the others on the surface. The colonists, including Leila, plan to relocate. Spock later admits to Kirk it was the only time in his life he had ever been really happy.

"The Devil in the Dark" (March 9, 1967) Directed by: Joseph Pevney Written by: Gene L. Coon Guest Stars: Ken Lynch (Chief Engineer Vanderberg), Janos Prohaska (Horta), Barry Russo (Lt. Commander Giotto)

Miners on Janus VI are being killed by a ghostly something that vanishes almost instantly. Kirk and Spock arrive to investigate and discover a large, rocklike creature is the killer. It emits an acid that can dissolve stone. After it is wounded by a phaser, Spock mind-melds with it and learns that it is a female, called a Horta, concerned that the miners are destroying her eggs, which they've mistaken for worthless silicon nodules. McCoy binds her wound with cement, and peace is made between the species. Soon the miners report the eggs are hatching and baby Hortas are burrowing happily, exposing rich new veins of ore.

This is the first time we learn that Spock can mind-meld with species other than humanoids.

"Errand of Mercy" (March 23, 1967) Directed by: John Newland Written by: Gene L. Coon Guest Stars: John Colicos (Commander Kor), Jon Abbott (Ayelborne), David Hillary Hughes (Trefayne), Peter Brocco (Claymare)

Kirk and Spock beam down to the primitive planet Organia to convince the neutral Organians to permit the construction of a Federation base. Permission is denied. Before they can leave, a Klingon task force arrives, forcing the *Enterprise* to retreat. Kirk and Spock attempt to disguise themselves, but the Klingon commander recognizes them. Spock survives a session with a Klingon "mind-sifter." Above, Starfleet and Klingon forces are moving into battle positions. Kirk and Spock are freed by the Organians, who want them with Kor, so they can explain: They are creatures of energy, far above humanoids in the evolutionary scale, possessing great powers and will not permit a war to occur. Weapons become too hot to hold; in space, ships are rendered immobile.

A peace treaty will be negotiated and enforced by them. Kor is chagrined that there will be no war: "It would have been glorious!"

This was the first episode to feature Klingons, although their ships were not seen. James Blish's Star Trek novel, Spock Must Die!, *is a direct sequel to this episode. However, because events in it have been shown impossible by later films and stories, it is now considered apocryphal by most fans.*

"The Alternative Factor" (March 30, 1967) Directed by: Gerd Oswald Written by: Don Ingalls Guest Stars: Robert Brown (Lazarus), Janet McLachlan (Lt. Charlene Masters), Richard Derr (Commodore Barstow), Eddie Paskey (Lt. Leslie)

The *Enterprise*, and the surrounding solar system, seem to blink out of existence for a moment. Investigating on the planet below, the crew encounters Lazarus, who claims the effect was caused by the arrival of his enemy. The enemy turns out to be an exact double of Lazarus from another dimension, who is evil. Only one of them can appear in either universe at any one time; if they ever meet in either, both will be destroyed. With Kirk's aid, the good Lazarus sacrifices himself to trap his double in the limbo between dimensions, where they will battle forever.

"The City on the Edge of Forever" (April 6, 1967) Directed by: Joseph Pevney Written by: Harlan Ellison Guest Stars: Joan Collins (Edith Keeler), Hall Boyler (Policeman), David L. Ross (Lt. Galloway), Bartell LaRue (voice of Guardian), John Harmon (Rodent)

The ship is examining an area of time displacement when McCoy accidentally receives an overdose of cordrazine, which causes him to go temporarily insane, and he flees the ship. Beaming down to the surface, the crew discovers an ancient, large, donut-shaped artifact among the ruins of a city. It speaks, identifying itself as the Guardian of Forever, displaying scenes from the past. McCoy leaps through it, vanishing into the past. When Kirk tries to contact the ship, the Guardian tells him it no longer exists; McCoy has somehow changed the past and the Federation never came to be. Kirk and Spock have no choice but to follow McCoy, hoping to arrive before he does and stop him. They arrive in Chicago in the 1930s, where they obtain temporary jobs in a mission run by Edith Keeler. Kirk soon falls in love with the gentle, farsighted woman. Using his tricorder and native electronics, Spock discovers that Edith was meant to die; if she lives, she will form a pacifist group that will delay America's entrance into World War II, allowing Hitler to win and effectively destroying all of the future. Obviously, McCoy somehow stopped her from dying. Unknown to them, McCoy arrived several days before, and when he sees Edith about to be hit by a truck, moves to save her. Kirk, hesitating only a split second, stops him and Edith dies. History restored, the Guardian brings them back, where a heartbroken Kirk beams his party back to the ship.

The Guardian of Forever appeared again in the animated episode "Yesteryear."

"Operation: Annihilate!" (April 13, 1967) Directed by: Herschel Daugherty Written by: Stephen W. Carabatsos Guest Stars: Craig Hundley (Peter Kirk), Joan Swift (Aurelan Kirk), Dave Armstrong (Kartan), Maurishka Taliferro (Yeoman Zahra Jamal)

Deneva is attacked by flying creatures that insinuate into the nervous system, causing insanity and death. Among those killed are Kirk's brother and his wife; his nephew is infected. Spock is also infected; although having a period of insanity, he manages to fight off the attacks enough to work. He and McCoy theorize that intense light will kill the creatures. Spock volunteers; the creature is destroyed, but Spock is blinded. Too late, McCoy discovers that only the ultraviolet spectrum is needed to kill the parasites, and the planet is bathed in it. Spock shows up with his sight restored; a protective "inner eyelid" indigenous to Vulcans protected him from permanent harm.

Second Season Episodes

"Amok Time" (September 15, 1967) Directed by: Joseph Pevney Written by: Theodore Sturgeon Guest Stars: Arlene Martel (T'Pring), Celia Lovsky (T'Pau), Lawrence Montaigne (Stonn), Byron Morrow (Admiral Komack)

Spock, who has been acting strangely for several days, is ordered by Kirk to report for a medical exam. McCoy finds that unless he gets to Vulcan, he will die. Spock reluctantly reveals to Kirk that he must return for the consummation of his marriage to T'Pring, a Vulcan female to whom he was bonded as a child. Defying orders to the contrary, Kirk heads for Vulcan, where he and McCoy are invited by Spock to attend the ceremony, presided over by the Vulcan patriarch, T'Pau. The bride has other plans, however, and chooses the ancient ritual of challenge. She chooses Kirk as her champion; he agrees to fight Spock without knowing it is to the death. Spock, deep in the throes of irrational Vulcan *pon farr*, tries his best to kill Kirk. McCoy gives Kirk an "oxygen" shot that causes him to collapse, appearing dead. Spock's rage vanishes with the satisfaction of bloodlust, as does his desire for T'Pring. McCoy beams up to the ship with the "body." T'Pring explains that she did not wish to be Spock's wife, and by choosing Kirk, she would be free to stay with her lover, Stonn, however the contest ended. Returning to the ship, Spock smiles broadly with astonished joy when he discovers that Kirk is alive.

We get our only glimpse of Vulcan seen in the series in this episode. Much of the speculation about Spock and Vulcan sexuality, life-styles, society, morality, and such have stemmed from this single episode.

"Who Mourns for Adonais?" (September 22, 1967) Directed by: Marc Daniels Written by: Gilbert Ralston and Gene L. Coon, story by Gilbert Ralston Guest Stars: Leslie Parrish (Lt. Carolyn Palamas), Michael Forrest (Apollo)

The *Enterprise* is seized in space by a giant energy hand formed by a being identifying himself as the legendary Greek god Apollo. He has been waiting for mankind to achieve the stars, and now he wants to again be worshiped by them. He forms an attachment to Carolyn Palamas (whom Scotty also desires). Although she falls in love with Apollo, she reluctantly helps Kirk destroy his source of power. Realizing mankind has grown beyond the need for gods, Apollo disperses his essence on the winds of space.

The original ending of this script, apparently censored by the network, had Carolyn pregnant with Apollo's child.

"The Changeling" (September 29, 1967) Directed by: Marc Daniels Written by: John Meredyth Lucas Guest Stars: Blaisdell Makee (Mr. Singh), Barbara Gates (Astrochemist), Vic Perrin (voice of Nomad)

A small probe identifying itself as Nomad has destroyed several planets, but halts when it decides that Kirk is its "creator."

Brought aboard the ship, it tinkers with the engines, wipes clean Uhura's memory, and kills, then revives, Scotty. Spock discovers via mind meld that it is a combination of an Earth probe (created by Jackson Roy*kirk*) and an alien probe of great power. It now feels its mission is to destroy all that is not perfect. Revealing that he is not Roykirk, Kirk convinces Nomad that it has made a mistake, and therefore must be destroyed. While the machine is locked in this conundrum, Kirk has it beamed into space, where it blows up.

Many fans feel that elements of this episode were recycled into Star Trek: The Motion Picture.

"Mirror, Mirror" (October 6, 1967) Directed by: Marc Daniels Written by: Jerome Bixby Guest Stars: Barbara Luna (Lt. Marlena Moreau), Vic Perrin (Tharn), Pete Kellett (Farrell), Garth Pillsbury (Wilson)

Kirk unsuccessfully negotiates for dilithium with the pacifistic Halkans. Beaming up during an ion storm, he, Uhura, McCoy, and Scott are interchanged with their doubles from an alternate universe. They find themselves aboard the Imperial Starship *Enterprise*, and greeted by a bearded Spock. In this ruthless society, promotion comes by assassination and treachery. Kirk must contend with attempts on his life by the mirror world Chekov and Sulu, as well as conceal his true identity from the "Captain's woman," Marlena Moreau, while coming up with a convincing reason to spare the alternate world Halkans. The others, led by Scotty, work to find a way back. Before they leave, Kirk urges the mirror-Spock to consider the illogic of an unstable Empire.

"The Apple" (October 13, 1967) Directed by: Joseph Pevney Written by: Max Ehrlich and Gene L. Coon, story by Max Ehrlich Guest Stars: Keith Andes (Akuta), Celeste Yarnall (Yeoman Martha Landon), Shari Nims (Sayana), David Soul (Makora)

Humanoids live in perpetual youth and health on Gamma Trianguli VI, thanks to the intervention of a godlike computer named Vaal, which they worship and feed radioactive rocks as fuel. When the natives begin emulating the loving actions of Chekov and Martha, the computer begins draining the power from the *Enterprise*. Kirk orders Scotty to phaser Vaal's defenses, draining its power, while he prevents the natives from "feeding" it. It finally "dies," freeing the natives to develop normally.

"The Doomsday Machine" (October 20, 1967) Directed by: Marc Daniels Written by: Norman Spinrad Guest Stars: William Windom (Commodore Matthew Decker), Elizabeth Rogers (Lt. Palmer), John Copage (Elliot), Richard Compton (Washburn)

The USS *Constellation*, commanded by Kirk's old friend, Matt Decker, is found derelict. A giant robot war machine from another galaxy is breaking up planets, then using the debris for fuel to destroy others. It killed Decker's crew while he watched helplessly; he is in shock. Kirk orders Decker sent to the *Enterprise* sickbay, while he and Scott try to repair the *Constellation*. A power failure puts them temporarily out of touch. When the planet eater returns, Decker, obsessed with the idea of destroying it, takes command and orders an attack that damages the *Enterprise*. Contact restored, Kirk removes him and orders Spock to leave the area. Decker steals a shuttlecraft and flies it into the machine's maw, hoping to destroy its interior. He's killed, but Spock notes the power dropped somewhat. Figuring more power is needed, Kirk himself pilots the *Constellation* into the creature, even though a malfunctioning transporter means he may not be able to escape. Scotty pulls him off in time, and the planet eater is deactivated.

Matt Decker is the father of Captain Will Decker, the man Kirk personally chooses to replace him as captain of the Enterprise.

"Catspaw" (October 27, 1967) Directed by: Joseph Pevney Written by: Robert Bloch Guest Stars: Antoinette Bower (Sylvia), Theo Marcuse (Korob), Michael Barrier (Lt. DeSalle), Jimmy Jones (Jackson)

A beautiful witch, Sylvia, and her warlock companion, Korob, capture Kirk and the crew in a medieval castle on Pyris VII. McCoy notes that it seems to be designed from racial memories of Halloween. Scott and Sulu are bewitched into serving them; as is later McCoy. When Kirk rebuffs Sylvia's advances, she casts him and Spock into a dungeon. Korob frees them, fearing Sylvia's emotional instability. Discovering them, she transforms herself into a giant cat, killing Korob. Kirk uses Korob's power source to destroy hers. The castle vanishes, leaving only two tiny life forms, which quickly die in the oxygen atmosphere . . . the real Sylvia and Korob.

"I, Mudd" (November 3, 1967) Directed by: Marc Daniels Written by: Stephen Kandel and David Gerrold Guest Stars: Roger C. Carmel (Harry Mudd), Kay Elliott (Stella Mudd), Richard Tatro (Norman), Rhea and Alyce Andrece (Alice series)

An android, masquerading as a new officer, jams the controls and heads the ship toward a planet populated by androids . . . and ruled by Harry Mudd. (He even has a special android duplicate of his shrewish wife that he can command to shut up.) However, Kirk soon learns that Mudd is actually also a prisoner; the androids feel such a need to serve that they will not allow him to leave. So Harry made a deal: the *Enterprise* in exchange for his freedom. The androids want more; they will use the *Enterprise* to spread themselves across the galaxy, making all men virtual prisoners. With Mudd's help, the crew manages to confuse the android computer interface with illogic, short-circuiting it long enough for Spock to reprogram them. The androids will now be content to build their own society. Kirk arranges for Mudd to remain as their "guest"—with hundreds of Stella androids to serve as his guards.

Harry Mudd returned in the animated episode, "Mudd's Passion."

"Metamorphosis" (November 11, 1967) Directed by: Ralph Senensky Written by: Gene L. Coon Guest Stars: Glenn Corbett (Zefrem Cochrane), Elinor Donahue (Commissioner Nancy Hedford)

Federation envoy Nancy Hedford is being shuttled by Kirk, Spock, and McCoy to the *Enterprise* for treatment of Sakuro's disease. The shuttlecraft is seized by a cloudlike creature, and forced to land on a planetoid. There they discover Zefrem Cochrane, the discoverer of warp drive, who vanished decades before. Amazingly, he is young and healthy. He explains that the cloud creature, which he calls the Companion, has kept him so by use of unknown energy; the creature also brought the shuttle down to provide him with permanent company. Attempting to communicate with it, Spock discovers that it is female and in love with Cochrane. He is horrified; and the Companion resultingly heartbroken. It merges its essence with Nancy Hedford's at the moment of her death, resulting in a healthy human body with both the Companion's and Nancy's minds. However, the Companion's life essence is tied to the planetoid; if she leaves, she will quickly die. Cochrane decides to remain; her love means more to him than all the wonders and honors waiting for him back home.

"Journey To Babel" (November 17, 1967) Directed by: Joseph Pevney Written by: D. C. Fontana Guest Stars: Mark Lenard (Sarek), Jane Wyatt (Amanda), William O'Connell (Thelev), Reggie Nalder (Shras), John Wheeler (Gav)

The *Enterprise* is serving as shuttle vessel for diplomats attending a Federation conference on Babel to decide if the Coridan system will be admitted. Among the last to board are Vulcan Ambassador Sarek and his wife, Amanda . . . Spock's parents. Spock and Sarek disagreed over his decision to join Starfleet and have not spoken for over eighteen years. Ambassador Gav, who openly argued with Sarek, is found murdered. Under questioning, Sarek has a heart attack. McCoy decides he needs an operation, and Spock must supply blood. Kirk is wounded by Thelev, an Orion spy posing as an Andorian, and the *Enterprise* is attacked by a super-fast and powerful ship of unknown origin. Because he is now in command, Spock refuses to stay in Sickbay. Sarek agrees it is the logical thing to do, but Amanda is outraged and heartbroken. Kirk makes light of his wound and returns to the Bridge, ordering Spock to Sickbay. Despite buffeting from the attack, McCoy manages to save Sarek's life. The attacker is defeated, and Kirk returns to Sickbay. Spock and his father make their peace, and McCoy, with everyone under his care, has the last word for once.

Mark Lenard next appeared in Star Trek: The Motion Picture *as a Klingon, making him the only actor to play all three major alien roles in Star Trek. He also returned in the role of Sarek in* Star Trek III: The Search for Spock. *This episode was the first mention of Spock's boyhood pet Sehlat, I-Chaya, seen in the animated episode "Yesteryear."*

"Friday's Child" (December 1, 1967) Directed by: Joseph Pevney Written by: D. C. Fontana Guest Stars: Julie Newman (Eleen), Tige Andrews (Kras), Michael Dante (Maab), Cal Bolder (Keel)

Kirk is ordered to negotiate mining rights on Capella IV with a people who worship bravery, honesty, and hospitality above all else. A Klingon, Kras, has arrived first, however, and is exerting undue influence upon Maab, a young chieftain. Maab kills the leader, then sets out to kill his pregnant widow before she can give birth. Kirk, Spock, and McCoy help her escape. While they battle pursuers, McCoy helps her give birth. Maab kills Kras when his treachery is discovered, himself dying in the process. The child, named Leonard James, is declared the new leader and, Eleen, as his regent, signs the agreement with the Federation.

"The Deadly Years" (December 8, 1967) Directed by: Joseph Pevney Written by: David P. Harmon Guest Stars: Charles Drake (Commodore George Stocker), Sarah Marshall (Dr. Janet Wallace), Beverly Washburn (Lt. Arlene Galway)

The *Enterprise* discovers that virtually all the colonists on Gamma Hydra IV have died of old age. Chekov is terrified when finding a dead body. Returning to the ship, Kirk, Spock, McCoy, Scott, and Lt. Arlene Galway all begin to age rapidly. Of the landing party, only Chekov is unaffected. McCoy desperately begins working on a cure. Kirk is the worst affected, but soon all the officers are too feeble to command. McCoy learns the aging is caused by radiation, and inhibited by adrenalins; Chekov's fright saved him from infection. Commodore Stocker, on board for a ride to Starbase 10, takes command, but in his inexperience with starship command makes the mistake of traveling through the Romulan Neutral Zone. When the ship is surrounded by Romulan vessels and ordered to surrender, Kirk insists that McCoy use a potentially dangerous adrenal dose on him. It works, restoring his youth, and Kirk pulls one of his famous bluffs, allowing the *Enterprise* to escape.

This is the first episode which mentions the pact between the Klingons and Romulans which resulted in Romulans utilizing Klingon ships and equipment.

"Obsession" (December 15, 1967) Directed by: Ralph Senensky Written by: Art Wallace Guest Stars: Stephen Brooks (Ensign Garrovick), Jerry Ayers (Ensign Rizzo)

Kirk is obsessed with destroying a cloudlike creature that killed his mentor, Captain Garrovick, and half the crew of the USS *Farragut* eleven years before by absorbing their red blood cells. Because he hesitated to fire at it, Kirk blames himself for their deaths. Garrovick's son, now an *Enterprise* crewman, does the same thing on Argus X, and Kirk berates him for it. When the creature attacks Spock, he gets a mind impression that the creature is intelligent, and intending to reproduce. The *Enterprise* follows it to its home planet, where a matter–antimatter bomb is set by Kirk and Garrovick, baited first by a jug of blood, then by themselves. They narrowly escape the explosion and escape. Thanks to Kirk, Garrovick is spared the years of guilt the captain himself suffered.

"Wolf In the Fold" (December 22, 1967) Directed by: Joseph Pevney Written by: Robert Bloch Guest Stars: John Fiedler (Hengist), Charles McCaulay (Jaris), Pilar Seurat (Sybo), Joseph Bernard (Tark), Charles Dierkop (Morla), Judy McConnell (Yeoman Tankris), Judi Sherven (Nurse), Tania Lemani (Kara)

On Argelius, a planet whose people are devoted hedonists, Scotty is suspected of murdering a dancing girl. He is found holding the weapon, a knife, but has no memory of the incident. Because of a head injury he recently sustained, caused by a woman, Scotty has shown hostility toward women, but was thought to be cured. Hengist, a professional bureaucrat, insists that Scotty be prosecuted. When Kirk asks a psychic to reconstruct the crime, the lights go out and she too is killed. Assembling everyone on the *Enterprise*, Spock uses logic to deduce that the evil entity once known as Jack the Ripper still exists and has been using Hengist to kill. The creature exists on fear; women are targets because they feel fear more intensely than men. The creature leaves Hengist's body and enters the *Enterprise* computers. McCoy gives everyone on board a tranquilizer. Having no fear on which to feed, the creature is forced to return to Hengist's body. Kirk orders it beamed into space at the widest angle of dispersal.

The creature returned in an issue of the D. C. *comics Star Trek book in 1985.*

"The Trouble With Tribbles" (December 29, 1967) Directed by: Joseph Pevney Written by: David Gerrold Guest Stars: William Campbell (Captain Koloth), William Schallert (Nilz Baris), Stanley Adams (Cyrano Jones), Whit Bissel (Mr. Lurry), Michael Pataki (Korax), Ed Reimers (Admiral Fitzpatrick)

Obnoxious functionary Nilz Baris orders the *Enterprise* to Space Station K-7 to guard a load of experimental grain. It is an open station; Klingons are also allowed docking privileges. Trader Cyrano Jones sells a furry little animal called a tribble to Uhura. It reproduces at a fantastic rate and before long the entire ship is filled with the creatures, who seem to eat everything in sight. Too late, it occurs to Kirk that they might be in the grain. They are, but all are dead—the grain has been poisoned. Kirk discovers the culprit, a Klingon agent, when a tribble spits at him— they love humans but hate Klingons, and the feeling is wholeheartedly reciprocated. Scotty gets rid of those on the *Enterprise* by beaming them onto the Klingon ship just as it warped out of orbit.

Gene Roddenberry has reported that the character of Captain Koloth, played by William Campbell, was intended to be a running foil for Kirk in the series' aborted fourth season.

"The Gamesters of Triskelion" (January 5, 1968) Directed by: Gene Nelson Written by: Margaret Armen Guest Stars: Angelique Pettyjohn (Shahna), Joseph Ruskin (Galt), Jane Ross (Tamoon), Steve Sandor (Lars)

Kirk, Uhura, and Chekov are captured by the "Providers," an unseen race who breed and train gladiators of all races and sexes, called Thralls. They are assigned "drill Thralls"; Kirk's is a beautiful young woman named Shahna; Chekov's a husky-voiced female named Tamoon. Going along with the training until they can devise a way to escape, Kirk romances Shahna. Kirk discovers the Providers are three glass-encased brains, kept alive by machines, who organized the games out of sheer boredom. Spock has traced them across many parsecs; the ship arrives, but is seized by the Providers. Kirk offers a wager for the freedom of his crew: himself against three Thralls. One of them is Shahna, who refuses an opportunity to kill him, allowing Kirk to win the battle. The Providers are chagrined, but Kirk convinces them that teaching the Thralls to build a civilization will prove immensely more interesting than endless wagering.

"A Piece of the Action" (January 12, 1968) Directed by: James Komack Written by: David P. Harmon and Gene L. Coon Guest Stars: Anthony Caruso (Bela Oxmyx), Vic Tayback (Jojo Krako), William Blackburn (Lt. Hadley)

A book about gangsters in the 1920s, left by the USS *Horizon* on the planet Iotia 100 years ago, has become the model upon which the imitative Iotians built their society. A gang boss, Bela Oxmyx, wants the "Feds" to help him eliminate his enemy, boss Krako. Krako wants the same deal, and the crew is caught between them. Finally having enough, Kirk and Spock, wearing snap-brim hats and double-breasted suits, "take over" the planet, consolidating all of the warring gangs under Federation control, in exchange for "a piece of the action." McCoy leaves behind his communicator, which contains a transtater, the energy source for all Starfleet equipment. Kirk wonders if the imitative and aggressive Iotians won't someday decide to renegotiate the deal.

"The Immunity Syndrome" (January 19, 1968) Directed by: Joseph Pevney Written by: Robert Sabaroff

The *Enterprise* is investigating the sudden loss of contact with solar system Gamma 7A when Spock feels in his mind the deaths of hundreds of Vulcans manning starship *Intrepid*. The cause is a gigantic amoeba from another galaxy, which emits negative particles, draining energy for food. Spock finds that it is ready to reproduce. The *Enterprise* penetrates the amoeba, but is unable to kill it. Spock uses a shuttlecraft to locate the most vulnerable point, so that an antimatter bomb can be exploded there, destroying the amoeba without splitting it. Though endangered by antibodies, Spock is rescued and the bomb exploded just in time.

"A Private Little War" (February 2, 1968) Directed by: Marc Daniels Written by: Gene Roddenberry, story by Judd Crucis Guest Stars: Michael Whitney (Tyree), Nancy Kovack (Nona), Ned Romero (Krell), Booker Marshall (Dr. M'Benga), Arthur Bernard (Apella), Janos Prohaska (Mugato)

On Neural, a planet where Kirk spent some time, the landing party is fired on by natives with flintlock rifles, a weapon generations beyond the culture Kirk knew. Spock is wounded and returned to the ship. Kirk returns with McCoy to visit Tyree, the leader of the hill people and an old friend. On the way, Kirk is attacked and wounded by a gorillalike, venomous Mugato. He's healed by Tyree's ambitious wife, Nona. The Klingons are providing the village people with the rifles, fomenting war for their own purposes. Nona urges Kirk to give Tyree better weapons, but he will only provide the same type of weapons, believing a balance of power is better than nothing. Nona steals his phaser and tries to give it to the villagers, but they kill her instead. Tyree, who has previously been pacifistic, vows revenge. Kirk sadly leaves the planet to its future of escalating warfare.

"Return To Tomorrow" (February 9, 1968) Directed by: Ralph Senensky Written by: Gene Roddenberry Guest Stars: Diana Muldaur (Dr. Ann Mulhall), Cindy Lou (Nurse), James Doohan (voice of Sargon)

On a cavern deep beneath the surface of Arrett, a barren planet, the *Enterprise* discovers three glowing globes containing the life essence of the last of the Arretians: Sargon, his wife Thalassa, and Henoch, their former enemy. Kirk, Spock, and Dr. Ann Mulhall agree to let the Arretians occupy their bodies while they construct androids to house them permanently. Henoch decides he will keep Spock's body, and plays upon Thalassa's desire to do the same. He destroys the globe containing Spock's essence. Sargon flees Kirk's body into the *Enterprise* itself, and tricks Henoch into leaving Spock, whereupon Sargon destroys Henoch. Spock's essence has been placed in Christine Chapel's mind, and is restored to his body. Sargon and Thalassa join their essences together and become one with the cosmos.

"Patterns of Force" (February 16, 1968) Directed by: Vincent McEveety Written by: John Meredyth Lucas Guest Stars: Richard Evans (Isak), Valora Noland (Daras), David Brian (John Gill), Skip Homeier (Melakon), William Wintersole (Abrom)

A routine check on planet Ekos shows the culture has somehow radically advanced. Kirk is shocked to learn that Federation historian John Gill broke his oath of noninterference and restructured the peaceful society of Ekos into a fascistic society patterned after Nazi Germany. His assistant, Melakon, has secretly seized power and is fomenting hatred and aggression against the neighboring planet, Zeon. Kirk and Spock, with the help of the underground, manage to free Gill, who goes on television to declare an end to hostilities and denounce Melakon, who shoots him. A coalition government is set up, supplanting the Nazi system, and peace between the two planets is restored.

* * *

"**By Any Other Name**" (February 23, 1968) Directed by: Marc Daniels Written by: Jerome Bixby and D. C. Fontana, story by Jerome Bixby Guest Stars: Warren Stevens (Rojan), Barbara Bouchet (Kelinda), Stewart Moss (Hanar), Robert Fortier (Tomar)

The Kelvans, a warlike race from the Andromeda galaxy, take on human form to usurp control of the *Enterprise* by transforming most of the crew into component elements. They are unused to human form, however, and the remaining crewmen take advantage of their unfamiliarity with human emotions and sensations. When the emotional reactions cause them to start bickering among themselves, Kirk is able to point out that they are becoming human . . . and in the 300 years that it will take to arrive at Kelva, their ancestors will be completely human and alien to their own race. The Kelvans agree to be placed on a Class M planet, and a robot ship is sent to Kelva with a message of peace.

"**The Omega Glory**" (March 1, 1968) Directed by: Vincent McEveety Written by: Gene Roddenberry Guest Stars: Morgan Woodward (Capt. Ronald Tracey), Roy Jensen (Cloud William), Irene Kelley (Sirah), David L. Ross (Lt. Galloway), Eddie Paskey (Lt. Leslie), Lloyd Kino (Wu)

The USS *Exeter* is found abandoned orbiting Omega IV, from which the *Enterprise* crew contracts a deadly virus. The planet's atmosphere confers immunity, so Kirk and others beam down. They discover Captain Tracey, the last survivor of the *Exeter*, who is convinced the immunity also stops aging in humans. He has taken the side of the Khoms against the Yangs, who have been fighting an ages-old war, hoping to discover the secret. Kirk and Spock are held prisoner with the leader of the Yangs. They escape and a final battle is held in which the Yangs are victorious. A U.S. flag is brought forth, causing Kirk to realize the planet is an instance of parallel evolution . . . here, the "Yanks" are still battling the "comms," communists. Tracey tries to convince the Yang leaders that Kirk and Spock are agents of the devil, and Kirk must defeat him in ritual combat. Kirk uses the "holy objects," the Constitution and Declaration of Independence, to point out that the laws and freedom are for all, even the Kohms.

Many fans prefer to view the Yangs and Kohms as being ancestors of colonists from Earth who brought their prejudices and war along with them.

"The Ultimate Computer" (March 8, 1968) Directed by: John Meredyth Lucas Written by: D. C. Fontana, story by Lawrence N. Wolfe Guest Stars: William Marshall (Dr. Richard Daystrom), Barry Russo (Commodore Robert Wesley), Sean Morgan (Ensign Harper)

The inventor of the *Enterprise* computers, Dr. Richard Daystrom, has his latest invention, the M-5 computer, installed on the ship for testing. The M-5 can completely run the ship without assistance—especially from Kirk. In a war game simulation, however, the M-5 exceeds its programming and begins to destroy Federation ships. It will not allow itself to be shut off. Daystrom, anxious to regain his former glory, has imprinted his own memory engrams into the computer, and inadvertently his own neuroses as well. Realizing what has happened, the remaining starships plan to attack; Spock fears that the computer will destroy them all. Kirk and Daystrom convince the computer that what it has done is wrong, murder, in fact, and it atones by shutting itself off, an open target for the starships. Kirk manages to contact them and the attack is halted.

"Bread and Circuses" (March 15, 1968) Directed by: Ralph Senensky Written by: Gene L. Coon and Gene Roddenberry, story by John Kneubuhl Guest Stars: William Smithers (Capt. R. M. Merik), Logan Ramsey (Claudius Marcus), Ian Wolfe (Septimus), Rhodes Reason (Flavius), Lois Jewell (Drusilla)

Investigating the wreck of the SS *Beagle*, the landing party is captured by Roman centurions in modern dress, who believe them to be part of a band of outlaw "sun worshipers." In this world, the Roman Empire never fell and is still in control of a twentieth-century level society. Kirk discovers that Captain Merik, now called Merikus, betrayed his crew into the gladiatorial games. The same fate is planned for the *Enterprise* crew. Kirk refuses to go along, and he, Spock, and McCoy are forced into the games. Scotty cuts off the city's power, and Merik, repenting, helps them escape. Back on the *Enterprise*, Uhura informs them that the "sun worshipers" actually worship "the son" of God; another parallel with Earth history.

"Assignment: Earth" (March 29, 1968) Directed by: Marc Daniels Written by: Art Wallace and Gene Roddenberry Guest

Stars: Robert Lansing (Gary Seven), Teri Garr (Roberta Lincoln), Don Keefer (Cromwell), Morgan Jones (Colonel Nesvig), Paul Baxley (Security Chief)

Using the "slingshot effect," the *Enterprise* is sent back in time to discover how Earth escaped nuclear holocaust during a particularly troubled few days in the late twentieth century. Just after arriving, the *Enterprise* intercepts a powerful transporter beam headed for Earth. Gary Seven, a handsome, middle-aged man, materializes, and immediately realizes the ship is from the future. He claims to be a twentieth-century Earth human, raised and trained by an unnamed race for the purpose of helping Earth survive. Kirk can't decide whether or not to believe him; computer records of this time are untrustworthy. Seven escapes, and Kirk and Spock follow. Seven is unable to contact his fellow agents and learns from an almost-sentient computer at his headquarters that they have been killed in an auto accident. He must complete their mission, which is to sabotage a weapons platform launch, causing enough of a panic to make the nations talk about disarming without actually scaring them into war. Roberta Lincoln, the secretary hired by the dead agents as cover, distrusts him and calls in the authorities. Seven makes his way to the rocket, but his adjustments are interrupted by Kirk, resulting in the missile going off course and threatening actually to detonate. Kirk decides to trust him, and allows him to redirect and detonate the missile. Spock promises that history has many adventures yet in store for Seven and Roberta. The *Enterprise* returns to its own time, having now determined exactly how Earth survived such a difficult period.

Seven was accompanied by an intelligent black cat with psionic powers named Isis. To Roberta's chagrin, the cat sometimes appeared as a beautiful and scantily clad young woman.

Third Season Episodes

"Spock's Brain" (September 20, 1968) Directed by: Marc Daniels Written by: Lee Cronin Guest Stars: Marj Dusay (Kara), James Daris (Morg), Sheila Leighton (Luma)

A mysterious, beautiful woman appears on the bridge of the *Enterprise* and renders everyone unconscious. When they awake, they discover Spock's body in sickbay . . . but his brain has been removed. McCoy devises a life-support system, which allows them to animate Spock's body. They pursue her ship to Sigma Draconis VI, where they discover an all-male culture living on the surface (Morgs) and females living deep beneath the surface (Eymorgs), using technology they are too unintelligent to understand. The woman who stole Spock's brain, Kara, is located, but has the mind of a child. Spock's brain has been placed into a computer that controls the machinery of the planet, and he tells them that "the Teacher," an electronic device, was used to boost her intelligence. McCoy is forced to use the Teacher on himself, and is able to begin to reunite Spock's brain with his body. Before the operation is completed, however, the knowledge fades, and McCoy is lost until Spock himself, now partly conscious, helps him complete the reintegration. The females are reunited with the males on the surface and will rebuild a civilization with the Federation's help.

"The Enterprise Incident" (September 27, 1968) Directed by: John Meredyth Lucas Written by: D. C. Fontana Guest Stars: Joanne Linville (Romulan Commander), Jack Donner (Sub-Commander Tal), Richard Compton (Romulan Technical Officer), Robert Gentile (Romulan Technician)

Kirk, who has been acting irrationally, orders the ship into the Romulan Neutral Zone without orders. It is immediately surrounded by three Romulan vessels using their new cloaking devices, and ordered to surrender by the lovely Romulan commander in charge. Kirk and Spock are ordered to the Romulan flagship, where Kirk is incarcerated while the commander tries to convince Spock to defect. Kirk seems to be becoming ever more imbalanced, and McCoy is ordered over to treat him. In a rage, Kirk attacks Spock, who instinctively defends himself with the Vulcan Death Grip, killing Kirk. McCoy beams back to the *Enterprise* with the body. Kirk is still alive, of course—his behavior and actions have all been part of a secret plot to learn about the new cloaking device. He has McCoy cosmetically transform him into a "Romulan," whereupon he beams back onto the flagship to steal the cloaking device. In the meantime, Spock pretends to go along with the commander's advances to stall for time. When the commander learns of the theft, she orders Spock killed, but again, he stalls for time by invoking his right under Romulan law to make a final statement. Scotty manages to install the alien device on the *Enterprise*; Spock, together with the commander, is beamed aboard, and the *Enterprise* narrowly escapes. The commander will be exchanged through diplomatic channels; Spock privately admits to her that he was tempted by her charms.

"The Paradise Syndrome" (October 4, 1968) Directed by: Jud Taylor Written by: Margaret Armen Guest Stars: Sabrina Scharf (Miramanee), Rudy Solari (Salish), Richard Hale (Goro), Sean Morgan (Engineer)

While checking out a planet that is soon to be struck by an asteroid the *Enterprise* plans to divert, Kirk, Spock, and McCoy discover it is inhabited by a tribe of mixed-heritage American Indians, who seem to worship a large obelisk inscribed in an unknown language. Temporarily alone, Kirk accidentally falls inside the obelisk, where an energy discharge causes him to pass out. Spock and McCoy are unable to find him, and Spock orders that they return to the ship so that they can reach the deflection point in time. McCoy doesn't like it, but cannot really disagree. Later, Kirk awakes with amnesia. His emergence from the obelisk is seen by the Indians, who think him a god, calling him Kurok. He is named medicine chief of the tribe, angering Salish, the former medicine chief, and required to take the maiden Miramanee as a bride. Meanwhile, the *Enterprise* is late reaching the deflection point, and damages the warp drive attempting to deflect the asteroid. Spock orders a retreat in front of the asteroid at sublight speed; which means it will take months to again reach the planet. McCoy rages at this, fearing for Kirk, but Spock ignores him, concentrating on the symbols of the obelisk. Kirk marries Miramanee, and falls deeply in love with her. His knowledge and intelligence are bringing the tribe out of the stone age, and his happiness is complete when he learns Miramanee is pregnant. But when the approach of the asteroid causes earthquakes, and he is unable to do anything about it, the tribe declares him a false god and stones him and Miramanee. They are saved by the beamdown of Spock and McCoy. Spock mindmelds with Kirk to restore his memory. Spock has figured out that the symbols are musical notes, and they have the key to get inside, as well as activate the obelisk's deflector mechanism. Miramanee was severely injured, however, and both she and the unborn child die.

* * *

"And the Children Shall Lead" (October 11, 1968) Directed by: Marvin Chomsky Written by: Edward J. Lasko Guest Stars: Melvin Belli (Gorgan), Craig Hundley (Tommy Starnes), Pamlyn Ferdin (Mary Janowski), Brian Tochi (Ray Tsingtao), James Wellman (Professor Starnes)

The *Enterprise* discovers that all of the adults in the Starnes Expedition on Triacus have died, but the surviving children seem not only healthy and happy, but oblivious to the deaths of their parents. Back on the *Enterprise*, the children use a chant to call up Gorgan, the beautiful "friendly angel," who uses the fears of the crew against themselves to wrest control of the ship. Uhura sees herself as a hag; Sulu sees giant daggers threatening the ship; Kirk cannot speak clearly to give orders. Kirk orders tapes of the children's parents shown on the viewscreen. These images of happier times delight the children, but when Kirk displays images of their graves, the children accept their deaths for the first time. Gorgan's power over them is broken, and he can now be seen for the hideous and corrupt being he truly is.

"Is There In Truth No Beauty?" (October 18, 1968) Directed by: Ralph Senesky Written by: Jean Lissette Aroeste Guest Stars: Diana Muldaur (Dr. Miranda Jones), David Frankham (Lawrence Marvick)

The *Enterprise* is assigned to ferry Medusan ambassador Kollos, telepath Miranda Jones, and designer Larry Marvick to a Medusan ship. Miranda is training to be Kollos's human contact, allowing Marvick to study Medusan technology. Although the thoughts of the Medusans are sublime, and they are the best navigators in the galaxy, their physical countenance is so hideous that any human viewing it will be driven hopelessly insane. Spock can look at Kollos, but only when wearing a protective visor. Miranda is envious of this, for she is blind, although she manages to disguise the fact from everyone but McCoy; she also has been unable as yet to form a complete mind link with Kollos. Larry Marvick loves Miranda, and is so jealous of the bond she will soon form with Kollos that he attempts to kill the Medusan. Kollos protects himself by opening his container and forcing Marvick to look at him. Driven mad, Marvick locks the controls, sending the ship into the energy zone beyond the edge of the galaxy. Only Kollos, merged with Spock, can navigate out. Miranda unconsciously causes Spock to forget to don the visor when disengaging, and he too goes mad. She regrets her action, and uses her telepathic power to help heal Spock, an action that proves her worth to Kollos and allows them finally to merge their minds completely.

"Spectre of the Gun" (October 25, 1968) Directed by: Vincent McEveety Written by: Lee Cronin Guest Stars: Ron Soble (Wyatt Earp), Bonnie Beecher (Sylvia), Rex Holman (Morgan Earp), Charles Maxwell (Virgil Earp), Bill Zuckert (Johnny Beehan)

A Melkotian warning buoy forbids the *Enterprise* to proceed, but Kirk orders a party beamed down anyway. A Melkotian appears, telling the party they will be punished for disobeying according to "their heritage." The party finds themselves in a stylized reproduction of Tombstone, Arizona, on October 26, 1881, the date when Wyatt Earp and his men killed the Clanton gang—and Kirk and his men are seen by everyone as the Clantons. Unable to convince anyone of their true identities or escape, they are forced into the showdown. However, Spock uses the mind meld to convince the others that what is happening is not real, and the bullets of the Earps pass harmlessly through them. Defeating the Earps in hand-to-hand battle, the crew again proves their worth as a species by refusing to kill helpless victims. The Melkotians approve, restore everyone to the point of first contact, this time allowing friendly contact to be made.

"Day of the Dove" (November 1, 1968) Directed by: Marvin Chomsky Written by: Jerome Bixby Guest Stars: Michael Ansara (Kang), Susan Johnson (Mara), David L. Rose (Lt. Johnson), Mark Tobin (Klingon)

Responding to a distress call, the *Enterprise* landing party is attacked by a small band of Klingons. The leader, Kang, accuses Kirk of attacking his ship without reason. Through a transporter trick, the Klingons are taken prisoner, but are helped to escape by a small but powerful energy being. It isolates all but an equal number of *Enterprise* crewmen belowdecks, then arms all of the combatants with swords and knives, as well as filling them with senseless bloodlust. The wounded quickly heal and no one can die. Kirk and Spock surmise that the creature feeds on hatred, and has set up a situation that will keep it sated for many years, perhaps forever. They manage to convince Kang, who somewhat reluctantly agrees that to fight without purpose is not the Klingon way. He joins with Kirk in literally laughing the creature out of the ship.

"For the World Is Hollow and I Have Touched the Sky"
(November 8, 1968) Directed by: Tony Leader Written by: Rick Vollaerts Guest Stars: Kate Woodville (Natira), Jon Morrow (old man), Byron Morrow (Admiral Westervliet)

McCoy discovers he has xenopolycythemia, an incurable, deadly disease at the same time the *Enterprise* encounters an alien generation ship built within an asteroid, called Yonada. The asteroid is on a collision course with an inhabited Federation planet. The people within are ruled by a computer, called the Oracle, spoken to by the high priestess, Natira. Kirk and Spock, looking for a way to change the asteroid's direction, are declared lawbreakers and ordered off. McCoy falls in love with Natira, and, knowing he has not long to live, decides to marry and stay with her. He discovers a way into the control room, and summons Spock and Kirk, even though it endangers his life to do so. The erratic course is repaired, and Spock discovers a wealth of medical knowledge in the computer—including a cure for McCoy's condition. He returns to the *Enterprise*, but promises to return to Yonada when its people find their new planet.

No mention is later made of the fact that McCoy is legally married to Natira, nor do we ever see her again. Most fans feel they had their reunion, but decided to annul and return to their respective duties.

"The Tholian Web"
(November 15, 1968) Directed by: Ralph Senensky Written by: Judy Burns and Chet Richards Guest Stars: Sean Morgan (Lt. O'Neil)

The *Enterprise* discovers the USS *Defiant* derelict, its crew all dead, apparently by each other's hand. While Kirk and others are on her in spacesuits, she begins to blink in and out of an interphase with another dimension. The transporter is not working correctly because of the power drain, and Kirk is stranded alone on *Defiant*. Before Scotty can pull him back, the ship vanishes totally. Spock charts the interphase occurrence and predicts they will be able to pull Kirk out in a few hours, with air to spare. Just at that time, however, an alien ship arrives, disrupting the interphase. It is a Tholian ship, and warns the

Enterprise away. Spock refuses to leave and is forced to disable the smaller ship. Another quickly arrives, and the two begin weaving an energy net around the *Enterprise*. Now it is a race against time to rescue Kirk before the web is completed or the energy drain renders the *Enterprise* immobile. They also must contend with the mentally debilitating effects of the interphase on the crew. At the last moment, Kirk is pulled back and the *Enterprise* breaks through the energy web.

It is in this episode that Spock and McCoy, thinking Kirk lost, play a tape of his "last orders." On it, Kirk urges them to work together and trust each other. Later, when he is found, they deny ever having played the tape. Many fans view this episode as the point where the two finally gained trust in each other as well as friendship, thereby completing the Triad.

"Plato's Stepchildren" (November 22, 1968) Directed by: David Alexander Written by: Meyer Dolinsky Guest Stars: Michael Dunn (Alexander), Liam Sullivan (Parmen), Barbara Babcock (Philana), Ted Scott (Eraclitus), Derek Partridge (Dionyd)

Responding to a distress call from Platonius, Kirk, Spock, and McCoy discover a group of psychokenetically powerful humans. Their leader, Parmen, is suffering from a wound that he wants McCoy to treat. Alexander, a dwarf without powers the others treat as a servant, assists McCoy and Kirk to take him with them, but a recovered Parmen will not allow the ship to leave . . . he has decided that a doctor is necessary for his people. Told by Alexander that the powers did not develop until the Platonians arrived on the planet, McCoy surmises that a natural substance in the food, kironide, gives one the power. It did not work on Alexander because of his dwarfism. McCoy gives Kirk and Spock double doses of kironide. Before their powers can develop, they and Christine Chapel and Uhura are forced to participate in humiliating games for the Platonians' amusement. Finally Kirk's power overwhelms that of Parmen, and the officers leave, taking Alexander with them.

This episode contained the controversial kiss between Kirk and Uhura, which caused many Southern stations to refuse to run the episode; the shot was also removed from early syndicated prints.

"Wink of An Eye" (November 29, 1968) Directed by: Jud Taylor Written by: Arthur Heinemann, story by Lee Cronin

Guest Stars: Kathie Browne (Deela), Jason Evers (Rael), Geoffrey Binney (Crewman Compton), Eric Holland (Ekor)

Answering a distress call from Scalos, the crew finds only a deserted city. A strange, insectlike buzzing is occasionally heard. One of the landing party vanishes after drinking from a fountain; the same thing happens to Kirk back on the ship when he drinks some coffee. He finds that his metabolism has been speeded up to a point where he is invisible to the others. Now he can see the Scalosians, who have followed them onto the *Enterprise*, and put the element that causes the speeding-up into his coffee. Their accelerated metabolism was caused by radiation from their planet, which also rendered the men sterile and killed all the children. Now the women must mate with males outside the race whom they lure to their planet. Unfortunately, such men are quickly "burned out" by the acceleration. Kirk, who really has no choice, makes love to Deela. In the meantime, Rael and the others install a freezing device in the engine room, which will preserve the other men until they are needed. Kirk manages to tape a report for Spock. McCoy concocts an antidote for the water, and Spock takes a dose himself in order to speak to Kirk. They halt the Scalosians' plan, and offer to help them via Federation science. Kirk and Spock return to normal speed, but not before Spock has performed weeks' worth of repairs to the ship in minutes at his accelerated speed.

"The Empath" (December 6, 1968) Directed by: John Erman Written by: Joyce Muskat Guest Stars: Kathryn Hays (Gem), Willard Sage (Thann), Alan Bergmann (Lan)

Stopping by a research station on Minara III to pick up research scientists endangered by a star about to go nova, Kirk, Spock, and McCoy discover they are missing. Falling unconscious, they too vanish. They awaken in a dark, underground cavern, where they discover the bodies of the scientists dead in labeled tubes, like experimental animals. Next they discover a lovely young woman who is mute. McCoy names her Gem. She displays empatic powers by healing a cut on Kirk's head. Two aliens appear, identifying themselves as Vians. They are testing Gem to ascertain the worthiness of her people to be saved from the nova. Their unusual method of doing so is to torture a human to see if Gem will sacrifice her love to heal him. Kirk is taken first, and healed by Gem when he is returned. Spock volunteers to go next, but McCoy slips him a hypo and goes instead. Spock and Kirk escape, finding McCoy at the verge of death. They bring him back to Gem, but are not allowed to try to convince her to heal him; the Vians insist she must be willing to do so on her own, for taking his pain upon herself may cause her to die. Their examples of self-sacrifice and friendship have taught her well, and she overcomes her fears and helps McCoy. Her race will be saved, and the three men are returned unharmed to the *Enterprise*.

Most fans consider this episode to be the ultimate expression of the Friendship between Kirk, Spock, and McCoy, as well as the prime example of how the dynamics of that friendship interact.

"Elaan of Troyius" Written and Directed by: John Meredyth Lucas Guest Stars: France Nuyen (Elaan), Jay Robinson (Lord Petri), Tony Young (Kryton), Victor Brandt (Technician Watson), K. L. Smith (Klingon Captain)

The *Enterprise* takes on board the Dohlman of Elas, the inner planet of the Tellun system, and Lord Petri, a diplomat from Troyius, the outer planet. The Klingons, who also covet the system, follow. Elaan is to be married to the Troyian leader in order to cement a peace pact. Petri is her escort and teacher of etiquette; the *Enterprise* chugs along at sublight speed to give him time to teach her. The haughty and somewhat wild Elaan does not desire the marriage; her unruly behavior culminates in her stabbing of Petri with a ceremonial knife. Kirk is forced to take over. He is successful until his skin comes in contact with her tears, which contain a substance that causes him to fall helplessly in love with her. Kryton, her guard, has been signaling the Klingons. He damages the warp drive, then commits suicide. The ship is at the mercy of the Klingons until Spock discovers Elaan's necklace of "common stones" is actually composed of dilithium crystals. The crystals are the reason that the Klingons are so anxious to possess Elas. Scotty installs the makeshift crystals and the *Enterprise* uses the element of surprise to defeat the Klingons. Kirk, although still feeling love for Elaan, does his duty by sending her on to Troyius. His example convinces her that she too must bow to duty and she will now try to be a good wife and representative of her people.

"Whom Gods Destroy" (January 3, 1969) Directed by: Herb Wallerstein Written by: Lee Erwin, story by Jerry Sohl and Lee

Erwin Guest Stars: Steve Ihnat (Garth of Izar), Yvonne Craig (Marta), Keye Luke (Donald Cory), Richard Geary (Andorian), Gary Downey (Tellerite)

Delivering a new medication to the only remaining insane asylum in the Federation, Elba II, Kirk and Spock discover it has been taken over by Garth of Izar, a former starship captain and idol of Kirk's. Using his shape-changing powers, Garth tries to trick them into allowing him aboard the *Enterprise*. Failing this, he tortures Dr. Cory, then Kirk, neither of which works. He also has Marta, a murderously insane green Orion girl, try to seduce Kirk. Garth then kills her simply to display his new explosive to Kirk and Spock. In a last-ditch effort to get the *Enterprise*, Garth takes Kirk's form. Spock, confronted by two Kirks, logically chooses the one willing to sacrifice himself to stop Garth, and knocks out the other. The crisis ended, Garth is given the new drug, which seems to moderate his madness significantly.

"Let That Be Your Last Battlefield" (January 10, 1969) Directed by: Jud Taylor Written by: Oliver Crawford, story by Lee Cronin Guest Stars: Lou Antonio (Lokai), Frank Gorshin (Bele)

A stolen shuttlecraft is captured by the *Enterprise*. In it is an alien who is solid white on his right side and solid black on his left. His name is Lokai, and he claims to be a political refugee from Cheron. Another alien appears, identifying himself as Bele, a police officer from Cheron who has been tracking Lokai for over 50,000 years. He is outraged when Kirk sees no difference in them: he is white on the left and black on the right, a condition that he considers makes him superior to Lokai and others of "his kind." Each claims justice and right is on his side, but Kirk stays out of it, offering to drop them off at a Starbase. Bele takes control of the ship, ordering it to Cheron. Kirk responds by activating the self-destruct sequence, and Bele releases the ship. Later, he deactivates the destruct mode and again takes control; this time the ship goes to Cheron. They discover it in ruins, long since destroyed; the hatred between the two races finally erupted in enough violence to destroy their world. Driven mad by the sight, Lokai and Bele both beam down to the surface, where they will continue to fight each other until one of them is dead.

* * *

"The Mark of Gideon" (January 17, 1969) Directed by: Jud Taylor Written by: George F. Slavin and Stanley Adams Guest Stars: Sharon Acker (Odona), David Hurst (Hodin), Gene Dynarski (Krodak), Richard Derr (Admiral Fitzgerald)

Kirk beams down to Gideon, a planet believed to be a germ-free paradise where no one ever dies, but Gideon officials report he did not arrive. Spock wants to institute a search for him, but is denied permission to do so. Kirk has arrived on what seems to be the *Enterprise*, but it is completely deserted. Exploring the ship, he discovers a beautiful young woman exulting in the open space of the corridors. Her name is Odona, and she explains that Gideon is so crowded that most people would kill for this much space. The lack of disease on the planet has caused massive overpopulation; Kirk gets a glimpse through the viewscreen of hundreds of people crowded together. Hodin, the Gideon leader, then appears and explains that Kirk has been captured in order that he could infect Odona with Vegan choriomeningitis, which he carries in his blood. She will then spread it among her people, causing millions to die, but allowing those remaining to have sufficient living space. Odona, his daughter, must die as a symbol. Spock beams them both aboard the real *Enterprise* and McCoy cures her, although her blood now carries the virus and will be used to spead the disease.

"That Which Survives" (January 24, 1969) Directed by: Herb Wallerstein Written by: John Meredyth Lucas and Michael Richards (pseudonym) Guest Stars: Lee Meriweather (Losira), Naomi Pollack (Lt. Rahda), Arthur Batanides (Lt. D'Amato), Booker Marshall (Dr. M'Benga)

A team beams down to a planet to examine strange seismic effects and is greeted by a hauntingly beautiful woman who kills an ensign with a touch, then vanishes. A power surge caused by her appearance flings the *Enterprise* almost a thousand light-years away; Spock calculates that it will take almost twelve hours for it to return. The woman, Losira, again appears, calling D'Amato by name and killing him with a touch. She also appears on the *Enterprise*, where she sabotages the engines. Only Scotty's instinctive "feel" for the ship allows them to escape being blown up. Meanwhile, the landing party discovers an ancient computer complex in a cave. Spock deduces that Losira is actually a construct of the computer, a sophisticated defense mechanism. Several of her appear, threatening all of them, and Kirk is forced to phaser the main computer. An image of Losira appears on a viewscreen, explaining that the planet was a colony of her people that was struck by a plague, which ships undoubtedly carried back to her home planet. The computer used this image to make the killing Losiras, but put too much of her into them: She hesitated to kill long enough for them to stop the computer. Her beauty has survived in more ways than one.

"**The Lights of Zetar**" (January 31, 1969) Directed by: Herb Kenwith Written by: Jeremy Tarcher and Shari Lewis Guest Stars: Jan Shutan (Lt. Mira Romaine), Libby Erwin (Technician)

Lt. Mira Romaine, with whom Scotty has fallen in love, is being ferried to her first assignment, on Memory Alpha, a planetoid where all the knowledge of the Federation is stored. A storm composed of strange, twinkling lights sweeps over Memory Alpha, killing all there. It soon reaches the *Enterprise*; although no one is killed, all experience some kind of neural disruption. Mira is most affected, and when she recovers, she seems to have developed the ability to see into the future. The storm returns and this time the lights invade Mira's body. Subsequent investigation shows that her brain patterns are becoming a match for the pattern of the lights' energy. This is possible, McCoy says, because her personality is unusually malleable by outside influence. They speak through her, identifying themselves as the last remnants of a long-dead race called the Zetar, and insisting that they be allowed to possess her form. Spock theorizes that the Zetar have become accustomed to the vacuum of space. Mira is placed in a decompression chamber, where increasing atmospheric pressure drives the Zetar from her body, and apparently destroys them. McCoy credits Scotty's steadfast love for her as a factor in her ability to resist the Zetar; even Spock cannot disagree. Soon, Spock, McCoy, and Scotty all agree that she is again fit for duty on Memory Alpha . . . agreement Kirk wryly terms "an *Enterprise* first."

It is accepted as fact by most fans that Scotty and Mira eventually joined together in an open marriage that allowed each of them to continue their respective careers.

"**Requiem for Methuselah**" (February 14, 1969) Directed by: Murray Golden Written by: Jerome Bixby Guest Stars: James

Daly (Flint), Louise Sorel (Reena Kapec), John Buonomo (Orderly)

Rigellian fever is spreading throughout the *Enterprise* crew, and Kirk orders the ship to an apparently uninhabited planet to secure ryetalyn, the only known antidote. Beaming down, Kirk, Spock, and McCoy discover Flint, a handsome, dignified man apparently in his late forties, who grudgingly allows them to stay at his house while his robot servant obtains the ryetalyn. In his study, Spock notes that an unknown painting by da Vinci was done with modern oils; similarly, the sheet music for an unknown Brahms waltz is of contemporary materials. Kirk is more interested in the appearance of a beautiful young girl, Reena Kapec, whom Flint identifies as his ward. His flirtations soon become serious, and are reciprocated; the two are obviously falling in love. Flint, who at first seemed to be encouraging them, is now crazed with jealousy, and orders his robot to kill Kirk. Reena stops it. Flint then spitefully reveals an entire room full of Reena bodies to Kirk—she is an android, constructed by him to be his perfect companion. He reveals he is from Earth and is thousands of years old. A genetic mutant, he does not age and cannot be killed; he was da Vinci, Brahms, and a thousand others. He eventually left Earth and settled here. But he was lonely and built a companion. The android was without emotion, however, and he used Kirk to awaken her feelings. Kirk is too much in love to care; he and Flint argue bitterly, then come to blows over Reena, despite Spock's warnings. Reena, loving both of them equally, cannot choose between them and short-circuits. Defeated, Flint allows them to leave with the ryetalyn. McCoy reveals that Flint's immortality was tied to Earth's complex fields, and that he is now aging normally and will eventually die. Kirk's grief, and Spock's apparent indifference to it, causes McCoy to flare bitterly at him. When the doctor leaves, however, Spock uses the mind meld to force Kirk to forget Reena.

Much controversy surrounds this episode. To mention only three items of contention: Many fans feel that Kirk fell in love with Reena too easily and too quickly, suggesting some sort of outside agent. Many fans also feel that Spock would not have used the meld in this manner under normal circumstances, partially confirming the first supposition. There is also great debate as to whether Reena simply "overloaded," or if she actually committed suicide, so great was her pain and confusion.

"The Way to Eden"
(February 21, 1969) Directed by: David Alexander Written by: Arthur Heinemann, story by Michael Richards (pseudonym for D. C. Fontana) and Arthur Heinemann Guest Stars: Skip Homeier (Dr. Sevrin), Mary-Linda Rapelye (Irini Galliulin), Charles Napier (Adam), Victor Brandt (Tongo)

The *Enterprise* beams aboard the passengers of the crippled ship *Aurora*, which has been stolen. They are Dr. Sevrin, a charismatic cult leader, and several of his disciples. Among them is the son of the Catullan ambassador, and Irini Galliulin, Chekov's former love. They have been searching for the mythical planet Eden. Sevrin, because he is a carrier of a disease as well as a wanted criminal, is placed in confinement, but the cult members are allowed the run of the ship, thanks to the presence of the Ambassador's son. Spock, who displays an atypical tolerance and understanding of them, actually finds a planet called Eden. Learning this, Sevrin orders his followers to help him escape. They steal a shuttlecraft and head for Eden, after unsuccessfully trying to kill the crew with ultrasonics. Following, Kirk and Spock find that everything on the surface of the beautiful planet is highly acidic and has burned the feet of the cultists. Sevrin kills himself by biting into a fruit, and the disillusioned others are returned to the ship.

Most fans refer to the cultists as "space hippies" because of their dress and attitudes. More important, this episode was suggested by D. C. Fontana's treatment "Joanna," which featured Dr. McCoy's daughter Joanna as one of Sevrin's followers. Needless to say, it was much better than the resulting episode.

"The Cloud Minders"
(February 28, 1969) Directed by: Jud Taylor Written by: Margaret Armen, story by David Gerrold and Oliver Crawford Guest Stars: Jeff Corey (Plasus), Diana Ewing (Droxine), Charlene Polite (Vanna), Fred Williamson (Anka)

The *Enterprise* travels to Ardana to pick up zienite, needed to stem a botanical plague. Ardanan society is divided into two groups: "citizens," who live in a city in the clouds, devoting themselves to art and science, and "troglytes," who work and live in the zienite mines, supposedly less intelligent and bestial. The troglytes refuse to give Kirk the zienite, thinking the *Enterprise*'s presence there a threat against their campaign for equality and better conditions. McCoy discovers that zienite emits a gas that inhibits intellectual ability. Kirk proves this by trapping both citizens and troglytes in a mine; soon, all begin to act emotionally and irrationally. Now shown that they are actually equal and of the same race, the citizens will work toward reuniting all their people.

Spock is obviously attracted, if only on an intellectual level, to Droxine, the daughter of the citizens' leader. He not only discusses politics and philosophy with her, but Vulcan biology as well!

"The Savage Curtain" (March 7, 1969) Directed by: Herschel Daugherty Written by: Gene Roddenberry and Arthur Heinemann, story by Gene Roddenberry Guest Stars: Lee Bergere (Abraham Lincoln), Barry Atwater (Surak), Phillip Pine (Colonel Green), Janos Prohaska (Yarnek), Bart LaRue (Yarnek's voice), Carol Daniels Dement (Zora), Nathun Jung (Genghis Khan), Robert Herron (Kahless)

Investigating a planet with a surface of lava, the *Enterprise* encounters the image of Abraham Lincoln. He is brought aboard the ship, appearing for all intents actually to be Lincoln, and he invites Kirk and Spock to the planet, where a large, Earth-like area has somehow formed. They agree, and upon arriving, meet Surak, the Vulcan who instituted the Reforms. Yarnek, a rock-like creature, tells them they are to battle images from their minds to test the strength of good versus evil. Representative of evil are: Col. Green, Genghis Khan, Zora, and Kahless, the Klingon "Surak." Yarnek holds the *Enterprise* hostage; if Kirk does not win, it will be destroyed. Surak refuses to fight, and is killed trying to make peace. Lincoln is also killed, as are Kahless and Green. Kirk and Spock defeat the remaining two, and are returned to the ship unharmed. They realize that their heroes were also taken from their minds, which is why they were so real, and acted just as they were expected to.

Because Spock instantly recognized the construct as Surak, there is no doubt as to Surak's appearance; and even though colored by Spock's expectations, we can assume that it acted as the real Surak did, as well.

"All Our Yesterdays" (March 14, 1969) Directed by: Marvin Chomsky Written by: Jean Lissette Aroeste Guest Stars: Mariette

Hartley (Zarabeth), Ian Wolfe (Mr. Atoz), Anna Karen (Woman), Kermit Murdock (Prosecutor)

Attempting to rescue the last inhabitant of Sarpeidon, a planet whose sun is about to go nova, the *Enterprise* discovers him in a large library-tape complex that also contains a time-travel device, the Atavachron. The librarian, who identifies himself as Mr. Atoz, tells them all of the people of his world escaped into the past. Thinking them of his own race, he tells them they must hurry and make a selection and be "prepared." Humoring him for the moment, they view scenes of the past. Kirk, hearing a woman scream, runs through a door and finds himself in the "seventeenth century." Unable to find his way back, he is arrested and put in jail. Attempting to find him, McCoy and Spock are thrown into an ice age. Lost, they are near collapse when found by a young woman, Zarabeth, who leads them to shelter. She tells them they cannot return even if they could find the portal, for to do so will kill them. She was sentenced to the isolation by a tyrant, and is thrilled at the company. Kirk, meanwhile, discovers the prosecutor of his case is also from the future, and convinces him to show him the way back, which the man does when Kirk tells him he wasn't prepared. Spock and McCoy have spent a relatively longer time with Zarabeth. Spock seems to be regressing: he eats meat, threatens McCoy with violence, and is becoming romantically involved with Zarabeth. When Zarabeth finally tells them they cannot return because of the preparation, McCoy knows that is why Spock is acting so strangely. Unless they return, they will soon die; if Zarabeth leaves the past, she will die. They make their way to the portal where they can hear Kirk calling. Spock attempts to remain with Zarabeth, with whom he has fallen in love, but McCoy cannot return alone. He and Zarabeth say tender good-byes and they return to the present. Spock is again his normal self. Atoz escapes to join his family in the past, and the *Enterprise* warps out of orbit just as the star goes nova.

A very popular sequel to this episode, Yesterday's Son, written by Ann C. Crispin, was published by Pocket Books.

"**Turnabout Intruder**" (June 3, 1969) Directed by: Herb Wallerstein Written by: Arthur H. Singer, story by Gene Roddenberry Guest Stars: Sandra Smith (Dr. Janice Lester), Harry Landers (Dr. Arthur Coleman), Barbara Baldavin (Angela), Roger Holloway (Mr. Lemli), David L. Rose, John Boyer (Security guards)

En route to Beta Aurigae, the *Enterprise* responds to a distress call from Camus II. There they discover Dr. Janice Lester and Dr. Coleman, the only survivors of an archaeological mission. Janice, a former flame of Kirk's, is very ill. She begs Kirk to stay alone with her while the others check the bodies. They discuss her failure to achieve starship rank (and their subsequent breakup); she blames it on chauvinism, but it is obvious she is unstable. Utilizing an ancient device, she effects a mind transfer with Kirk, then tries to kill him (in her body), but is interrupted by the return of the others. Kirk, in Janice's body, collapses and is taken by McCoy to the ship for treatment. Coleman, who is party to the switch, tells Janice that it might not last. Taking command, Janice orders a diversion to Benecia, ostensibly to get treatment for Dr. Lester. Spock is puzzled, noting that a starbase would be much better and on their course. Kirk awakens and manages to talk Spock into a mind meld, convincing the Vulcan of his true identity. Learning of this, Janice orders Spock tried for mutiny. During the trial, McCoy and Scott become convinced of the switch, and they too are ordered court-martialed. When Janice hysterically orders them all killed, the rest of the crew become convinced as well. The stress causes the transfer to break, returning each to his/her own body. Janice's mind snaps, and she collapses. Dr. Coleman, who has been in love with her all along, asks to be allowed to look after her. Kirk agrees, feeling that her condition is partly his fault.

In the scene where Kirk tries to convince Spock to test his identity via mind meld, he mentions events from earlier episodes, one of the few times in the series when other episodes are referred to.

THE NEGLECTED WHOLE—OR, "NEVER HEARD OF YOU"— PART TWO

By Elizabeth Rigel

We never cease to be amazed at the insights our writers find in the characters of the Star Trek regulars. Last volume, Elizabeth took a close look at the female regulars, and offered some startlingly new opinions and observations about their characters and their place in the Star Trek world. Now she turns her attentions to the two junior officers, with equally fascinating results.

In Part One of this article (*The Best of Trek #10*), you met the supporting ladies of Star Trek. Now let us introduce two of the gentlemen:

(Pavel) Chekov
First Appearance: "Amok Time"
Rank and post: Ensign, navigator, backup Science Officer
Rank and post by *The Search for Spock:* commander, First Officer/Science Officer.

Pavel Chekov first appeared among the Bridge crew of the *Enterprise* in Star Trek's second season. The *Star Trek Guide* outlined Chekov as "reliable and dependable, with a good head on his shoulders in spite of his youth." He was one of the few minor characters given adequate (if not overwhelming) screen time to live up to his description, surviving despite the rigors of Starfleet and fickle television rating systems.

Chekov was born to a middle-class family near Moscow and is an only child ("Day of the Dove"). He has apparently always been their "nice boy," the one who still cries after receiving his mother's proud letters and fruitcakes. Thus he was well prepared to assume the pecking-order position (vacated by fellow youngster Janice Rand) of "the Bridge baby." He bears the common burden of youth: no respect. He lacks maturity, so he will be made better by being watched, bothered, and left behind. He has talent but is too green to understand it. If he does a job right, another person receives credit. And if he does something wrong . . .

He is introduced in "Amok Time," but his earliest filmed episode was "Who Mourns for Adonais." And according to Khan Noonian Singh, Chekov was around as early as "Space Seed." This identification must be accurate. The *Enterprise* was alone in "Space Seed," and no ship visited Ceti Alpha V thereafter. Chekov was indeed aboard the *Enterprise* at that time or they never would have met. Chekov was already twenty-two by the time of "Who Mourns For Adonais?", so he could have graduated from the Academy early.

However, raw genius alone cannot earn a starting position on Kirk's "crisis bridge" team. Kirk requires additional on-the-job training for rookies and transfers, which is why he has the finest ships in the fleet. He required it of Sulu and Uhura sometime between "Where No Man has Gone Before" and "The Man Trap." For everyday duties such as navigation, the training period is brief. But Chekov has been personally groomed by Spock to be the backup Science Officer. Because Spock is the best Science Officer in the fleet, it is entirely reasonable that it took Chekov a year of training (in one of the two (eight-hour) or three (six-hour) off-shifts on the Bridge) before he was allowed to relieve Spock of the position. In an emergency he would be in charge of auxiliary control. He was also never seen off-duty because he was up to his eyeballs in "homework." (Obviously, Spock learned his teaching methods from his mother.)

There's no question Pavel learned his lessons well. As Kirk said in "The Ultimate Computer," "Chekov could do his job with his eyes closed." There are days when Spock is not even missed. Chekov adopted the science duties with complete confidence in "Catspaw," "The Immunity Syndrome," "Friday's Child," and "The Enterprise Incident," to name just a few.

He is equally skilled on ground assignment, as in "Who Mourns For Adonais?" This show in particular emphasizes Chekov's logic and talent. (He didn't scream, either.) First, he made the connection between Apollo and his mechanical energy source. Second, he volunteered himself into danger to protect his superiors. Third, his task was complicated by the fact that no one, especially Scotty, did anything useful. And fourth, Chekov was probably scared to death. Apollo had threatened several times to kill the landing party. (And the crew, as well; the ship could not be contacted, so how could anyone know he had not already done so?) Until the final commercial, it looked like Chekov was on his own—he would have to destroy Apollo himself. Now, logically, the expendable ensign should have been the one to bear the brunt of Apollo's anger. Chekov tried to point this out to Kirk, and encountered Kirk's actual modus operandi: "If I don't do it, it isn't done right." The captain is willing to die to prove his point. So although Chekov was presented well in "Who Mourns?", it is a shame that he looked so good only because everyone else did so badly.

Although Chekov was never intended to make his screen debut in "Amok Time," the episode is an indication of things to come. One of his first lines is the eloquent, "I think I'm going to get spacesick." Don't doubt it—Chekov is forever falling victim to the malice of man and nature. He is first to become ill in "The Immunity Syndrome," "The Tholian Web," and "Day of the Dove." A particularly painful moment is the bewildered, trusting expression on his face just before the coldhearted Kelvans evaporate him into a teething toy.

It has been truthfully said that if McCoy is loose when the action starts moving, he is going to get clobbered. But it's even worse for Chekov, who is frankly expendable in story terms, regardless of how popular he became. Now and then a writer may generously nail both of them, as in "The Deadly Years." (Chekov was spared from deadly radiation so that McCoy could pull him into taffy in Sickbay, instead.) This is not the only similarity between Chekov and a major character. His struggling imitation of Spock is obvious, but as a person he is much like his other heroes, McCoy and Kirk.

McCoy has been called the embodiment of that chaotic element, emotion. Chekov is even more emotional; his spirit is young and not yet very organized. McCoy has the advantage of maturity and a stable career, plus self-control—which, admittedly, he doesn't always use. He has come to an age and viewpoint that enable him to channel emotions to definite goals.

Chekov cannot do even this much; and the only thing he's learned so far is that when he acts like Dr. McCoy, either the enemy or the boss whales the tar out of him. Maybe McCoy torments Chekov, not because he objects to his exposure to Spock, but because he reminds the doctor of himself in younger days.

The education of the ensign must be an interesting hobby for his stern tutor, Spock. When Chekov is feeling logical, he drives even McCoy nuts. Yet Chekov is hopelessly emotional, by Vulcan standards a lost cause. It must please Spock no end that someone even worse off than McCoy is being successfully "rehabilitated."

In the long run, though, Pavel is much more like Jim Kirk. They share a particularly fascinating problem: a powerful love/hate relationship with authority and The Job.

Kirk's contempt for Headquarters and Federation bureaucrats is well known. When he encounters an alien race, he educates them until they suit him. He takes badly to a power that proves stronger and/or more ethical than he is. Kirk *must* be in charge; he craves power, and with a starship at his command, he usually gets it. This is when he loves his job. But there are days when things do not go his way. Perhaps he has orders he does not want, or his friends are mad at him for doing something stupid. Some nights he lies awake hating the long hours and missing the loving women and happy homes he's thrown away. At such times, he hates his job. He does not quite know how to solve his problem, but when presented with a solution, he cannot go through with it.

Apply this to Ensign Chekov. Pavel is proud to have an envied posting on the heroic *Enterprise*. The work is stimulating, his folks adore him outer space is breathtaking, and the people are the best. At times he feels the invincible, "what, me worry?" life is upon him ("The Apple," "Friday's Child"). He enjoys the company of Sulu the gossip and Uhura the big spender. And Chekov's favorite commander has got to be Scotty. Scotty is a party on legs—for instance, he starts bar fights with Klingons. But the best thing about Scotty is that he lets Chekov work in peace. He doesn't do babysitting. If Kirk lets Chekov on his Bridge, the fellow must know his job. Scotty (gasp!) respects Chekov. So do Uhura and Sulu. Their support is his only comfort.

However, a disturbing thought must occasionally cross his

mind: Is it better to be highly regarded on a mediocre cruiser led by nobodies, or to just be nobody on the *Enterprise*?

Is "just being there" worth all the baiting and condescension? What reward has he gotten so far for his hard work? He is afraid of the kind of "blood brother" friendship that Kirk has with Spock and McCoy, so he doesn't open up to anyone. Oh, Uhura and Sulu *seem* to like him, but they probably just feel sorry for him. He is, after all, their inferior. Kirk and Spock have told him so. Everyone he works with is in the chain of command—how important could the pressures on a mere ensign be? If Uhura is as calm as Spock, and Sulu never takes that blasted grin off his face, then what could his "friends" know about loneliness? He is frankly afraid of them. Even the temporary help, like DeSalle of "Catspaw," treat Chekov as if all he really needs is a bottle and a diaper. As for Kirk or Spock, Chekov seems resigned to his belief that he will never please them, and resigned to their belief that they are doing him a favor by teaching him patience. He bottles up his feelings too often, hoping to please them, but he ends up hating them and himself. He can't even attract female companions, with the dubious exceptions of yeomen, security, or some alien's leftovers. Is it any wonder he fights Spock ("The Tholian Web"), Kirk ("The Children Shall Lead"), and the Klingons (any opportunity) so fervently?

An excellent example of the contrary Kirk/Chekov relationship can be seen in "The Trouble With Tribbles." After a minor error draws a lecture, the friendly captain informs the ensign that his memory stinks. ("Ivan Burkov/John Burke" obviously was, like "Jeanne d'Arc/Joan of Arc," common in American textbooks) a convenience of the Russian translator, and no excuse for Kirk's bad manners.) Later, when the Klingons insult Kirk, Chekov is the first (and only) one who defends him. Scotty holds back because Kirk isn't worth the trouble. But when the captain lines up the transgressors, he first blames loyal old Pavel for starting the fight. Nice guy, huh?

"The Gamesters of Triskelion" were obviously aware of Chekov's suppressed anger. If they could tap and channel that aggression, they could have a truly brilliant gladiator, one who might even defeat Kirk someday. They selected him out of a crew of 430 capable crewmembers, gave him a woman of his very own, and severely punished his uncooperative boss. If

Chekov really hates the service, this should have been enough to win him over.

It is not. The military may stink, but it does issue paychecks, promotions, and doors that lock from the inside. One of the reasons Kirk seems to like Chekov so is that the ensign has a short memory. They decide to escape.

Chekov has an amusing relationship with his woman, Tamoon. She seems a nice enough young gladiator, but she's not his type. He does not like her any more than he does captivity, but he doesn't take it out on her. He never lied to her, and he made a point of politely tying her up during his escape attempt. (Kirk, however, cracked Shahna's jaw.) Chekov also didn't care for Sylvia ("Spectre of the Gun"), but he defended her to the death. It is Chekov, not Kirk, who "doesn't go around beating up beautiful women." True, Chekov isn't much exposed to beautiful women. But he will defend himself.

This incident was still not enough to resolve his love/hate problem with authority. By the time of "The Children Shall Lead," it was once again volatile enough to become dangerous. This "beast" was ideal for Gorgan's plans, which require getting rid of the meddlesome Kirk and Spock. Chekov has heard from Starfleet Command, he says, and the Captain and First Officer are to be arrested. It is something he has always fantasized about doing. If only, just this once, he could get back at them! Never again would he feel inferior or intimidated; now someone would respect his abilities and needs. To his credit, Chekov admits that he does not wish to kill them, although he will if he must. If anyone on the *Enterprise* has the capacity to kill Kirk, it would be Chekov—and Gorgan, who has killed before, would send the most dangerous person for the job. However, Kirk saw that even then Chekov was not controlled deeply enough to succeed, and he was able to stop him

It is ironic that Kirk has assembled the best crew in the fleet by giving no more than a pat on the head for effort. He has been warned by now that the natives are restless, and it is surprising that he hasn't done something about it. Chekov has once again made clear that he wants better, and again he is ignored. Compare this with the ambition of Chekov-2 ("Mirror, Mirror"), who wanted a raise so badly that he would kill Kirk to get it. (From what we saw of Kirk-2, we almost hope he got it.)

Probably Chekov's most controversial role was in "The Way

to Eden." Fans complained vigorously that their teeny-bopper hero has turned into just another stuffy military man. Pavel was supposed to attract young viewers—in this show he sounded like their parents. True, this is not how Pavel Chekov was first introduced, but that is because he has outgrown the description. He is entirely the Chekov we have recently seen.

Pavel originally loved his job. No doubt his family did, too. For all we know, it may have been their idea. But because Chekov was the one who had to live with it, the starry-eyed idealism finally faded. He discovered that the outwardly glamorous *Enterprise* was a real drudge factory. His bosses (and many crewmembers have only one) proved to be perfectionists and workaholics. They did not understand why he did not share their passion for solving problems or "work as play." The conflict developed and he did not, could not, solve it. On top of all this, he had served only three years. There was no legal way to get out of the military. He is wondering whether he has made a mistake.

Into this troubled scene strolls a serene soul named Irina, an Important Person from his past. He had broken off their relationship when she dropped out of the Academy to become a swinging hippie. He did want to continue the relationship, but on his own terms. Pavel Andreivich Chekov would never be associated with a hippie, no matter how much the free life-style might appeal to him. His common sense (or traditional pressures) won out, and he was convinced of his own correct position, all the way through Starfleet Academy.

Pavel used the same arguments on her that his parents would have used on him: The work ethic (industriousness, loyalty, paying taxes for services) is a good thing. If she would not work, she would starve. On a primitive planet, she would have little medical care. She would find the morals of the hippies degenerate, their goals selfish and shortsighted. He knew that he could not bear to see her inevitable final decline, such as befall the dregs of society. Instead, he would go forth into the galaxy and become a hero.

Imagine how Chekov felt when Irina met him again on the *Enterprise*. His dire warnings have come to nothing. All his emotions come crashing down on him: envy for her simple life, and her happiness. Shame, that he was afraid to follow. Anger, that she makes her living by sponging and stealing from people like Chekov who earn their bread. But above all, pride. He was wrong. He would like to escape this crushing career and make peace with her. But not on his life would he admit it.

He feels cheated. He has done everything he was supposed to do, and it doesn't work. It is all garbage.

However, Irina too has changed. She did not accept his word as a friend that he would find her Eden, because he was no longer a friend. He loathed it, and it humiliated him, but he tried. She responded to his assistance by taking over the ship. She gave the *Enterprise* and the lives of her crew into the hands of a thief, a lunatic, and an attempted murderer. Irina knew fully well what she was doing, and what her unstable leader would do. Well, Chekov may have been wrong about her the first time, but he was right in the long run.

He does choose to bid her farewell. He can now distinguish between Irina and her life-style, though he hopes she will practice it legally. And he has learned that environment alone does not make a person err, but the choices he makes do, as well. It's no different from the understanding that Kirk is temperamental because he chooses to be, not because he's Irish.

"The Way to Eden" was crucial to Chekov's self-esteem and the solution to his problem. He is no longer on the *Enterprise* because he "should" be there, but because he wants to be there. He is still young, but he has grown up.

By the time of *Star Trek: The Motion Picture*, Chekov has become a lieutenant (note that Kirk was *not* there) and secured an additional post as weapons officer. And in *Star Trek II: The Wrath of Khan*, he is a full commander on the *Reliant*, all ready to assume the "Jim Kirk School of Strategic Thought." Of course, *Captain* Terrell and *Commander* Chekov are the ones to beam down on a routine survey to be caught by Khan. It would seem that after Chekov's eyewitness observations of what happens to valuable *Enterprise* personnel who beam down into danger, he would never leave any ship again. Some things never change: Chekov being tortured and screaming himself blue; Chekov being in a position to blow Kirk's rear end off and then somehow not doing it. Even under Khan's influence, Chekov refused to harm Kirk; Terrell's will was not as strong, so he killed himself. Pavel never lost his weapon or was attacked, so nothing could have prevented him from killing Kirk. But Chekov still had his will, and he simply would not do it.

(It would be interesting to see how Chekov would actually run operations if he had his own ship. Would he turn cautious? After all these years, it must have occurred to him that the "Jim Kirk School" does not have many living followers.)

It is logical that Chekov would so quickly join the renegade *Search for Spock*, no questions asked. Chekov owes as much to Spock as he does to Kirk, and he would prefer to express his gratitude in the typically silent but active Vulcan manner. Chekov also respects McCoy, mostly because Spock did. Pavel and the doctor never did get along very well on their own; both thought Spock had some bad effect on the other. As the reviewers in *Best of Trek #8* pointed out, (1) Chekov does not need a reason to do the right thing, so long as there is a right thing needing to be done, and (2) the man is sick. He should be home in bed. The Ceti Eel supposedly derives nutrition as a parasite, so either his poor brain was starved for food and air, or it was just chewed a bit. If McCoy had been the least bit well, he would never have let Chekov run loose, but he must have believed he could call the commander back to Sickbay later. No question, Chekov did not need the extra aggravation.

It was up to Chekov and Scotty to almost recreate a battered, *big* ship. Their talents were less emphasized, and far more important, than any other effort in *The Search for Spock*. After all, you can't exactly walk to Genesis. Everything else done, although important, cannot be considered to be in the same league. As Star Trek proved countless times, Kirk can bust out of jail anytime. Characters are invincible and immortal. Ships are honest to their nature and break down. Ships die.

Chekov is in a delicate position, though, one that may be to Kirk's advantage in the fourth film. Unlike Scotty and Uhura, Chekov was not on duty when they left for Genesis. And unlike Kirk and Sulu, Chekov got onto the *Enterprise* early and undetected. This means that *no one saw Chekov leave Earth and/or go to Genesis, therefore no one can charge him with anything*. Legally, that is. And only Saavik and the Vulcans of Mount Seleya know how he got to Vulcan.

Can the Federation convict him of conspiracy on circumstantial evidence? It isn't impossible—McCoy was being sent to an asylum without so much as a hearing—but just this once he might get away with it. Kirk may badly need a spy in high places in the months to come. (Of course, there's always Saavik, but she has not learned to keep her mouth shut; her honesty could put him away.) However, Chekov does stand a better chance of being acquitted than Uhura does. Too many fans are making the assumption that "Mr. Adventure" will keep *his* big mouth shut.

One more thing: Consider poor Pavel's clothes. "Buster Brown," they've been called (although in 1985 his stirrup slacks mysteriously came into fashion among junior high students). Chekov may not be quite as flamboyant as Kirk, but it is generally believed that the man does have taste. Obviously he was dressed blandly in order to ditch Petty Federation Officials in Charge Of Two-Month Debriefings and the everloving *Federation Enquirer*. So don't shoot anyone in Wardrobe, unless it happens again. Chekov may look good in Klingon armor.

(Hikaru Walter) Sulu
First appearance: "Where No Man Has Gone Before"
Rank and post: Lieutenant; astrophysicist, helmsman
Rank and post by *The Search for Spock*: Captain of the USS *Excelsior*

It is astonishing that Sulu has been given so little attention on screen and in print. Surely a young man so elegant, so dashing, so essential to the safe operation of a Federation starship deserves better.

His history is certainly unique. The closest he ever got to a romantic encounter was his, ah, welcome of the Deltan Ilia, but he is not lonely. When he is insulted, he can shrug it off; but challenge him to a contest and he will win it, without malice or pride. Unlike some of the regulars, he takes care of himself and enjoys doing it—exercising, eating properly, taking recreation. He has no fear of dying, and he isn't afraid of living. He not only strives to be happy, he *is* happy. Perhaps his lack of exposure arises from the problem some writers have to relating to characters who are at peace—it is far easier and more fashionable to expose a person's weaknesses, or even choose a villain as the target for sympathy. By this standard Sulu's only fault is being too nice to possibly be considered interesting. So Hikaru fires the phasers, steers the ship, and similarly stays out of trouble that would help his popularity.

It isn't obvious how much Kirk appreciates Sulu. For one thing, Kirk rarely says so. His steady hand can easily be taken for granted, so it is. Indeed, the helmsman is one of Kirk's favorite targets when something goes wrong. Originally, the fact that Sulu was a lowly lieutenant was excuse enough, but now he is a convenient scratching post for another reason: he doesn't care. He knows his work is good and Kirk is not mad at him personally. Even if he was, and had good reason to be, Hikaru would mend the situation without fuss. Sulu is able to humor the Captain, and he acts as a buffer between Kirk's unthinking temper and those crewmembers who are sensitive to it. It is not a pleasant position to be in, but as long as Kirk acts as he does, it is necessary. No one else will play this game: McCoy and Scotty yell back, Spock coolly informs the captain that he's being silly, and the others grind their teeth and slink away. Kirk needs Sulu desperately; without him he would lose every friend he has. The helmsman's patience, tact, and acting are nothing short of amazing.

He utilizes his ease with people in another important task—breaking in the rookies. Bailey, Stiles, Kevin Riley, and Pavel Chekov are just a few of those left in his care. He knows all the front duties better than anyone, and he makes it clear that there is no embarrassment in asking his help. Of course, the youngsters look to him for cues as to when the Captain's anger is to be taken seriously and when he's just blowing off steam.

Even in life-or-death situations, Sulu is an uncommonly stable presence for the rookies to cling to. From "May the Great Bird of the Galaxy bless your planet" to "Don't call me tiny," he always has a succinct observation, soothing their nerves with lively chatter, gossip, and wag, but in turn he absorbs a good deal of information from them. Sometimes his gossip's tongue is required to save lives—Hikaru knew in "Day of the Dove" that Chekov was an only child (he claimed to be avenging his dead brother), and therefore that Chekov was dangerously mad.

Sulu was almost ready for a promotion in the series. As an astrophysicist in "Where No Man Has Gone Before," he had little screen time, but enough to establish his competence. He was qualified to command the *Enterprise* in an all-out war against the Klingons ("Errand of Mercy"). This indicates that Sulu is more highly trained in fleet operations than is Scott—which is no slur against Scotty, who is as capable in solo engagements as he is with his engines.

Sulu proved quite competent in handling security in "The Man Trap." To his good fortune, Kirk never followed up on it by appointing him security chief, for if he had, Sulu would have: (1) been killed; (2) been regularly in hot water until he was removed; (3) been brilliant, which would destroy a convenient plot device.

The Sulu of "Mirror, Mirror" is predictably everything the real Sulu is not. In that other reality, he has a position worthy of his talent, but not his ambition. Sulu-2 has no intention of waiting twenty years to be the captain of his own ship, and dastardly as he was, one certainly could sympathize with that. Had his selected targets not been from another universe, his well-laid plans may have worked. (Perhaps not . . . Kirk-2 must be pretty good himself not to have killed a single security chief in two years of Federation-reality, and most certainly he can take care of himself.) Had Sulu-2 not been so bloodthirsty (not to mention a twin to the crewman Kirk already had), he might have made that ideal security chief that Kirk was always looking for. (But, if our Sulu couldn't get the job, perhaps Kirk subconsciously didn't want a good one.)

Incidentally, Sulu-2 had a ladyfriend, or at least he thought he did. In the canon universe, Sulu and Uhura are affectionate friends, so whatever the other fellow did to earn the woman's enmity, he certainly did a good job. The real Sulu never even gets far enough for offense to be taken.

In "The Enemy Within," Hikaru assumed leadership of the stranded landing party. Having completed a survival course taught by Spock, Sulu was able to save all his people despite their lengthy stay on the planet. Sulu made light of the difficulties, limiting his complaints to, "Where's room service? The rice wine is taking too long." Also, because he sent up the doglike animal, the problem was revealed to Scotty before other people could be harmed.

Sulu also has advanced engineering experience, as indicated in "Day of the Dove." Because Klingons have cut off life support to the Bridge, Kirk sends him to auxiliary control to *repair* it. Kirk did believe that Sulu actually fixed it, so he must have had the experience to do so. So we'll postulate—when George Takei disappeared during the second season to film *The Green Berets,* Sulu was Scotty's apprentice in Engineering. At this time, Scotty was losing his old hands and assistants (such as DeSalle) to promotions and transfers, but the Academy graduates were not enough to meet his personnel needs. Thus Scotty asked for and received Sulu's help in breaking in *his* new kids. The opportunity was also good for rounding out the helmsman's skills for future command.

Surprisingly, Hikaru really doesn't care much about his work. He gives every effort to ensure the best possible job, but when the deed is done he forgets it. He is not a victim of one of Star Trek's (and America's) greatest neuroses—addiction to his career. He never lets a mere job become a prop for his identity. When he is on duty it is his top priority, but when it is time to relax, he relaxes. He is free of the snake pit that workaholics such as Kirk or Spock throw themselves into.

Kirk and his followers developed as people as their positions demanded. Sulu, though, brought a stable and satisfied personality into his worldly circumstances, and the result is that circumstances have no control over him. He will not gamble with his sanity by investing his identity in the effort of his hands or in a job that could be gone tomorrow. Take Kirk or Spock off the *Enterprise*, even for a vacation, and they are bereft of their purpose for existence. *Star Trek: The Motion Picture* proved that conclusively. Without the specific place of the *Enterprise* and the time "prime of life," they melt away, because they've persuaded themselves they are good for only that. Sulu, on the other hand, would be happy as a stockbroker or a dishwasher. He is more mature than either of them in that he does not limit his head and hand to what he is paid for.

To a great extent, this gives him his appearance of agelessness. This does not mean that he will never grow old, but that he has no fear of growing older. Age may someday fetter his ability to work and play, but it will never rob him of his enthusiasm for life. A far cry from Kirk and Uhura, who will do almost anything to keep their fair faces but distressed minds frozen in time, as if this is a good thing. In reality, denial and stalling set them up for a cruel shock later.

There is a lot of little boy in Sulu. He plays harder than he works, but his play does not exclude family, friends, or happiness, as work often does. Recreation develops the character, refreshes the mind, gives one grace in both winning and losing, and attracts curious company. Janice Rand shared his love for plants; although to his amusement, she insisted that they would one day prove (upon her person) to be carnivorous. Kevin Riley would hang around despite his voluble objections to Sulu's repeated attempts to "educate" him. The helmsman is generally believed to be precariously off-balance, but he has never lost an audience. If the others would rather be boring or bored, or work too much and goof off, this is their problem. Since they are dissatisfied now, when "work" is all they live for, what will they do in retirement? Is this maturity? Then children are far wiser. Sulu, for one, has not let maturity evict his childlike curiosity, freedom, and playfulness. It is appropriate that Sulu sees the value of "play" in "Shore Leave," although he doesn't get to enjoy much of it. Ask him how he can always be so happy (and Chekov has probably done so many times), and he will quote, "My friends, you stress very unimportant matters" (E. Sandoval, Omicron Ceti III) and go on transplanting his weeping willows. Sulu is mentally healthier than most, and he is far from crazy.

Fortunately, even when he *is* crazy, he is rarely dangerous. "Return of the Archons," "This Side of Paradise," and "Wolf In the Fold" show a loopy Sulu, or as George Takei describes it, "with pongs." In these instances he is no more disturbing than usual. As Sylvia's tool ("Catspaw") he was less help than she thought him to be. When Sulu is sane he can wipe the floor with anyone in the gym. But Sylvia knows nothing of the martial arts, so he loses his "edge," his control, and his struggle with Kirk. Sulu was unstable in "And the Children Shall Lead" only because Gorgan played on his fear of responsibility; what would happen to 430 innocent people if he fell asleep at the wheel? He dares not travel into "unsafe" space, so Gorgan has him under control.

For an insanity that is truly close to his character, review "The Naked Time," wherein he believed himself to be d'Artagnan of Dumas' *The Three Musketeers*.

D'Artagnan was a young Gascon gentleman who went north in 1625 to seek his destiny among the Royal Musketeers. On the day of his arrival, he gracelessly offended all three musketeers of the title and found himself challenged to three consecutive duels of honor. The Inseparables were highly amused by this turn of events, and when he stayed to fight their common enemy, the Cardinal's Musketeers, the three accepted him into their friendship. All of them looked forward to the day when he completed his apprenticeship and became their true comrade-in-arms.

Athos was the eldest Musketeer, a solemn nobleman said to be embittered by a lost love. Porthos was a babbler and a self-proclaimed ladies' man. Aramis considered himself a churchman at heart and insisted that someday he would sheathe his sword for a Bible. They served the King against the forces of Cardinal Richelieu, the real power in the land. It was d'Artagnan who approached the Inseparables with an unfolding adventure that finally involved the governments of both France and England. The four Musketeers thwarted the plans of the Cardinal by capturing his agent, Lady de Winter, who was revealed to be Athos's thought-dead wife. For her international crimes she was put to death by the public executioner of Lille. Athos gave the letter of safe conduct she carried, signed by the Carindal, to d'Artagnan. When d'Artagnan was brought before Richelieu as the ringleader of the executioners, the letter was produced and his life was spared. Impressed by the gentleman's cleverness, the Cardinal granted d'Artagnan a lieutenancy in the Musketeer corps. Soon after, Aramis disappeared to a monastery, none knew where, and Porthos married a wealthy widow. Athos served under d'Artagnan for seven years, then returned to his estate.

In some ways, Sulu is very much like d'Artagnan. Certainly he is skilled in the sword, and his position in Starfleet often involves the safety of many lives. He interrupted a circle of three great friends, but was accepted because of his daring and integrity. (However, it took the three longer to accord a junior officer more than professional respect.) The "Big Three" friendship fell apart in *Star Trek: The Motion Picture*, even as d'Artagnan's friends separated.

So it's not surprising that he should fall into the role when affected by the virus. When the crewmen first ran from Sulu, he knew them for the cowards of the Cardinal. When Uhura rejected his offer of protection against them ("Sorry, neither"), he recognized her for the villainess Lady de Winter, the fair-but-no-maiden who spurned d'Artagnan and was executed. (Apparently, "woman" is as unpredictable, and therefore deadly, in Star Trek as in romantic France.) Good thing for Uhura that d'Artagnan had never had a Vulcan nerve pinch before.

For some reason, Sulu was never again seen to wield his swords. He turned his attraction to guns ("Shore Leave"), and Kirk took that away from him. No doubt this explains why the normally fearless helmsman was upset when an enraged samurai (also created out of his own thoughts) charged after him. Sulu's yearning for the gun did make it possible to stop McCoy's black knight, but aside from that no one saw fit to let the man enjoy his hobby.

Sulu is rarely upset by anything, but when he is, it usually involves the safety of others, as in "The Children Shall Lead." He told Janice Lester/Kirk that she could execute Starfleet personnel literally "only over my dead body." And Khan's surprise attack was all the more upsetting to him because the expletive-deleted shields would not go up.

But personal danger rarely distresses him. This doesn't make him unrealistic—on the contrary, he is far more realistic than some. Kirk, for one, believes that if he bluffs death, stares it down, then it will go away. Sulu, though, has come to terms with the possibility that he really might die at any moment. His console could electrocute him, life support might fail, Klingons might make a sneak attack, or he could drown in the bath. All life is borrowed, so why cry about the inevitable? Why not simply enjoy each day and be thankful to have made it this far and seen so much? Sulu is the only one who looks forward to birthdays, and he'll continue to celebrate as long as he can afford to buy the candles with his pension. If death is no longer feared, there is no harm in tossing off jokes about Balok or Khan—they can't hear, they don't care, and it makes the children feel better.

Sulu and Kirk will have a better chance to become friends if they end up cooped up in the Bird of Prey. Sulu already has quite a crush on that small batlike ship, and even if Starfleet exonerates them, it's doubtful he would let the designers touch it. Let's hope Kirk at least lets him keep his toy and stays with something he knows, like convincing Maltz to join them. It would be a golden opportunity for Sulu, easily replacing his loss of a ship with talking turbolifts.

Sulu's source of inner peace is never mentioned, nor are many of his interests, achievements, or goals in life. It is possible that he has a strong religious faith to strengthen him both in health and hot water. By circumstance he has an American accent, admires a French musketeer, and is presented to an audience that began as approximately half Christian. There is no solid evidence that Sulu holds a Christian faith, but from his attitudes and actions, he could. His life is dedicated to doing good and not expecting good in turn. He does not have many vices, and he tries to eliminate those he does have. Hikaru Walker Sulu would sacrifice his own life to protect another, and he would do so without regret or (usually) fear. He is "in the world but not of it" and knows where to place his priorities. And he observes the phrase, "Be ye kind to one another, tenderhearted, forgiving of one another, even as the Lord hath forgiven you." Above all, Sulu is good with people, often kinder to them than they are to themselves. He might be Christian or Buddhist or Shinto, but unless he says so, there is no way to know. There is Oriental and Filipino blood in him, and there are many other beliefs in the world (not to mention the many other worlds known in Star Trek's time).

Whether or not Sulu has a religious conviction, he plays an important part in understanding man in Star Trek's (and our) time. Kirk and company are not the only ones capable of making profound statements, but as they are the stars, they get the attention. Thus, something very important is neglected.

If Kirk/Spock/McCoy represent the spirit of man, then Sulu/Uhura/Chekov are the source of man's strength: faith, hope, and love.

Faith is Sulu. Faith is the unshakable conviction that nothing can stand against a being that is right with its Maker. A man can have hopes without faith, but they will not be *hope*—they will be unworthy of his true nature and destiny. And he cannot have the *agape*, the love for all beings regardless of their worthiness, without faith. Faith is the bridge between the world of sinful, stumbling mortals and the holy eternity where they belong. Faith is a creature of this life, ceasing at life's end; but in its domain it is supreme among men. Sulu heads this forgotten triad: His strength and purity are the powerful link between the purely-mortal and the purely-eternal impulses of man.

Hope is Chekov. Hope is transient, a product of fleeting man as he struggles to achieve his goals. In timeless eternity, hope, which implies a progression in measurable human time, has no meaning or being. Hope is active; it takes action to achieve its desires; when the object of effort is gained (or lost), hope ceases and a new goal is chosen. Yet without love, hope's goals are often frivolous and without benefit. Chekov is the active, even impatient, driving force, that must have results while still in the mortal world.

Love is Uhura. Love is the whole being of Almighty God. This *agape* force does good to all men; but men, beause of their impurity, are unable to truly return it. Therefore love, although the final word in the soul, does not translate well into the realm of mortals. Love needs faith to be welcomed into a man, and love needs hope to be its hands, building that faith. Uhura, like the power she represents, had difficulty "translating" into her imperfect world, and she will take longest to come into her strength. But in the end, she will command the forgotten triad. "And now remain these three, faith, hope, and love; but the greatest of these is love" (1 Cor 13:13).

Star Trek III: The Search for Spock was one of the better vehicles for expressing the unity of Sulu/Chekov/Uhura (not to mention putting the tense, electric, shattered threesome in the spotlight). Sulu was tempted by the splendid if odd-looking *Excelsior*, truly a once-in-a-lifetime chance, and in his faith he let it go. Kirk was called upon to sacrifice his ship, and he did so, but considering his misery in *Wrath of Khan*, it's hard to believe he was losing much. What would he have done if called upon to give up the *Enterprise* at the *beginning* of his career, when that career had some meaning for him? Sulu had reached that marvelous point in time. All his dreams were finally coming true. Yet he let it all go to do what he knew was right. He didn't have to; despite his concern, this mission had nothing to do with him personally.

Chekov was the force of hope's power for action when he aided Scotty in repairing the crippled *Enterprise*. As ever, Chekov needs a concrete goal, one that he can reach in a reasonable period of time, to be satisfied. Kirk, like Chekov, is mostly a creature of hope: creating, striving, achieving (or failing), and living throughout in great impatience. But Chekov has the talent to repair the ship as well as command it; and Kirk, frustrated with idleness, envies him. His own hands ache to take action, but command will not permit it.

Uhura demonstrated her love for the others in both of these ways, with mixed results. In choosing McCoy's life over duty, she showed her faith in Kirk's task. By sabotaging Starfleet's commuication system, she gave the crew the hope of success. But she had to remain behind to do these things, and it is very obvious that given the chance, she would have gone with the men. It was indeed love that caused her to endanger herself, when surely Janice Rand, Winston Kyle, or some other such loyal soul would have volunteered to take that position—and be turned in by Heisenberg. Rather than cause another to be punished, Uhura took the questionable honor upon herself.

Oh, the friendship of Sulu, Chekov, and Uhura still needs major development, but even now it is clearly more affectionate, peaceful, and stable than that of Kirk/Spock/McCoy. Chekov still needs some patience lessons, but not just now. Why take all the life out of him? Uhura is rather too shaky for her role and will take some years growing into it. Sulu for now is their natural leader, but it is a comfortable, almost lazy leadership. When Uhura has grown up a little, there will be some dynamic changes, and Sulu will be then content to follow her vision.

Even Kirk is beginning to notice the strength of these people. Until now, he has shied away from showing affection for them because it would be unprofessional, too intimate for a great captain and his meek underlings. Never before would he have considered joining them for a drink for any occasion, let alone invite them to his home. But he is beginning to understand that they are not children any longer, and that perhaps he still is. It is disturbing to him, but he is doing his best to work it out. It is his last hurdle in aging—the "calendar syndrome." (This is the tendency of parents never to see their children as growing up, or the mental rut of an employer who sees his employees as never older than the day they were hired, because if they age, then so do their elders. It's a curable ailment but still quite persistent, especially in somewhat vain persons like Kirk.) Yes, it hurts Kirk in some small way that his "kids" don't need him anymore.

This article will conclude in *The Best of Trek #12* with Part Three—"The Engineer and the Doctor."

SPECULATION: ON RELATIONSHIPS, RESPONSIBILITIES, AND RISK

By Sharron Crowson

One of the continuing debates in human relations is about responsibility. How much do we owe to society? What are the rights of the individual? When do these come into conflict? These questions, and others raised by them, also apply to the convoluted and finely detailed world of Star Trek. Indeed, many episodes and recent films have themselves raised such questions. There are no sure answers, but Sherry Crowson offers some observations about whose needs outweigh whose.

Every relationship entails rights and responsibilities as well as risks. Star Trek has always relied on the exploration of relationships to give it depth and meaning. *Star Trek III: The Search for Spock* is no different, and perhaps a better example of such exploration than some earlier works. There are many interesting relationships in this film; between organizations, between cultures, and especially between individuals. These relationships all have something in common, layers of interlocking responsibilities, rights, and risks.

To begin, let's examine the relationships surrounding Starfleet. We need to consider Starfleet both as a branch of the United Federation of Planets and as a collection of individuals working together within a specific framework.

Starfleet is responsible for defending and protecting the Federation, for exploring new territories and discoveries, and for carrying out the directives of the Federation Council. To fulfill its obligations, Starfleet has the concomitant right to expect competent leadership, some understanding of how such an organization must function, and the funds and material necessary to its task.

The Federation is responsible for providing direction and seeing that Starfleet gets what it needs to operate properly and efficiently. It has the right to expect a certain level of professional conduct from Starfleet officers and cooperation with the Council and its objectives. It's a reciprocal arrangement that ties both organizations together and requires them to work toward common goals by fulfilling mutual responsibilities.

The relationship between Starfleet and its officers shares many aspects common to the relationship between Starfleet and the Federation; they also share common goals and common responsibilities.

Yet, in *The Search for Spock*, there seems to be times when these relationships are strained, when responsibilities go unrecognized and unfulfilled, while rights are still insisted upon. For example, Starfleet lets itself be dictated to by a panicked Federation Council. It does not stand up to the political pressure and support its officers.

In the novelization of the film, Sulu is slated to command the *Excelsior*, but is ordered to step down in favor of Styles because the Federation is in a state of panic over the theft of Genesis. Sulu had been ordered aboard the *Enterprise* for the training cruise and had no choice but to go along when the ship was sent to investigate Genesis. He performed his duties in that perilous situation well enough to earn a commendation. However, Starfleet bows to political pressure and replaces him as commander of *Excelsior*. Starfleet does not support him the one time Sulu had every right to expect that support. Therefore, it fails to fulfill its responsibilities to Sulu just as the Federation fails to supply Starfleet with competent leadership.

Starfleet fails other officers—Kirk, Spock, and McCoy—in the same manner. It has the responsibility to value their lives and their contributions to the service and protect them, if at all possible. McCoy and Spock have the right to expect that the sacrifice of their lives should have some meaning, some purpose, and not be thrown away out of fear or panic.

Kirk is responsible for his crew and goes to Commander of Starfleet Harry Morrow to get help to fulfill his obligation. He has the right to expect cooperation and help; his request is not so bizarre, so outlandish as to be outside the realm of possibility.

But Morrow is prejudiced, in the truest sense of the word. He prejudged Kirk's request by letting the Federation, in its turmoil, unsurp Starfleet's perogatives. Morrow makes no effort to determine the facts of the case Kirk presents. He finds it difficult to deal with abstracts of soul, loyalty, and risk with the Federation breathing down his neck about security and the system-wide upheaval caused by Genesis. It's easier, *safer*, to say no to Kirk, although it is likely to cost McCoy's life and Spock's soul. What amazes me is that Morrow, who claims to know Kirk well, should think that saying no to him would be the end of the matter.

We also witness the relationships of individuals to the society at large. David Marcus is part of the Genesis team, as that team is part of a larger segment of society not directly under Starfleet influence. The Federation puts Starfleet officers and ships at the disposal of the team to help with Genesis. Though it's an uneasy relationship at best, both sides benefit and seem to work together with a minimum of disruptive friction.

David is the biologist of the team; it's his responsibility to see to it that the forms designated and encoded by the other members of the team generate life. When problems arise in this area, David chooses to risk the use of protomatter to solve them. Protomatter is inherently unstable and David's peers deemed its use unethical, because there was no way to determine what effects its lack of stability might cause. Without using protomatter, David felt it might be years before Genesis could be tested—or that it might prove impossible altogether.

Saavik says to David, "Like your father, you changed the conditions." It's true that Kirk changed the conditions of the *Kobayshi Maru* simulation—however, nothing but his pride and a test performance were at stake. He truly believed the test was arbitrarily designed to limit his choices in a way contrary to the real world. David, on the other hand, had sound scientific data indicating that protomatter was dangerous and unpredictable, yet he used it to solve his problem—an easy answer. He wanted Genesis immediately—he was unwilling to wait or work to see if there might be a safer, more effective way to deal with the problem. He did not expect the project to directly involve so many lives, but he was willing to risk a reaction he had no way to predict or control. He did not act responsibly and took advantage of the close relationship of the team to get away with something that he knew was wrong.

The Genesis team, as a whole, took their responsibilities seriously. They did not want to see their work taken from them or used as a weapon. They were willing to risk hiding it while they tried to discuss their position with the Federation, rather than blindly hand over a potentially devastating discovery to Starfleet, who they believed would take it illegally and by force. When they realized how Khan, who had commandeered the *Reliant*, would use it, "they bought escape time for Genesis—with their lives."

Kirk is responsible for trying to keep Genesis out of the Klingon Commander Kruge's hands and it costs the life of his son, David. This is one time when the needs of society had to take precedence over personal needs. The decision comes down to numbers and potential, but it is not made lightly. Though everything happens so quickly and there is little opportunity for Kirk to do *anything*, I cannot imagine him trading Genesis for David's life. I don't believe David would have allowed it, once he understood that the Klingons were not interested in the creative aspects of Genesis but only its power of destruction. David feared, a soul-deep fear, that his team's work would be "perverted into a dreadful weapon." Though he was irresponsible in the method of building the process, he would not have been party to turning it over to Kruge. He had come to understand several things about his father and Starfleet, and the need to protect the innocent from the results of the Klingon mentality and lust for power was something he understood well. He gives his life to protect Saavik and Spock—he is much like his father.

Sarek, representing Vulcan as its ambassador to the Federation, had the responsibility to carry out the wishes of the Vulcan people with dignity and respect. He also has the right to call upon his society to give him what he perceives as a need—the refusion of Spock's *katra* with his living body. Sarek risks being thought aberrant and, logic forbid, emotional, but takes that chance to give Spock back his life. His years of service and the value of an individual life give Sarek the right to demand whatever help the Vulcan Masters can give him. Their knowledge and years of training also make the masters responsible for handling the problems their area of expertise qualifies them to deal with.

It should have been possible for Vulcan, as a member of the

Federation, to get permission to retrieve Spock's body; but Sarek has been to the Federation Council and seen the state it was in. He knew there was no way that the Council would be able to handle a request dealing with Genesis in time to be of any help to him.

So, Sarek goes to see Kirk, demanding to know why Kirk did not fulfill his responsibilities as a friend and bring Spock's body and essence home to Vulcan. He did not know that Kirk had not received Spock's *katra*, and, knowing the relationship between Kirk and Spock, he found it hard to credit Kirk's denial. His abrupt request for the mind meld is unusual in the extreme. He has to be desperate, if such a state can be attributed to a Vulcan, to be willing to hurry such an extremely painful process—painful for both of them. Sarek has to lower personal barriers and experience Kirk's grief and his son's death; he has to open that wound in Kirk again, just when it was beginning to be bearable. Sarek's own sense of responsibility makes him expend every effort; he puts aside his own pride and pain to explore every possibility. Kirk consents to the meld; he knows the risks and what it will cost him in grief, but he, too, must have the answers and assurances that are possible only through the meld.

When they later discover that McCoy holds Spock's *katra*, Sarek asks Kirk to find a way to do the impossible, to get both Spock's body and McCoy to Vulcan so they may install Spock's spirit in the Hall of Ancient Thought. In essence, Sarek is asking Kirk to balance personal relationships against his responsibility to Starfleet and the Federation.

Kirk risks the disapproval of his peers, his position, his power, and his prestige if he tries. If he doesn't try, he risks lives, loves, soul, and honor. That's some choice.

Here is the essential area of conflict; of rights, responsibilities, and risks. Which should take precedence?

There will always be a gray area where matters of conscience have to be decided by the individual. Even within the Federation, there are different views of what is considered moral and what is culturally acceptable. Yet there are commonalities among all those who espouse Federation ideals.

Humans and Vulcans may not agree on what is considered polite or even reasonable, but they do agree on a respect for life and for the value of each contribution. Both cultures are willing to set aside convention, in the pursuit of life, and a quality of life that makes such a choice possible. Although Vulcans may be slightly more rigid when it comes to custom, they are not subject to the same kind of emotional pressures that cause both Starfleet and the Federation Council to fail to live up to their own ideals in a moment of crisis.

Spock's human friends risk everything to bring him back to Vulcan, to give him a chance to have a whole life, not to be just a shadow in the Hall of Ancient Thought. They might have settled for that if there was no other option, but by their sacrifice they make their own eloquent plea to Vulcan in the presence of the Masters, though it is Sarek's voice that asks for *fal tor pan*, the refusion.

Out of necessity, or possibly because of Vulcan ritual, the humans are excluded from the ceremony, except for McCoy who must be there. There is no explanation of the ceremony given to those who must wait through the long Vulcan night, beyond the nonspecific warning that McCoy is endangered by the process, as is Spock. Vulcan culture is not adept at dealing with emotional impacts and so must seem cold and indifferent to us, who look at the ceremony with Human eyes.

As Vulcan is known for its respect of life, honor, and truth, concepts Human worlds also understand and value, other aspects of the culture are given their rightful place—as minor trials and tribulations. Two alien cultures must risk being misunderstood for the sake of a relationship that brings exchange of knowledge, ideas, and companionship on the way to mutually beneficial goals.

Kirk and his friends choose to take the many risks, impelled by personal ethics, that will allow them to continue in their relationships with each other and the absent Spock. This choice may be at odds with society at the moment, but clearly they were listening to that still, small voice that tells a being what is right—and what *is not*. When people stop listening to that voice, no matter how softly it speaks or how loudly society shouts, that's when you have established the potential for catastrophe— for rule by a Stalin or a Hitler.

Kirk and company will never use the excuse, will never say, "I was only following orders." However, they might say, "If I'm in trouble now, at least *I* know what I did was *right*." Spock asks Kirk in the confusion aftermath of refusion, "Why did you do that (come back for me)?" Kirk answers simply, in perfect faith and trust, knowing it to be true as he knows little else, "You would have done the same for me."

And if it comes time to pay for listening to conscience rather than the dictates of society, for not betraying that trust, I have no doubt Kirk and the others will pay the price and never stop to count the cost. They know there are principles, lives, and relationships that are worth whatever you have to risk to keep them.

THE CLASSIC STAR TREK

By Linda M. Johnston

The word "classic" is bandied about pretty freely these days . . . The word has even popped up in these collections from time to time. But what is a "classic," really? How is it defined? Who decides? And, most importantly, can Star Trek truly be termed a "classic"? Linda Johnston answers these questions in the following article, as well as offering a short course on what "classic" actually means.

Thanks to a local independent television station, I've been watching some of the old shows I watched when I was a teenager or thereabouts, shows like "Mod Squad," "Combat," and "Star Trek." Even in my youth, Star Trek was my favorite, but the three were more equal in my esteem then than now. This second time around, twenty years later, I began to wonder, personally, why the older I got the better Star Trek got, and the less satisfying the others were. And, by extension, I began to wonder why Star Trek seems to be quickly becoming a classic and other shows apparently are not.

I teach English in college, so the word *classic* is quite familiar to me, yet that a work is a classic is, like a lot of religion, simply to be taken by faith because it has stood the test of time. *Antigone* is a classic because it has survived since mid-400s B.C. *Canterbury Tales* is a classic because it has survived since the 1300s. *Huckleberry Finn* is a classic because it has survived since the late 1800s. But is Star Trek a classic because it has survived since 1966? Is twenty years enough time to establish something as "a classic"? How does one predict what will survive the test of time or know when classic standing has arrived?

"Now wait," you may be saying. "You're comparing apples with oranges, written literature with visual television. Star Trek already is a classic within its own medium, having survived almost half as long as television itself." That may be true, and I, personally, believe it is. But comparing one TV show with another seems somewhat pointless when we try to capture *classic* in the classical literary sense. A classic is, by definition, something "of the highest rank or class; serving as an outstanding representative of its kind; model; having lasting significance or recognized worth." How can one call any television show a "classic" when (1) the medium is so new that there have been devised only recently standards by which to judge what makes a good series (I am, for the moment, excluding old movies made before the advent of TV, and do not include in this discussion technical matters such as editing, directing, special effects, etc.); (2) something so novel cannot yet have proven lasting significance; (3) there are so few apples in the barrel—what other science fiction TV series, exactly, are you going to compare Star Trek with?

So, in the traditional sense, Star Trek cannot yet be called a *classic*. But when it can be, fifty or one hundred years hence, whatever that vague and arbitrary number of years is that something must survive, will it have survived? Will it be a classic?

I think the answer is yes, and I have several specific reasons for this belief.

First, a classic is something that, like influenza, spreads throughout the world, unstoppable, affecting rich and poor, educated and uneducated. And, like the flu, some get a mild case, others a bad case. Nearly everyone has heard of *Huckleberry Finn*, for instance; whether they've read it or not can tell you the author, at minimum, they've heard of it. The name pops up in the oddest places—there's no immunity.

We saw this invasion of Star Trek begin to happen not long after the last episode was aired. In *The Star Trek Compendium*, Allan Asherman states, "By 1978 Star Trek had made syndication history. The series was being seen over 300 times per week worldwide in 134 markets in the United States and 131 international markets located in 51 countries. Star Trek was being seen translated into forty-two languages. At the start of 1978, there were 371 Star Trek fan clubs and 431 fanzines being produced, and approximately thirty Trek conventions were being held each year."

Today, Star Trek references have spread to the general population. In 1984, Nena, a German secretary, recorded "99 Red Balloons," an extremely popular song that has an explicit Star Trek reference: ". . . every one a Captain Kirk." For me, the clincher came last spring. I hate to admit it, but when I choose a textbook, I don't always read every word of it. I had two new texts and, much to my amazement, found that both had one or more specific references to Star Trek—and these for 1984 college freshmen!

Let me clarify a point here. Contemporary popularity is not necessarily a harbinger of classicism, often just the opposite; what is "popular" is often critically poor. However, when something popular also becomes pervasive through various media, especially through allusion in scholarly literature, it is well on its way to becoming "a classic." Star Trek has entered this stage.

In the humanities—music, art, literature, theater (television?) —another test of what climbs to classic stature seems to relate again to the very word *classic*. "Of or in accordance with established principles and methods in arts and sciences" is another dictionary definiton of *classic*. Just where were these principles and methods established? The first body of material to be considered classic in the Western sense was that of ancient Greece and Rome. A "classic," then, conforms to what ancient philosophers and critics themselves said an exemplary work should be.

It is not my intention here to get into a lengthy discourse—as the Greeks would say—on ancient philosophy, nor am I going to take every Star Trek episode and movie and try to explain how it conforms to the ideal of Greek thought, though I will say, there are some episodes and some movies more "classic" than others, *Star Trek II: The Wrath of Khan*, for instance, being almost a perfect Greek tragedy, with Khan as a tragically flawed man not all evil like Kruge and whom we can simultaneously admire and despise (i.e., creative tension, a major Greek standard for drama).

There are, however, two Greek principles of literature/ drama/ art against which Star Trek can easily be measured because one is so obvious to any fan and the other is so much discussed in Star Trek literature.

Greek playwrights believe that to be effective a play should be cathartic, figuratively cleansing the emotions. That is, one should be so drawn into the play that he laughs, cries, rages, and so on, at the appropriate places. Vicariously, he becomes part of the action. He forgets that he is seeing a play, an illusion. Any fan will tell you that more episodes than not pull the viewer into them—to laugh or cry or rage. Is there anyone who did not shed a tear at Spock's death?

I often find a kindred spirit among my students, someone who loves to come in and talk Trek. It always amuses me when he begins to speak of Kirk and Company as if they actually existed in the flesh. Sharron Crowson's *Best of Trek #9* article "Speculation: On Power, Politics, and Personal Integrity" is a perfect example of this real/unreal confusion that marks a classic. She asks, "whom and what did the Federation send to deal with the most explosive crisis of the century?" as if the Federation actually existed to send anyone anywhere. Writer Harve Bennett sent the *Grissom*, yet we are so drawn into the *Enterprise* world that we forget it isn't real. The first rule of reading a short story is that nothing exists before the first word or after the last one, or, in the case of Star Trek, between episodes, yet fans are constantly filling in the gaps, speculating, about the "actions" of nonexistent beings in a yet-to-be world. I'd find the tendency ludicrous—if I didn't do it myself.

Realism, thus, is one classic method for developing cartharsis. Another is concealment. An artwork must be so well crafted that one forgets it is contrived. Good art never draws attention to the artistic process. Seldom in Star Trek does anything spoil the illusion. The smoking operating table in "Journey To Babel" and the elevator scene between Kirk and Saavik in *Wrath of Khan* are the only exceptions I can think of, and they are technical problems more than plot or character development. (How many takes did they do in the elevator, anyway, that Shatner and Alley were in stitches?)

Character development is another technique for assuring catharsis. We identify with a filled-out character. In talking with fans, I, like Joyce Tullock, in "Brother, my Soul . . ." (*Best of Trek #9*), have found that every person has a favorite character, usually because that character has qualities the fan himself lacks. This "opposites attract" theme is central to Greek, specifically to Platonic, philosophy. The degree to which a work of art successfully handles this "incomplete man" theme seems to me directly proportional to the degree to which that work will attain classic stature.

Plato believed that man strove constantly to live the "good life." To him, the good life had nothing to do with leisure or money. A man was living the good life, or was *virtuous*, when he fit into the purpose for which he was created in two areas: society, and his own totality of soul. In Star Trek, we see the Triune characters—Kirk, Spock, and McCoy—and, to a lesser extent, the other characters—constantly seeking this classical "good life."

In Plato's ideal society, there were three basic functions that needed to be fulfilled. These functions are typified by the teacher, the soldier, and the worker. I do not find it by chance that at the beginning of *Star Trek II: The Wrath of Khan* Spock is a teacher. He has always functioned as the one who acquires, preserves, and imparts knowledge. Kirk, of course, is a natural-born soldier. He is often also the diplomatic arm of the political system, a part of the classical soldier function he does not really enjoy but performs adequately. McCoy, though not an artisan who crafts metal artifacts, nonetheless functions as the worker. His skilled hands are always busy.

Without stretching logic too much, we can see also that the other characters have found their ideal places within the *Enterprise* microcosm. Chekov is Spock's protégé, and on the *Reliant*, he is the knowledge-gatherer. Sulu, with his love for weaponry, is the soldier, who, if Genesis had not intervened, would have been captain of the *Excelsior;* with his warm, ready smile and humor, he could easily act as diplomat. Uhura and Scott, both members of the engineering section, are workers, constantly using their hands to keep vital ship functions operational. As a nurse, Chapel, like McCoy, is also a worker. Rand's position is difficult to explain in Platonic terms—perhaps he forgot the category I shall euphemistically call "companion," although that certainly falls into the worker class. No wonder her role did not survive.

Philosophically speaking, the crew of the *Enterprise* is living the good life: everyone is performing the task he was created for. No bickering, no shoving, all harmonious. Plato's ideal society.

Until a niche is jeopardized. Many of the episode plots are based on a disruption—from within or without—of this ideal society. In one show after another, each Triune character is offered a chance to change his role in the *Enterprise* society. In "The Galileo Seven," "The Tholian Web," and "The Paradise Syndrome," Spock moves from second in command to become the highest ranking officer present and, though he always saves the day, he is never comfortable with this higher role, nor is he very good at it. More than once, he reminds McCoy that he has no desire to command a starship. McCoy, of course, is quick to let everyone around know that Spock is in over his head.

In "For the World Is Hollow and I Have Touched the Sky," McCoy is given the opportunity to live out his dying days in a different society, doing nothing. At first, he thinks this would be wonderful, especially because he is in love, but he realizes, even before he's cured, that medicine is his whole life and that his place in society is as Chief Medical Officer of the USS *Enterprise*.

Kirk's position as captain is the one most often threatened, either by other men, aliens, machines, or by strife within Kirk himself. "The Enemy Within" is the first episode in which we see Kirk losing control of his ship as the splitting of his own personality in two makes him incapable of leadership. Immediately thereafter, in "The Naked Time," Kirk's position is again jeopardized from an internal personality change. Charlie X, Harry Mudd, and Khan are some of the people who try to dispossess Kirk of his rightful social position. The most powerful displacement episode, though, is "The Ultimate Computer," for the other enemies he could at least fight. But his position is within Starfleet and it is this very system that is trying to replace him. Fortunately, machines, although valuable in their own places within society, as Spock says, are not ready to rule humans. "There are certain things men must do to remain men," said Kirk. (Perhaps Star Trek's adherence to this classical standard of "the good life" with each community member contributing his unique talents explains why Kirk seems always to be destroying paradise societies, for example, "The Apple" and "Return of the Archons.")

But by far the most obvious enactment of this theme of man's place in society comes at the beginning of *Star Trek II: The Wrath of Khan*. Captain Kirk is now Admiral Kirk, and for once McCoy and Spock agree—Kirk is a man out of his societal niche. "You should never have given up the *Enterprise* . . . Get your ship back. Get it back before you really do get old," advises the doctor. "Logic does reveal . . . that you erred in accepting promotion. You are what you were: a starship commander," says Spock. Kirk is absolutely miserable with a desk job. Despite all the horrors of Khan and Kruge, Kirk is happy commanding the *Enterprise*. His place in society is the command chair. I shall be extremely surprised and disappointed if Kirk is not demoted right off in *Star Trek IV*. He deserves the reward of being captain again, of returning to "the good life."

Two other themes based on Platonic ideal of society should be mentioned. Plato believed in equity of wealth. There should be no extremes of wealth or poverty. "The Cloud Minders" emphasizes this theory. Plato was also an advocate of women's rights, believing they had a legitimate right to hold any position they were capable of, even the top political office. Unfortunately, there is never a female captain in Starfleet. "Poor Janice Lester," "Turnabout Intruder" seems to say at the end, "If only she'd been content with her place as a woman obviously inferior to men." Even Uhura never gets to lead an expedition. Only in the last movies do we see that Saavik has a shot at her own command. Vulcans, however, have apparently read Plato's *Republic*, for T'Pau obviously is in her rightful place. In *Star Trek IV*, I hope we see some women wearing pants figuratively as well as literally.

Not only must man seek his intended place in society, but, Plato says, he must also seek harmony among the parts of his own being. Throughout his life, Plato tried to define the pieces that comprise the thing we call *man*. Basically (and I mean bare-bones basic, for no one can pretend to condense Plato's ideas into a short essay), Plato said that man could be divided into two major parts, the body and the soul. Somewhere in between the two is the intellect, which could itself be divided into reason and the senses. Together, reason and the senses gain knowledge or wisdom. When all is working in harmony, man is said to be *virtuous*. The four chief virtues of the soul extending from the man as a whole are wisdom, justice, courage, and temperance.

Many protagonists in classical literature are incomplete. They are always seeking some missing part of themselves. Much has been said about the relationship of the Triune. This relationship, this interdependence, is a symbolic literary representation of

Plato's philosophy. It takes Kirk plus Spock plus McCoy to make one complete man.

If we can't compare Star Trek with another science fiction series, we can compare it with something fairly similar, the fantasy, *The Wizard of Oz*, which, with little argument, has established itself as a classic, having passed all the aforementioned criteria. In *The Wizard of Oz*, we have a heroine who is a complete human being. She is wise, just, courageous, and temperate. She is, thus, virtuous. However, classically, and literally, she is displaced. She is looking for the way home, for her ordained place in the universe. It is the other three major characters—another Triune—who are each fragmented. The scarecrow lacks reason (a brain). The tin man lacks feeling, senses (a heart). And the lion lack courage (a brave-acting body). At the end, each receives the missing ingredient, and the three taken together represent one unified whole.

Again, without consideration of technical aspects of film, *The Wizard of Oz* is a classic partly if not entirely because it so beautifully interweaves these two classic ideas of man's search for his place in society and his search for his whole self. Thematically, this classic is closely paralleled by Star Trek, a potential classic.

We have seen that on numerous occasions plot conflict arises because someone's place in the *Enterprise* society is threatened. Now let us see how plot and theme make use of man's search for completeness, for virtue.

Like the Oz characters, within the Star Trek Triune, each person represents only a part of Plato's complete man, but instead of having a fourth person who magically supplies the missing parts, each Star Trek person supplements the other two.

Spock, as has been well documented, represents reason. He deals in abstractions, in theories, in the invisible, the universal, the changeless. He relies primarily on logic, both deductive and inductive. (Logic, by the way, comes from the Greek word *leg-*, meaning "to gather.") In "Shore Leave," for instance, Spock gathers evidence that suggests someone is fabricating reality from mental images. In "Courtmartial," he gathers evidence, including a test of the computer, and concludes that someone has tampered with the computer's program and that Ben Finney is not dead. He enjoys gathering information.

Often, though, Spock cannot see what is plainly under his

nose: that the primitive creatures in "The Galileo Seven" had no logic of fear; that Minerva Jones ("Is There In Truth No Beauty?") is blind.

McCoy, on the other hand, is the senses of the Platonic Man. Much of Star Trek literature states or implies that McCoy is the embodiment of emotion. To Plato, however, there was a distinction between sensual and emotional. To him, the worst sin against mankind was an act of unbridled passion (emotion). Such a "wild" man was called vicious. Even at his most caustic, his most agitated, McCoy never loses control (often because of his dependence on the other two). He is never Plato's evil man. If he were, he would never have killed the creature in "The Man Trap"; he would have wallowed in self-pity in "For the World Is Hollow . . ."; and so on. By *sensual*, Plato meant the use of the five senses and worldliness of experience. McCoy is of Southern gentility. He enjoys fine drink and fine food, and he has an eye for beautiful women. Whereas Spock deals in abstractions, McCoy deals in concretes. McCoy is a "seer." His gift is not logic but intuition, a word based on the Latin *intuere*, "to look at or toward."

Because McCoy relies on the tangible evidence of his senses, he has a difficult time believing that the creature in "Man Trap" is not Nancy Crater. His faith in what he sees also makes him the first victim of the illusionary world of "Shore Leave."

Plato recognized a certain antithesis between reason and sense. Much has been made in Star Trek literature of the feud between Spock and McCoy. True, they seldom agree on anything, primarily because their incompleteness makes each view the world differently. They are not so much men in a mirror (as Joyce Tullock stated in her article "Brother, My Soul: Spock, McCoy, and the Man in the Mirror," *Best of Trek #9*) as pieces of a shattered mirror angled differently. Yet Plato says that reason is dependent upon the senses for data, and that the senses are dependent upon logic for self-control. In the series we see the feud, but we also see the mutual dependence. It is evidence of the senses—McCoy's white sound device—that proves Spock's deduction right in "Courtmartial," that knows how to deceive those very senses in "Amok Time," and that provide inspiration for illogic in "The Galileo Seven." Conversely, it is logic (Spock's urgings) that causes McCoy to shoot the deceptive salt creature, that convinces McCoy that Kirk is alive in "The Tholian

Web," that is able to depose Decker when McCoy cannot in "The Doomsday Machine." Constantly we see the feud between reason and sensation, but we also see their classic cooperation, and it is this last which is so often overlooked in Star Trek analyses, yet so vital to predicting a classic.

Both reason and sense are part of the intellect. Intellect is for Plato the highest natural faculty of Man, guiding and directing the body. Kirk is very definitely the body in Plato's complete man. Undeniably, he is the sex symbol of Star Trek. Being both naive and a McCoy fan, I was not aware just how many women had wild fantasies about Kirk until I saw the near-brawl over very explicit pieces of Kirk artwork at a recent Star Trek convention. Kirk is definitely a lover (remember the boots scene in "Wink of an Eye"?) He takes every opportunity to remove his shirt. Also, he does physical battle with the Squire of Gothos, the Gorn, the Klingons. He acts.

But Kirk acts only after consulting Spock (reason) and McCoy (sense). There's an old cartoon that shows a character with an angel on one shoulder and the devil on the other. Although Spock and McCoy may not be quite that extreme, though the direction is Platonically right, there are countless scenes of Kirk caught (by choice, usually) between Spock literally on his right and McCoy on his left.

Triune, meaning three in one, is a perfect appellation. The Triune is one Complete Man, having reason, sense, and body. Thus, all combine to make the soul, which, in harmony, has virtue. If one character is missing, the soul becomes unbalanced. ("Plato's Stepchildren" is, of course, an explicit rendering of this theme.) That is why Spock's death is not only emotionally upsetting for Kirk and McCoy; it shakes their very essence. They are hopelessly incomplete without reason. It is not only Spock's soul they seek to reunite with his body but also their own soul which has been shattered. It happens to be Spock who died, but the search would have been necessary were it Kirk or McCoy.

In the *Trek Roundtable* section of *Best of Trek #9*, some fans could not understand Kirk's decision to destroy the *Enterprise*. Others felt that Kirk had "matured." Here we see a classic dilemma: The Klingons are trying to usurp Kirk's social position, symbolized by the *Enterprise*, and, in so doing, are thwarting his effort to reunite his soul. It is not strange, though it may be sad, that Kirk chose totality of being over social standing, truly the good of the one for the good of the many (a concept that will be vindicated in *Star Trek IV*).

Thus, if the use of classic philosophy as a basis for theme, plot, and characterization is one more mark of a future classic, Star Trek is well on its way here, too.

Now, if this crash course in Greek philosophy was confusing, let me take the one episode which, to me, epitomized the best use of man's place in society and man's search for completeness as thematic material. Instantly, several fans will say, "Oh, 'The City On the Edge of Forever.' " This episode seems to be the most critically acclaimed, and I cannot think of a better tabloid of the Triune as perfect Platonic symbol than the final old Earth scene: Reason (Spock) standing behind and directing the Body (Kirk) to willfully and deliberately act to restrain the Senses (McCoy). The scene is virtuous because we vividly see wisdom, courage, temperance, and justice.

For me, however, the episode most true to Platonic ideals is "The Empath." It is often criticized for its excessive, senseless violence. And I suspect that, because of the ending lines, the episode is often misinterpreted as being a statement of the value of emotion *over* logic. McCoy says, ". . . with all their scientific knowledge and advances, it was good, ol' fashioned emotion they valued most." Scott then wonders if the Vulcans know that, and when Kirks asks if Mr. Spock will take them the news, Spock says, "I shall certainly give the thought all the consideration it is due," and it truly isn't due much. The point of the episode, just like *Star Trek: The Motion Picture* is not that one part of man is better than another but that all parts—reason, sense, and body—must operate in harmony.

Let's begin at the beginning, for even before Gem is introduced, we wee Platonic philosophy in operation.

First and most obvious, it is the Triune only that is brought underground by the Vians, totally isolated from the *Enterprise*—Spock first, then McCoy, then Kirk. But Kirk (the Body) wakes first; then he "comes to his senses" by awakening Spock and McCoy.

The three stumble upon Gem simultaneously, but each immediately reacts differently, and almost exactly as they did in "City." McCoy impulsively approaches the girl—ahead of the others. "She seems (looks) harmless enough," he says. Kirk acts to physically restrain him as Spock, again slightly behind the two, gives a logical reason: "The sand bats of Maynark IV appear to be inanimate creatures until they attack." The Man is in perfect harmony.

Immediately the Body demands information. At least half of Kirk's lines in this episode are questions. "What is it, Spock? Analysis."

Spock gives a logical answer. "From what we know," he begins, ". . . a life form such as hers could not have evolved here."

Then Kirk turns to the doctor. "Bones, what's wrong with her?"

From his examination of Gem, McCoy "jumps to the conclusion" that all her species are mutes. "That's my observation, for whatever it's worth," he says, denigrating his input.

To act rightly, the Body must have the input of both reason and sense. Only after this exchange does Kirk move toward Gem.

Not surprisingly, it is Kirk, the physical man, the soldier/diplomat who receives the first three physical abuses—the cut from his fall in the surface laboratory, the jolt from the Vian weapon, and, later, the "torture experiment" (with his shirt removed, of course).

The next part shows Spock and McCoy operating on different levels of reality. The three men find the underground laboratory. "Fascinating," says Spock abstractedly. "*Look* at this stuff," says McCoy. The Vians appear and McCoy says, "We've just *seen* the results of your tests." (italics added) Outside, McCoy *sees* Scotty and the search party. When they disappear, the doctor, mystified, asks Spock, "Where did they go?" "I believe they were never present," says Spock. McCoy believes in what he sees. Spock does not. In a later scene, he and Kirk are surrounded by a force field. It is Spock who is able to get around "reality" to a higher abstraction. "In spite of what we see . . ." he begins, then suppresses all emotion to kill the force field and walk out. Here, then, we have *three* scenes in one episode that show the interaction of sense and reason.

Then, as if that isn't enough, the Vians state the parameters of a test: there is "an 87 percent chance the doctor will die —sensory function will cease; there is a 93 percent chance Spock's brain will be damaged, resulting in insanity" —the reasoning function will cease. Notice that the chances are about equal that each will lose his function, thus, logically, that each one contributes an equal but totally different element to the complete Man.

Plato's theory of man's place in society disrupted is demonstrated in the scene where a choice must be made as to who will be the guinea pig. At first, each man is in his proper role. Kirk, as captain, will go and, because he is rightfully in command, that is his prerogative. No one can argue with him because his decision is within his right as commander. In his proper role as physician, McCoy unintentionally upsets society by knocking Kirk out. It is important that the action is unintentional, for he can be forgiven for upsetting the societal balance.

Now Spock is in command, so he will go with the Vians. Because the displacement is accidental, Spock's succession is just, and McCoy should not question it. However, McCoy, deliberately and premeditatedly, knocks out Spock. Before he succumbs to "the good doctor's hypo," Spock makes a statement Plato himself would have said: "Your decision is highly unethical." McCoy's deliberate disruption of the law of man's place in society is, indeed, highly unethical, and, in a sense, he is now to be punished for it, and it is this impulsive, intuitive, sensual part of the Triune which was immoderate who suffers most.

If this "decision" scene shows Man out of harmony in society and the subsequent punishment, the "dying" scene shows Man's internal discord. When one member of the Triune seems hopelessly lost, the others attempt to compensate. Instantly, Spock becomes more sensitive ("good bedside manner"); Kirk becomes more logical, deducing that Gem is the focal point and solution to their problem.

In my opinion, the final scene with the Vians is the best summary of what Star Trek is all about and why it will become a classic.

Here we have the Total Man—the Triune—juxtaposed sharply against the Incomplete Man—the Vians. One Vian gives Plato's definition of virtue (harmony of soul). "You were her teachers," he says, having taught her "the will to survive [courage], love of life [wisdom/the Good Life], passion to know [temperance/justice]. Everything that is truest and best in all species of beings has been revealed by you." The Vians recognize the Triune as the ideal, complete, Total Man.

To the Vians, Kirk says, "You've lost the capacity to feel the emotions you brought Gem here to experience. You don't understand what it is to love [the Platonic "good life"]. Love and compassion are dead in you. You're nothing but intellect." Despite McCoy's illogical remark at the very end, it is not that intellect per se is evil. It is that any part—reason, sense, or body—without the others causes imbalance of the Man.

Few of us real live humans are "virtuous" in the Greek sense. Perhaps we have not found our niche in society. Or perhaps we are weak in one of the key areas of the Complete Man. We are, thus, forever searching for our perfect place in the universe and/or for our soul. The *Enterprise* is a world in harmony and, together, its characters represent the ideal man. We have, if only temporarily, found the Good Life. That is why we have such an insatiable appetite for anything related to the show, why we spread its message of brotherhood like the gospel to the world, why we identify so strongly with the characters, why we want to serve on the *Enterprise*, why we laugh and cry as we watch the show, why we hate to come back to anything less than that good life.

Of "the will to survive, the love of life, the passion to know," the Vian says, "these are the qualities that make a civilization worthy to survive." A firm foundation on this premise of virtue is also what makes Star Trek worthy to survive, worthy to become a classic. I am convinced that it will be—or is.

THE JOURNEY TO—AND BEYOND—
THE SEARCH FOR SPOCK

By Hazel Ann Williams

Why did events in the last two Star Trek films unfold in the fashion they did? What were the forces that shaped the death and resurrection of Spock, the destruction of the Enterprise, *and the trials faced by Admiral Kirk? In the following article, Hazel Williams takes a look at some of the behind-the-scenes machinations that possibly could have made it inevitable that both films turned out the way they did. And she offers a few speculations on the direction* Star Trek IV *will take.*

From "The Cage" through *Star Trek III: The Search For Spock*, the world of Star Trek has been through many changes. New characters have been introduced, only to die off or disappear. The *Enterprise* has been redesigned three times, and the uniforms are as changeable as the weather. Change is the essence of life, but nothing wreaked as much havoc as the drastic events of *Star Trek II: The Wrath of Khan* and *The Search for Spock*. At the end of *The Search for Spock*, the *Enterprise* has been destroyed and most of the major characters are at grave risk. How did we get into this situation? Where *can* we go from here? Since the future is grounded in the past, let's look back and analyze the findings.

Star Trek II: The Wrath of Khan began by putting the characters in perspective to their universe. When Kirk was Captain of the *Enterprise*, he was portrayed as brash, daring, brave, and in all ways extraordinary. A man sure of his abilities and confident of the people around him. He ably led a group who proved they could think their way out of every situation an unpredictable universe could present. Why Kirk considered, much less accepted, an Admiralty position is not revealed in *Star Trek: The Motion Picture*. That he hated the job, hated being away from a command position and the *Enterprise*, is painfully obvious. The Kirk who takes a new *Enterprise* out against the threat of V'Ger is a desperate, driven man who bears only the slightest resemblance to the self-confident Captain of the episodes.

Slowly, over the course of the movie, Kirk regains most of those well-remembered qualities. *Wrath of Khan* picked up ten years after V'Ger. Again, we are faced with a desperate Admiral Kirk, but this is a quieter, bleaker desperation. He is fifty years old and in the grip of a devastating midlife crisis. Looking back, the Admiral sees all his best and brightest years behind him. To Kirk, his questions about his own future seem sensible. What more could—or in his view of reality, should—he do? Kirk's line, "Galloping around the cosmos is a game for the young" isn't sarcasm, it's his new belief, or what he feels he *should* believe. It is this attitude that causes his friends' concern, and inspires McCoy's warning, "Get back your command before you turn into one of these antiques, before you really do grow old." In this disoriented state of mind, Kirk must face some of the greatest challenges of his life.

Spock, too, has changed, but this is the change of growth and maturity. As the episodes progressed, Spock showed more of his humanity. Yet, when *Star Trek: The Motion Picture* begins, we see he has retreated to Vulcan to purge his human half. Spock's way has never been easy; as Amanda explained to Kirk, "Neither Vulcan nor human; at home nowhere, except Starfleet." Whether in reaction against his own "weakening" to emotional humans, or simply tiring of the constant struggle to control his feelings while denying he had any, Spock was driven to Gol and *Kolinahr*. He is just as desperate as Kirk to find, or rediscover, something neither can, or will, name.

STTMP gave Spock a vivid picture of logic and the sterility of the Vulcan Way carried to extreme. His experience with V'Ger allows Spock to accept that he no longer must hold his Vulcan and human heritages in dichotomy. He can merge both to create a greater uniqueness that *is* Spock. The complex simplicity of IDIC (Infinite Diversity in Infinite Combinations) is a lesson Spock can now fully appreciate. *Wrath of Khan* shows us that Spock used the years since V'Ger to apply that lesson to himself.

The tense rigidity of his battle stance and the quick, tight, stress-revealing movements are gone. This Spock can relax, even to the point of lighthearted word play with his protégé or closest friend. He is sure of his place in the universe and the placement of his soul. All the best facets of Spock are now combined into a mature being.

Except for the quiet aura of competence created by experience and survival, the rest of the *Enterprise's* regular senior officers are comfortably familiar. McCoy, with his feet still solidly planted in his belief of humanism. Scotty, still a devil on shore leave and bursting with pride at his engines and his nephew. Sulu, bright and wonderful, happy to get back to the *Enterprise*, whatever the reason. Uhura, more beautiful than ever and secure in her own abilities. Chekov, now first officer of the *Reliant*, but still Chekov. They provide a solid background to bounce back the shattering reflection of a shaken Admiral Kirk and the solid, concerned Captain Spock. An almost happy family reunion, but then the real problems begin.

Instead of rehashing the plot, let's look at five major events. Because both *Wrath of Khan* and *The Search for Spock* depend deeply on Kirk's actions/reactions/decisions, we'll deal with these events as influences upon him.

The return of Khan is a master stroke. The cataclysm that struck Ceti Alpha IV made survival almost impossible, and advancement of Khan's "master race" merely a pipe dream. The deaths of his wife and people and his own terrible sense of failure combine to put more pressure on that great mind than it can tolerate. The arrival of Terrell and Chekov, with the chance for escape and a return to power, pushes Khan over the edge. He becomes evil and madness personified.

Khan's thirst for vengeance exceeds the boundaries of quest. It becomes an all-consuming obsession. Even with Genesis aboard (and there's little doubt that these brilliant people won't understand it and be able to duplicate the process), and Kirk supposedly entombed in Regulus, Khan must finish the task personally and destroy the *Enterprise*, Kirk's ship and love. Khan is more than a physical threat, he becomes a symbol of past sin and past error that haunts the future, Kirk's future. Khan is the ultimate random factor in Kirk's one-time orderly universe, and it is he who starts the chain reaction of events that ends in tragedy.

Where would evil be without power? *Star Trek II: The Wrath of Khan* provides power to spare in the form of Genesis. As proposed, it would help alleviate the problems of population and food production by force-evolving life-giving conditions on lifeless planets. Yet it has military potential, too. The "discussion" between Spock and McCoy of the Genesis Effect aptly points out the vast potential for a novel form of destruction that would create new life as it was destroying the old. To control this power is to control the universe, and the struggle for control is the battle line of the film. For Khan, it is not only the key of release from his own personal hell, but the key by which he can avenge himself upon Kirk, and to once again be Master. Kirk, again on the side of the angels, must keep Khan from possessing the device and save the Federation from Khan's evil domination. A classic confrontation, and one that intensifies the final Khan-Kirk showdown.

The person responsible for creating Genesis is Dr. Carol Marcus, Kirk's one-time love, and the mother of his son. Although we know very little about this relationship, Kirk's reaction to her name shows that the parting, at least, was painful. She and her project are threatened by Khan's madness. Kirk arrives too late to save the rest of the research team, but just in time to help Khan get Genesis, and without enough preparation to spare himself an abrupt and painful introduction to his son, David. With blood and death behind them, and the threat of Khan and Genesis before them, Kirk and Carol's bittersweet reunion is necessarily brief. In many ways, this scene raises more questions than it answers, but its effect on Kirk is unmistakable. He feels even older and more confused than he did at the beginning of the movie.

The introduction of Kirk's son, although not of major importance to the plot, is an event in Kirk's life. David, with his strong aversion to the military and Starfleet, is almost a stereotype of the brave scientist doing battle glorious with the nasty, evil armed forces. His shock and resentment at finding out one of *them* is his father is therefore understandable. Kirk is hurt by his son's rejection, and this feeling adds to his growing list of problems. By the end of the film, David has vividly learned what real evil is, and the price that must be paid to stop it. He can then begin to accept his father as a human being, a man, and not a false image of a Starfleet authority figure. Before this change,

Kirk bears a heavy burden of guilt about David's reaction to him, and grieves for their life that could have been.

Hunted by a madman with the potential to destroy the universe, embroiled in personal problems, trying to fight with a crippled ship managed by "children," Admiral Kirk manages to beat the odds again. Even when a dying Khan sets off the Genesis Device, Kirk and the *Enterprise* survive to witness the birth of a new world. Yet Kirk still has to face his biggest crisis: the death of Spock.

Spock, with his slightly higher tolerance to radiation, has done what no one else (*almost* no one else) could have done—repaired the main engines and saved the *Enterprise*, Kirk, and the trainee crew. This time the price of salvation was Spock's life. Kirk witnesses his friend's final agony and death, but is cut off by a wall of glass, unable to touch, unable to give or receive the comfort of embrace. The sacrifice, grand and noble as it was, is almost too much for Kirk. Spock was more than a friend. He was Kirk's right hand, his balance in all things, especially rash and foolhardy things . . . almost Kirk's other half. For the first time, Kirk must face the harsh lesson of mortality. As he explains to David, "I've cheated death . . . and patted myself on the back for it . . . but I've never faced it, not like this." Kirk listens to David's words of comfort without real acceptance, although he allows himself some joy at David's gesture of conciliation and embrace.

Something happens to Kirk on the way to the Bridge—he loses the hard edge of his grief. When faced with the new planet, he is filled with wonder; he feels young again. In Engineering and at Spock's funeral, Kirk grieved, but now something is numb, something vital has been stilled. Even with his moist, shining eyes and the throwaway line of, "I can't believe his questing spirit is at rest . . . ," something is missing. Kirk has too quickly seemingly accepted Spock's death, something that should happen at a very late stage in the grief cycle. The voice of Spock and the final scenes of the movie give fans hope for our favorite Vulcan, but what of Kirk?

There is no real ending to *Wrath of Khan*, for very little has been resolved. Khan has been blown to bits along with the *Reliant*, and that threat is removed. Genesis works better than expected; it was intended to develop a lifeless world or moon, not create a new planet. Genesis is more potent than ever and this can only lead to controversy. Who can be trusted to administer such power? Can the Federation survive the moral, economic, and military side effects? How can it be adequately protected?

Because Doctors Carol and David Marcus are the only members of the Genesis team left alive, it's reasonable to assume they will take charge of whatever group explores the new Genesis Planet. Kirk and Carol seem to have made a tentative step toward renewing their relationship, but that was in the midst of crisis, when people cling to each other out of desperate need. They still occupy different worlds. Do they *want* a relationship of that nature, or are they more motivated to part as friends? David has begun to change from childish stereotype to human being. It poses interesting possibilities for the future. Can he establish his own personality?

The biggest problem is, of course, Spock. As was noted earlier, the final scenes of *Wrath of Khan* gave hope for Spock's return. It has to be tied up with the Genesis Effect, of life from lifelessness. Related to this is Kirk's strange reactions. Will he suppress the pain he must feel and slide through the rest of his life? Will he come to grips with his feelings, and problems, and face the future, taking his friends' advice to follow his own first, best destiny. No, *Star Trek II: The Wrath of Khan* does not end, it merely pauses.

Fandom circulates many stories that should more fairly be called rumors. One such states that, at the cast party after the premiere of *Wrath of Khan*, Leonard Nimoy said he couldn't wait to see how Spock would come back in *Star Trek III*, and Harve Bennett almost had a coronary. As James Blish says in his book of episode adaptations, *Star Trek 4*, a writer should not inflict his technical problems on his readers. However, fandom explores every aspect of the Star Trek Universe, and to understand the direction *The Search for Spock* took, it seems we have to seek a partially technical explanation.

Except for a gifted few, most writers must begin their work with clear and definite goals in mind. Then either the characters or the circumstances will dictate how the writer accomplishes these goals. An examination of *Star Trek III: The Search for Spock* seems to reveal three major objectives. First, as the title states, Spock must be found and revived. A second goal is to completely discredit Genesis. If, as further analysis will bear out, the Genesis Planet must be destroyed, an easy explanation is that it exceeded its programmed parameters and we're damned lucky that it held together this long. A functioning Genesis would raise too many problems. It would pose as big a threat to the Federation as Khan, albeit a more obscure and insidious one. Genesis is too well-known to ignore, as so many new devices and discoveries were in the episodes. Although it is the obvious key to Spock's resurrection, it must be discredited and destroyed. The third goal, even though it seems cruel to fans, is the destruction of the *Enterprise*. It could have been avoided, written around, if it was not a goal. The "why" is unknown. Mr. Bennett's supposed explanation that he simply wrote himself into a corner is totally unacceptable. The written word has always been vulnerable to erasers.

Star Trek III: The Search for Spock acknowledges the nonending of *Wrath of Khan* by revamping the important final shots of *Wrath of Khan* in its opening sequence. However, we do see changes. Kirk says most of his trainee crew has been reassigned, and David and Saavik are on the *Grissom*, en route to the Genesis Planet. Because the *Enterprise* has not yet reached dock, this must have been accomplished by a ship-to-ship transfer. Another ship has gone to Ceti Alpha, gods know where Carol is, and Kirk now feels the full weight of Spock's absence. Now he is uncomfortable, even morose, saying he has left the best part of himself behind, and that they have paid for their victory with their dearest blood. Kirk notes the crews' obsessive reaction to Spock's death, but he doesn't associate it with his own. McCoy is acting strangely, although we later understand his change, and more than enough clues are provided. Everyone is burdened by Spock's death, an event no one ever conceived as possible.

To further complicate the picture, certain conditions are imposed. First, every other member of Starfleet must appear dull of wit—to put it kindly. Admiral Morrow, if he is the friend the film implies, must have realized Kirk would not take calmly the retirement of the *Enterprise* and the refusal to allow them to return to the Genesis Planet. Even if he knew Kirk only by reputation, did Morrow really believe he'd so easily dissuaded Kirk from an obviously important task, especially one that involved Spock and McCoy? When Kirk left the officer's lounge, Morrow should have had red alert sounding in his head loud enough to deafen him. Another point: Just because Morrow "never really understood Vulcan mysticism," is that any reason to brush it aside as if it didn't exist? Does the Admiral *really* understand human (or alien) psychology or physiology, warp physics, theoretical mathematics, or stellar evolution? If not, do these too not exist?

As an officer, Styles is a bit more believable. His overbearing pride in his ship, and his own abilities, will never make for a happy ship. His crew will obey him, or suffer the consequences of a blotted permanent record and a rough trip, but they'd never follow *him* into the mouth of hell. Styles's reaction to yellow alert in space dock is a nice theatrical bit, but ludicrous. The alert could have been sounded as a drill, due to a fire or accident on his ship or another ship, or the dock itself, due to sabotage, outside threat, a ship coming in disabled or out of control, and so on. If we can think of all these things, why can't a trained Starfleet officer—the *Captain* of the Fleet's fastest, newest, and most powerful ship—think of at least one?

There are two ways to make a character, or a set of characters, appear extraordinary. The first, and admittedly the most difficult, is by careful choice of dialogue, action, and reaction that *is* extraordinary. The second, easier and simpler, way is to play down all other characters in the film, making them dull and vaguely stupid. Unfortunately, *The Search for Spock* used the second method. The character of Esteban, the Captain of the scientific exploration ship *Grissom*, is entirely unbelievable. He and his crew must be experienced, and have seen quite an array of the strange and unusual, or they would not have drawn this assignment. Esteban is so stiff and by the book, it's easy to understand his poor showing as a battle commander—it's his refusal to take any initiative that's ridiculous. Only the character of "Mr. Adventure" has any link to reality. His behavior can be written off to inexperience, youth, and a phaser pointed at his chest.

Besides making everyone at Starfleet imbeciles, a second condition is, that in order to place Spock's essence at rest, Spock's body must be returned to Vulcan. The reason for this is not brought out in the movie, except that it is responsible for further narrowing the possibilities. The novelization cites the duality of mind and body, good enough for a plausible cover story, and fairly reasonable philosophy. A point to mention: Sarek must have known Spock's tube had been found or he'd simply have asked Kirk to bring McCoy to Vulcan, or even simpler, have done it himself. Kirk believed Spock's body burned on entering the Genesis Planet's atmosphere. Remember David's line to Saavik: "The gravitational fields were in flux. It could have soft landed." Sarek had read Kirk's report, which surely included the disposition of Spock's remains, so Sarek knew it was Kirk's intention to burn his son's body. Sarek would not have asked Kirk to return a body that no longer existed. Whether the process would have worked without Spock's body is unknown, but apparently as long as the body existed, it was as necessary to the ritual as the essence in McCoy's mind.

This brings us to the third condition, McCoy's reaction to the death meld. Although it would have been safer to bring McCoy to Vulcan first, and thus protect Spock's essence, the good doctor's mind was in confusion. Parts of Spock's needs and thoughts kept sliding into McCoy's consciousness. McCoy's reaction led him on a desperate path of indiscretion and, finally, imprisonment as a nut case. Even at this point, the story could have developed along different lines had an alternate route to Spock's revival been sought. Sarek could have appealed to the Federation for McCoy to be brought to Vulcan for "treatment." Surely the Federation Council couldn't have been as bigoted as Admiral Morrow. Sarek could have also used his enormous influence to get Kirk to the Genesis Planet, or simply requested the return of his son's body with the greatest possible speed, citing Federation laws and Starfleet regulations guaranteeing personal religious freedom. The only way to negate these possibilities is the fourth and final condition. Simply stated, it is "time is of the essence," and needs no further explanation.

In consideration of the story goals and imposed conditions, what results is a precise series of events that constantly narrows Kirk's choices until the final result is achievable through no other means. The Klingon threat has been a slowly tightening coil during the whole movie. Beginning with a theft of basic information, it progresses to violation of Federation space, discovery of the Genesis Planet, and the "accidental" destruction of the *Grissom*. With the *Grisson* gone, David, Saavik, and a living Spock are alone and vulnerable on a spectacularly dying planet. The second story goal, discrediting Genesis, is fulfilled by David's admission to having used protomatter, a wonderfully vague catch-all substance able to hide all problems under a scientific umbrella. Although tying the aging of Spock to the aging of the planet stretches science fiction almost to the border of pseudo science-fantasy, it presents an interesting, if not well handled, set of side-bar problems.

Kirk arrives at the Genesis Planet to find the Klingons already there. The brief battle leaves the *Enterprise* burned out, unable to maneuver, run, or fight. She is, to all respects, dead and trapped in orbit around a dying planet. That the Genesis Planet is going to explode very soon is vital, or the threat is lessened to a degree where the destruction of the *Enterprise* is not a necessity. Kruge, the Klingon commander, plays a hunch and reveals his hostages. For Kirk, finding his son, and a living Spock in the hands of the Klingons on a dying planet, raised the stakes to almost impossible heights.

To force Kirk's surrender, and prove his ruthlessness (an unnecessary gesture, fandom knows the Klingons don't play around, and the movie has more than proved the point by having Kruge kill his spy and her ship, kill one of his own crewmen for disobeying an order, and kill a giant worm with his own hands, just for fun), Kruge sacrifices one of the hostages, secure in his knowledge that Genesis can be found in the *Enterprise's* computers, or at least in the surviving hostages. David, jumping the Klingon about to kill Saavik, is killed instead. Why David instead of Saavik? Neither, to this point, is indispensable, but David's death provides goals that would not be accomplished by Saavik dying. First, David is the scapegoat for the failure of Genesis and his own stupidity. Now there will be no disgraceful trial, investigation, and so on. It was all David's fault; David is dead, therefore the case is closed. Second, it also closes the questions of Kirk's responsibilities toward his son. Third, it adds a touch of revenge and another notch of desperation to Kirk's actions, as if that were needed.

David is dead, Saavik and Spock are held by the Klingons on a self-destructing planet, the Klingons have more of an advantage than they realize in the impotent *Enterprise* and Spock, and Kirk is left with few options. Making the only real choice that enjoys even the slimmest chance for success, Kirk sets the *Enterprise's* self-destruct, invites the Klingons over, and beams everyone down to the Genesis Planet. This plan has several things going for it: It greatly reduces the number of Klingons, it protects the hostages—now Kruge's only link to Genesis, the hostages can be freed with relative ease—Kruge won't be expecting a rescue force, he believes he just saw 400 plus crewmen and his own boarding party destroyed, and the shock of *Enterprise's* destruction should stun Kruge to inaction for a few precious minutes. The basic problem now is to rescue Spock and Saavik, and get aboard the Klingon ship, preferably in a position of control. As McCoy says, Kirk has turned death into a fighting chance for life; not a guarantee, a chance. If it had not worked, they'd be no worse off, for they were dead men without the Klingon ship.

Disposing of the remaining Klingon guard is child's play. The next step is more difficult. Using words sharply reminiscent of his futile challenge to Khan, Kirk dares the Klingon commander to beam up his party. Kruge answers by beaming down to face Kirk and brings the brilliant pacing of the Klingon threat to its inevitable and very final conclusion. With all but Spock, Kirk, and Kruge safely aboard the Klingon ship, Kirk joins Kruge in hand-to-hand combat—a brief, violent melee that brings the level of the movie back to basics. Kirk has offered his career, his son, his ship, and now offers his life for a chance to recover his friend.

Killing the Klingon in a satisfactory manner, Kirk escapes with Spock to the refuge of the Klingon ship. The finale of a reborn and whole Spock is almost anticlimax to the sheer beauty of the final scenes of the Genesis Planet. With all hell literally breaking loose, Kirk holds Spock in a safe, sure embrace as they beam up at the last possible second. After that, no one believed Spock would not be fully recovered. Anything less after such great sacrifices from so many would have been ludicrous, if not violence-producing.

The destruction of the *Enterprise* is a thorn in the side. As the story is written, Kirk could have done nothing else once the Klingon demanded his surrender. Examination of a few alternatives proves that point. What if Kirk wiped the memory banks (if it's possible to do so in their limited amount of time), killed the Klingons as they beamed up, and had then gone to the planet? This would reduce the number of Klingons, but doesn't necessarily protect the hostages. If Kruge killed Spock and Saavik before he had the *Enterprise's* Genesis tapes in his hands, he would not be the first Klingon to jump the gun. Also, when his boarding party didn't call or respond, Kruge would realize he'd been tricked. He'd probably then destroy the *Enterprise*, and take his hostages, leaving Kirk and crew stranded on Genesis. This is not a good plan.

Kirk could wipe the memory and simply beam down, leaving the Klingons to find out as best they could that they'd been tricked. This has all the disadvantages of the first plan, with the added problem of leaving a larger number of living, angry Klingons to deal with. We've already established that Klingons aren't the most tolerant race in the universe. This would give Kirk and party time to get to Spock and Saavik, but leaves them in a bad bargaining position. Kruge has all the good options, and that makes this another bad plan.

A third alternative is that Kirk could refuse to surrender, but that is irrational. The trouble with aliens is that they think differently than you do. Kruge might kill the hostages just to prove he could or would, he might attack the *Enterprise*, and in her condition, kill them all. If Kruge was willing to play out his hunch on the *Enterprise's* condition, and feeling he couldn't get Genesis from Kirk, he would have simply taken his hostages and gone home. The *Enterprise*, unable to follow or escape, would have been destroyed with the Genesis Planet. Good-bye, everybody . . . not a satisfactory ending.

Finally, Kirk could have tried one of his infamous bluffs. Something to the effect that if Kruge kills the hostages, Kirk will wipe Genesis, or blow up the *Enterprise*, and so forth. It's not even improbable that Kruge would then feel justified in his estimate of the *Enterprise's* battle abilities by this ultimatum. The Klingon's most obvious move, because they believe the *Enterprise* holds over 400 people—an amount his small group could never overcome by force—would be to take his hostages and go, again abandoning Kirk and the *Enterprise* to its fate. Kruge, indeed any Klingon, would like to bring home an intact Federation starship, but Genesis is clearly the more important prize. Even incomplete information is better than nothing.

Even with the chosen plan there were a few problems. Kirk took a chance with the delicate timing of the rescue by pausing to watch the fall of the *Enterprise*. We must, however, concede that it would have been almost impossible for Kirk to *be* Kirk and not watch. He must have bet that Kruge would not react instantly and that they had a bit more time to effect the rescue and still finagle a way onto the Klingon ship. Also, at any given point, Kruge could have taken the hostages and left. It seems unlikely that he would have risked taking the whole *Enterprise* group, as there are only two Klingons to guard the other seven. These points can be easily set aside by Kirk's always extraordinary luck, and Klingon psychology and cultural training. This way we are treated to a couple of moving, potent scenes.

At the end of *The Search for Spock*, Kirk's nether parts are grass and all of Starfleet eager lawn mowers. Sulu, Uhura, Scotty, and Chekov are in similar shape, although McCoy may be excused by pleading temporary insanity, an out it's doubtful he'll use. Genesis is exposed as a sham and a failure, and can be safely relegated to never-never land. David is dead and the *Enterprise* has been destroyed. Now it's time to speculate what might happen next.

Although David's admission to the use of protomatter and the inherent instability of Genesis have made it useless in providing worlds to colonize and exploit for minerals, food, and other production, it is still a potent weapon—or is it? What remains of Genesis, the device and the research?

If the material detailing Genesis had been in Regulus I's memory banks, Khan would have found it. The actual device would have been icing on the cake, for Khan and his people could have developed a new device from the complete research material, just as they could've reconstructed the material from the device. Therefore, the lab's banks were wiped clean. The *Enterprise's* memory banks had the bare bones on Genesis in its proposal form. When Regulus's banks were wiped, Carol or David must have kept at least one copy, and the might or might not have supplemented *Enterprise's* tapes. It doesn't matter, because the *Enterprise* is gone. The Klingon information could not have been very complete, or Kruge would never have risked entering Federation space on such a desperate search for information. Carol may have had a copy with her, or there may be a required depository for top secret scientific projects. The latter is highly unlikely, because the more copies of anything that exist, the harder it is to guard or keep secret. So the only probable complete set of information on Genesis is with Dr. Carol Marcus, wherever she is. Being a sensible, bright lady, she may (and probably will) choose to hide or destroy it. Genesis has brought only pain, death, and destruction. It did revive Spock, but only his body and only under a set of unique, impossible to recreate, circumstances. Genesis's only use now is military. Further research will be impossible without complete records. It may prove impossible to fix all of Genesis's problems even with Carol's records. Other teams may rediscover Genesis after many years of painstaking research, but my impression of the original team is that they were the best and brightest. Genesis is now only the vaguest of possible future threats.

For the *Enterprise* there can be no future. She is gone and an era is over. Technically, the ship was dead when Kirk and party beamed down to the Genesis Planet. They could not have repaired her in time and still have completed their desperate mission, but her final death throes gave them life. It was a poetic balancing of Karma, for as Spock gave his life for *Enterprise* and her infinitely precious cargo, so *Enterprise* gave its existence for Spock and his rescuers. Her death was glorious, bright, and beautiful, much preferable to scrapping or mothballing. But to me, *Enterprise* was the embodiment and soul of Star Trek and fandom, my own personal vehicle to the stars. I neither apologize for my tears, nor look forward to a universe populated with pregnant guppies.

We must also consider Spock. Here the only acceptable result is for him to recover completely and be the Spock we know so well. Whether he returns to Starfleet, stays on Vulcan, or finds another course for his life path will probably depend on the fate of his friends, who did so much on his behalf. Logically, he should not approve of their actions, but neither Spock nor his responses are totally logical. While McCoy carried Spock's essence, Spock occasionally spoke through the good doctor. It is my belief that McCoy's line, ". . . what you had to do. What you've always done, turn death into a fighting chance for life," is not McCoy's alone. It is a statement from both McCoy and Spock, trying to comfort their anguished friend, Jim Kirk. This has always been one area where Spock and McCoy could agree. As Spock sorts out his memories, he will find all the times of his joining to McCoy, and he will find this time. He will continue to give Kirk comfort and support, friendship and honest love, in whatever the future holds. Even if this is not the "proper" interpretation, Spock is logical enough to realize that the deed is done and he can't change it. He is Spock enough to feel the irrational warm glow of friendship, and the lengths we will go for that bond. Whatever track is taken, Spock will be there for all his friends.

Kirk and his faithful crew have saved Genesis from the Klingons, brought home an intact Klingon ship, and returned McCoy to sanity and Spock from the dead, but they broke, or severely dented, almost every Starfleet regulation doing so. Kirk's future seems to hold only three possibilities:

First, he may be court-martialed and publicly disgraced. This seems unlikely. Starfleet would have to make Genesis and the Klingon violations public. Because Khan's actions also deal with the proceedings, his taking of the *Reliant* would also come out. None of this is likely to please Starfleet's PR department. Public opinion would, in all probability, shift to Kirk and his friends as the people who saved the Federation. Even in the military, public opinion, and funding, are important enough to make a difference.

Second, Kirk may be "allowed" to quietly retire rather than face a general court. Although Kirk may feel his actions are wrong and deserve punishment, he may still demand a court-martial rather than let his friends sink into oblivion. Again, this is something Starfleet would want to avoid.

Third, Kirk may be bumped upstairs, promoted to a strictly advisory, noncommand position. Here Starfleet benefits from Kirk's experience without having to air its dirty laundry. Kirk can't protest a promotion, so he can choose either to accept this exile or resign. (This is similar to the "court or grounding" choice Kirk was given in "Courtmartial," but they're unlikey to offer a choice this time. Also, Kirk *was* innocent in that instance.) Whatever happens, it seems that Captain Styles's warning, "Kirk, if you go through with this, you'll never sit in the center seat again" seems all too true.

The future of Kirk's co-conspirators is tied up with his. If there is a general court, for whatever reason, they will stand it together. If Kirk retires, they may be allowed to resign their commissions, or they may also be placed in safe, advisory, or simply boring positions. It seems most likely that Starfleet would want to keep the experience of Scotty and McCoy available, but the simple fact of having survived a five-year mission may keep Sulu, Chekov, and Uhura in the service.

There are a string of less likely, and more bizarre possibilities. *Star Trek IV* could start with, "Having been completely exonerated by a little known Starfleet rule, the crew of the *Enterprise* gets a new ship and . . ." They could all quit and join the twenty-third century version of the merchant marine, or start their own fleet, or . . . On the slightly more serious side, they could stay on Vulcan. Starfleet might be persuaded to leave them alone if they stayed there in exile. Perhaps Vulcan could refuse to extradite them. Of course, that would effectively end the series, and then there's Vulcan logic and Kirk's sense of honor and duty to deal with . . .

Here's my personal favorite, and the only scenario I can come up with to keep Kirk and friends in Starfleet as fully functioning individuals. Starfleet, in order to keep various and sundry eggs off its collective face, looks the other way and Kirk, and such are allowed back into the big, happy Fleet. Pressure could be brought to bear by certain Vulcans, and others, threatening to make the entire affair public. Or perhaps Admiral Morrow isn't as dumb as we thought. He had read Kirk correctly, but could see no official way to sanction the act. His silence was tacit permission. Styles must have been in on it, too, for he knew it was Kirk on the *Enterprise* and seemed to know what Kirk was up to. Thus, Admiral Morrow only has to say *"secret mission,"* or at least claim that was the case. Very secret, even Kirk didn't know (or did he?), but he and his crew can be trusted to keep the secret—for the good of the Fleet, of course. This way they are returned to the Fleet without prejudice. Their official records won't carry the real story, for the secrecy must be maintained, and they will therefore be just as eligible for promotion and duty positions as any other member of the Fleet.

There is precedent for this. If you will recall the only two-part episode, "The Menagerie," *Spock* stole the *Enterprise* and violated the only General Order that still carried the death penalty by taking it to a proscribed planet. All was forgiven because Spock's actions gave a valued Starfleet officer the only possible chance for a viable, tolerable life. Yes, he broke the rules, but no real damage was done, and good came of it. Spock was not disciplined in any way; he retained his rank, his position as first officer, and eventually became the captain of the *Enterprise*.

The only negative result of Kirk's actions is the destruction of the *Enterprise*, and she was to be scrapped anyway. The pluses include the capture of a Klingon ship and the repulsion of a clear and present danger in the form of the Klingons and Genesis, the returning of two very valuable Starfleet officers to active, productive duty, and the incidental rescue of Lt. Saavik. This is an even better score than Spock racked up. If Kirk, Scotty, McCoy, Uhura, Sulu, and Chekov are to appear in any future stories, some variant on this explanation must be used, and having a precedent in an episode only makes it easier and more attractive.

Star Trek, like V'Ger, must evolve. As the actors portraying the major characters age, we must prepare ourselves for their gradual replacement and eventual demise. I've always favored moving the senior officers up to advisory positions and familiar junior officers taking over the command duties. This will be accomplished by introducing new—but interesting and competent—crew members. I want to see these people replaced with love, not disposed of and tossed aside. Yet the ongoing fan (and fun) argument of replacing Kirk versus replacing Shatner may be canceled out by the next movie. Will *Star Trek IV* simply tie up loose ends and explore another aspect of the Star Trek universe with a new ship and new characters? Will it be the final chapter for people who have loved and faithfully followed the series for twenty years? Something in my mind, my heart whispers no. Where *can* we go from here? Anywhere. There *are* always possibilities. This article brought up a few, but more exist. I will wait to see Mr. Bennett's magic, humbly suggesting he remembers Star Trek is love, friendship, and all the best man is and does . . . But most of all it is the people who hold these values dear, and follow this life-style.

THREE BY DEBBIE GILBERT

Once again we are pleased to present a series of three short articles by a new writer. Debbie tells us she's been a faithful follower of our Best of Trek *series since its inception, but it's only recently that she decided, "Hey, I can write this stuff, too!" Indeed she can, as you will see in the articles below.*

Galactic Terpsichore?

It is an affirmation of the depth and richness of the Star Trek universe that nearly every facet of our twentieth-century life can in some way be tied into it. As a former ballet dancer, I thought it would be interesting to explore the use of dance in Star Trek.

To the disappointment of those of us who are patrons of the arts, Star Trek never treated dance with the same respect it accorded music, drama, and painting. In every case, dance in Star Trek served as either a pleasant entertainment or a sexual lure—never as a legitimate art form. Star Trek also presents a problem in analysis because it's often difficult to say just what is dancing and what is not. The exotic costumes, the lushly atmospheric music, the aura of sensuality that pervades the show all combine to create a *feeling* of dance even if no one is actually moving. An outstanding example was provided by Kathryn Hays as Gem in "The Empath." Because the character is mute, her role is essentially one long pantomime, but the actress clearly conveys her emotions, in a exquisite and poignant manner, without need for words.

Roddenberry's view of women as sex objects (he admits this

and does not consider it necessarily a bad thing—so long as the *men* are allowed to be sex objects, too!) is nowhere more evident than in his portrayal of dancers. All the people seen on Star Trek who use dancing as more or less a means of making a living, are, without exception, female. Every man's private fantasy is embodied in the notorious Orion slave girls, whose dancing is said to excite men into a frenzy of passion. Vina, in one of her guises in "The Menagerie," performs the erotic dance for Captain Pike, and Marta of Elba II ("Whom the Gods Destroy") does a similar version for Kirk. (Actually, it is probably the lascivious eyes of these women, and not their dancing, which makes them seem irresistible.) The pub dancers on Argelius II perform a variation of Near Eastern belly-dancing which has less sexual overtones than that of the Orions (but which Scotty finds agreeable nonetheless). On the Shore Leave planet, McCoy dreams up two cabaret girls who seem to be direct descendants of the can-can dancers from the days of *Gaité Parisienne*. The good doctor has very old-fashioned tastes!

From several examples, we know that social dancing is still practiced in Star Trek's time. Dr. Helen Noel mentions dancing with Kirk at the ship's Christmas party. Yeoman Ross waltzes with Trelane, the Squire of Gothos, to the accompaniment of Uhura's harpsichord. Later in the series, in "Requiem for Metheuselah," Kirk waltzes with Reena Kapec, Flint's protégé, to an unpublished Brahms work. (It's rather odd that this twenty-third-century man is so proficient at a dance form that is already a lost art to twentieth-century Americans.)

Dancing among primitive tribes is so common that it's surprising the *Enterprise* didn't encounter more of it on planets in the early stages of development. Seems to me that the people of "The Apple" would have performed some type of sacrificial dance for Vaal. We know for a fact that dancing is a part of Vulcan's long history. Spock remarks that Marta's dancing is reminiscent of that done by Vulcan kindergarteners. Obviously the Vulcans recognize how important dance is for development of total coordination in mind and body. Spock's movements during his *Kal-if-fee*, although not really dance, do indicate training in a stylized fighting art such as kendo or fencing.

And then some of the dance in Star Trek is just plain silly. In "I, Mudd," everybody does the ubiquitous waltz, this time to nonexistent music. In "Plato's Children," the Platonians force Kirk and Spock to perform a ridiculous little do-si-do, and they transform Spock into an expert flamenco dancer (whom we all know was not played by Nimoy). The most irrelevant, inexcusable use (abuse?) of dance occurred in "The Way to Eden," where the hippie dancing of the sixties was merely transplanted a couple of hundred years forward. In that episode, Star Trek reached the epitome of bad taste.

There has been no dance at all in the Star Trek movies so far, mainly because we are never given the opportunity to observe another culture. I had hoped that the vestal virgins might perform during Spock's *katra* ceremony (it certainly would have enlivened the scene), but they merely stood like statues. Perhaps there will be dance in *Star Trek IV* . . . after all, Kirk is going to have to do some fast stepping to get out of the fix he's in!

The Minerals of Star Trek

One of my earliest hobbies was rock collecting, which I began at age seven (perhaps that's why I never caught Star Trek during its prime time run—I must have been out looking for specimens!). Many years later, when I became a Star Trek fan, I did some research and came up with twenty-eight substances or alloys that were created solely for the purposes of the TV series.

The most vital and often-mentioned material is dilithium, which in its crystalline form provides power for the *Enterprise's* warp drive in a manner similar to the way that laser beams are crated through rubies. It is not known whether this is a new form of lithium, or a totally different element. We know of two crystal types: reddish-gold blocks, used in the ship's energizers; and translucent octahedrons (a six-inch quartz "pencil" was used to simulate the latter). Dilithium crystals are common stones on the planet Troyius, where they are called radans and are used in jewelry. Once, in an emergency, crude radans were used in the engines, and they proved adequate to achieve warp power.

One substance is merely a figment of Captain Kirk's fertile imagination, yet it has an episode named for it: "The Corbomite Maneuver." Kirk (who is apparently an excellent poker player) has twice bluffed his way through enemy territory by saying that his ship's hull contains corbomite. This mythical mineral reflects dangerous radiation back to the source and then self-destructs, with the backwash of the explosion killing the enemy as well.

Neutronium is the densest alloy in the Galaxy. It formed the hull of a "doomsday machine" that almost swallowed the

Enterprise. On Argus X, tritanium can be found—a mineral or ore which is 21.4 times harder than diamond. That seems incredible enough, but tritanium isn't the hardest substance known to the Federation. Rodinium allegedly holds that honor, though the Romulans' photon torpedo managed to pulverize shields composed of it.

Star Trek even presented us with mineral life forms. The peaceful, intelligent Horta is a silicon-based creature that can burrow through solid rock. She deposited millions of basketball-sized silicon spheres—which were later discovered to be her eggs.

Some substances were never given a name. On Alfa 177, a crewman slipped on a soft yellow ore. It is so magnetic that when he beamed up, the transporter was severely damaged, causing Kirk to be split into two entities as he beamed aboard. There is a rock on Gamma Trianguli VI—containing uranite, hornblende, quartz, and other elements—which explodes when dropped. What are those other elements, I wonder? TNT?

There are many more substances—celebium, muranite, irrillium, topaline—the names of which sound so real that I had to double-check my rock identification books to make sure they didn't already exist. In the Andromeda Galaxy, however, there exists a mineral with an even more poetic name. In the words of one inhabitant of the planet Kelva: ". . . crystals which form with such rapidity that they seem to grow. We call them . . . *sahsheer*."

The Great Bird Has Impeccable Taste

Gene Roddenberry has said that *Star Trek III: The Search for Spock* is the best Star Trek yet made.

He's right! *If* by "best" you mean true to its original vision. *The Search for Spock* is what Roddenberry would have done with the series if he had had the money. Even in this third, big-budget film, the sets look fake and the lines are sometimes corny, but that's the way Star Trek has always been; that's part of the reason we love it. While Robert Wise tried for galactic extravaganza, and Nick Meyer used naval battles and Dickens quotes, Nimoy simply gives us the characters and lets them tell the story. Nimoy's influence is pervasive; every frame of this film reflects his love and understanding of Star Trek. It is the first movie created especially for *us*, the die-hard fans.

Viewed strictly as a work of cinema, *The Search For Spock* is definitely flawed. It has much in common with *The Empire Strikes Back* (incidentally my favorite of the *Star Wars* films): somber mood, emphasis on characterization and mysticism, and a lack of structure (like *Empire*, it is probably the middle third of a trilogy). Whereas *Empire* distributes its action throughout, in *The Search for Spock* the excitement is scrunched up in the middle, making the ending seem anticlimactic. Both films end "up in the air," leaving you feeling vaguely dissatisfied. My *only* serious criticism of *The Search for Spock* is that it ended too soon. I disagree with certain critics who have labeled the movie dull and boring. Naturally they would think so—they had just seen *Indiana Jones and the Temple of Doom* the previous week, and after that rollercoaster, *any* movie would seem slow. When will the critics learn not to compare Star Trek with other SF blockbusters? Star Trek is *not Star Wars*, nor has it ever tried to be; its goals are entirely different.

The plot of *Star Trek III: The Search for Spock* lies somewhere between a good fanzine story and the best of the TV episodes. Some people have derided Harve Bennett for what they see as absurdities, but he handled the material remarkably well, considering the situation he was left with at the end of *Wrath of Khan*, and actually this story contains far *fewer* plot holes and inconsistencies than did *Wrath of Khan*. Spock's "refusion" is believable to me, but only because he is an alien, with a vastly different physiology and culture. Who's to say what is possible for his species? There is precedent for the feasibility of a mind/body separation; recall Sargon in "Return to Tomorrow." What I found much harder to swallow was Spock's regeneration on Genesis. How did his body shrink back to a one-celled organism, then grow into a fetus and child and adult? And why did *pon farr* come so early, if the "original" Spock was in his thirties when he experienced his first one?

As for the film's most controversial aspect: I did not find the destruction of the *Enterprise* to be sensationalistic or manipulative. Consider the ship's circumstances: obsolete (in Starfleet's opinion), she had been decommissioned and was headed for the scrap heap. Even if she had still had a future, Kirk could no longer be a part of it, because he is now a criminal. Thus, as the ship hangs in space, empty, powerless, broken with no hope of repair, Kirk knew he had nothing to lose. If the *Enterprise* must go to her grave, better for her to die by Kirk's own hand, and go out in a blaze of glory, than to be ignobly dismantled by a Starfleet salvage crew, or worse yet, fall into the hands of the Klingons.

Kirk had undergone quite a remarkable transformation since the events of the last film. Jolted from his petty, self-centered obsession with aging, once again he thinks of others before himself. This is a Kirk stripped down to his basic self, more human and vulnerable than we have ever seen him. Grief, frustration, and desperation have left him too weary to maintain a facade any longer, and for the first time, he breaks down in front of the crew. His reaction to David's death floored me (though not quite so literally as it did Kirk!). Kirk continues to grow as a person because William Shatner continues to extend his boundaries as an actor, and the result is a joy to watch.

Mark Lenard, in the small but vital role of Sarek, delivers the film's most powerful performance. Beneath the granitelike Vulcan mask, he is clearly seething with passion. The mind meld scene in Kirk's apartment, with both actors at a peak of emotional intensity, is exquisitely done.

Third-place honors for best actor go to Christopher Lloyd, who as Kruge makes the perfect Klingon. Unlike previous commanders such as Kor and Koloth, Kruge makes no attempt to be charming. At times he is shrewd and cunning, yet at others he is incredibly pigheaded. Like all the Klingons in the film, he is barbaric and ruthless, but one can't help admiring his warrior race for their preference of death over a life without honor. The scene in which Kruge strangles a "microbe," then remarks that nothing much is happening, is a tongue-in-cheek classic. And giving him a "dog" was a stroke of genius; it adds another dimension to his personality. The fiery battle between Kirk and Kruge is truly impressive, with a mythic, archetypal quality, as if symbolic of a struggle between Good and Evil at the edge of Hell. It reminds me of Darth Vader's alleged duel with Obi-Wan at the lip of a volcano; now, if George Lucas ever actually films that scene, he will be accused of ripping off Star Trek!

DeForest Kelley's McCoy is marvelous, as are all the secondary characters (with the exception of Chekov's embarrassingly fake Russian accent), and the actors make the most out of their expanded roles. I am still unable to reconcile Robin Curtis's version of Saavik with my memories of Kirstie Alley. Robin, though apparently a capable actress, did not quite seem to understand what the character was all about, and seemed only to be following the director's orders.

Of the new characters, my favorite is the bizarre alien who confronts McCoy in the bar. In him we have another believable humanoid, in the Andorian tradition (but what species is this guy, anyway?). I didn't care for Admiral Morrow; he didn't seem authoritative enough to be Kirk's superior, and he has an annoying habit of nodding his head every time he speaks. James Sikking was hilarious as the effeminate Captain Styles, a "tin-plated dictator with delusions of godhood" if there ever was one. Mr. Adventure looks like a carbon copy of our old pal Kevin Riley—could he be his son? On the other hand, the young men chosen to play Spock at various ages did not bear nearly enough resemblance to Leonard Nimoy.

As for the spacecraft: It was a nice touch to name a ship after the late astronaut Virgil "Gus" Grissom. The vessel carrying Valkris looked rusty and disreputable, as a smuggler's ship ought to look. (By the way, I wish we could have seen more of Valkris and her relationship with Kruge.) We are *supposed* to hate the *Excelsior*, of course—and it's easy to do. She lacks grace; her line is not aesthetically pleasing; and on her Bridge, the technological overkill is enough to make one laugh out loud. By contrast, the Klingon Bird of Prey is a thing of beauty, soaring with wings outstretched like a condor in flight.

The musical score is a disappointment, being mainly a reiteration of the Spock and Genesis theme, but James Horner cannot be blamed for this, given director Nimoy's near-obsessive repetition of Spock's death scene. Horner did write a new Klingon theme, and its discordant percussion seems more appropriate than the clean, smooth French horns used by Jerry Goldsmith in *Star Trek: The Motion Picture* (the Klingons don't deserve such noble music).

In essence, *Star Trek III: The Search for Spock* is a film that takes itself seriously, yet has the presence of mind to laugh at itself as well. And don't worry about the *Enterprise*—our gallant crew will find a solution (it happens all the time in fanzines). Instead of complaining about the details, Star Trek fans should consider this movie on occasion for rejoicing, for indeed Star Trek *does* live!

THE ROAD TO THE *ENTERPRISE* (AND BEYOND)

By David Gardner

The new ships, the Reliant, *the* Grissom, *and the* Excelsior, *seen in the last two Star Trek films, were a welcome addition to the Fleet . . . or so you'd think. But David Gardner presents something of a different viewpoint in this article, one that might make you think twice about admiring these spiffy new vessels. Also, David has a few thoughts about the real age of the* Enterprise, *and why everyone seemed to forget it in* Star Trek III.

Several facts from the Star Trek motion pictures have been perplexing me for years, but none have occupied my mind more thoroughly than the various inconsistencies (or, more correctly, seeming inconsistencies) surrounding the use of the Starship *Enterprise* and the other representatives of the Fleet.

To begin with, there is the question of the *Enterprise*'s age. In *Star Trek III: The Search for Spock*, Admiral Morrow states that the *Enterprise* is "over twenty years old," and, therefore, ready to be scrapped. It is quite easy to prove that the *Enterprise* is well over thirty years old, and may be approaching the age of forty when Kirk is forced to destroy it. Furthermore, we are forced to wonder why the Federation would spend all the millions of credits to refit the *Enterprise* with the best existing technology only to relegate her to serving as a training ship, a second-rate posting at best, only a few years later.

Before continuing, we must discuss the concept of a "five-year mission." Was Kirk, in his famous introduction, speaking of the mission length as a minimum assignment time, maximum assignment time, average assignment time, or only the amount of time he would like to spend "in the area," as it were? I believe we can safely discount the latter, as the Star Trek intro is too reminiscent of Kirk's impassioned speeches, not an area to be taken lightly. A maximum cruise of five years would not give a ship captain the time to get to know his ship, crew, or patrol area well enough to justify the transfer. A minimum time of five years begins to appear logical if one considers that by the time of Star Trek, life expectancy is also certain to have increased dramatically; if one is to believe the Medical Reference, humans live well beyond their one hundredth year. For the purposes of this article, I have, however, assumed an average mission to be of five years' duration.

Given this argument, let us work out the age of the *Enterprise*. The events of *Star Trek II: The Wrath of Khan* and *Star Trek III: The Search for Spock* all take place within a very short time frame, apparently during the space of a week, so they can be counted as negligible for the purposes of establishing age. We know, however, that approximately eight years pass between *Star Trek: The Motion Picture* and *Wrath of Khan*, and evidence suggests that about two and a half years pass between the end of the *Enterprise's* original five-year mission (portrayed in the televised episodes) and the beginning of *STTMP*. (This is never actually confirmed; Decker states that Kirk hasn't "logged a single star-hour in over two and one half years," and Kirk himself states that he has been Chief of Starfleet Operations for two and a half years.) The events related in the animated episodes are generally thought to take place during the "fourth year" of the five-year mission under Kirk, and because the technology, terminology, and uniforms are all as they were in the live-action series, this can be believed; so they, too, will be discounted for our purpose. Our total so far is seventeen and a half years.

Spock relates to us in "The Menagerie" that he served under Captain Pike for over eleven years. Before that Captain Robert April had the *Enterprise* for at least one five-year mission. That gives us a minimum age for the *Enterprise* of thirty-three and a half years. If one assumes at least two years for the refit after April and before Pike, this total goes up to thirty-five and a half years. If one allows that April is very likely to have had two voyages aboard her, one as a shakedown cruise (which we'll arbitrarily limit to two years), the total goes up to thirty-seven and a half years. There is also the possibility that there was another, unknown commander between April and Pike; his five-year mission would bring the *Enterprise's* age to forty-two and a half years. As you see, Morrow was way off.

Why? Although on the surface it appears to be, to coin a phrase, "very illogical," I believe that Morrow had several motives for making these particular statements. To begin with, the problem of Genesis was first and foremost in his consciousness. Not only would he have to worry about sealing it off from the Federation, but he would be certain to realize that the Federation's enemies would be trying to learn everything they could about this "ultimate weapon." Furthermore, Morrow has been ordered to get the *Enterprise* away from Kirk, primarily because Starfleet cannot afford to have its model Captain traveling into more new danger. We get several hints from all three movies that the Klingons are increasing their activity at the Federation border, and, in view of the treaty between the Klingons and the Romulans, doubtless Romulan activity is increasing as well. Kirk's experience, as well as his example, is to be called upon in case of intergalactic war.

But that isn't the entire answer, and here we have to delve into the inner workings of Starfleet, including that organization's earliest beginnings. Carol Marcus says in *Wrath of Khan* that Starfleet has kept the peace for more than a hundred years, so I believe that we can take this as a rough estimate of the age of Starfleet itself; about three times the age of the *Enterprise* (or perhaps as little as twice her age, if some of the upper estimates are true).

During its first thirty years, Starfleet probably suffered from the same bureaucratic red tape and funding shortages as all new organizations. Consider that in a very short time, by relative standards, those in charge of Starfleet would had to have established at least the beginnings of a peace-keeping force, a military force, an exploration force, and the Starfleet Academy, not to mention logistics and support for all of the above. This force would've had to be sufficient until new, better-designed units could be brought on line, at which time they could be retired to backup forces. These ships were probably forced to be far more flexible than the capital ships with which we are familiar, and had none of the resources that we associate with the *Enterprise* and other ships of her time period, yet were more often than not called upon to perform many of the same functions. In short, Starfleet was probably originally composed of whatever the fledgling service could draft from the planetary navies it would be replacing, with whatever original construction ships it could afford.

After fifty years things had probably stabilized for Starfleet, and Command began to think about supplementing their forces with a comprehensive construction program featuring vessels that were truly able to handle a variety of roles. It is therefore not surprising that when it came time to design a ship, Starfleet Command wanted it all, and, to be fair, they deserved it.

The design and testing period for the *Constitution* Class heavy cruisers was probably the most intense in the history of any spacefaring race, in the Federation or out of it. All technologies relating to starship function and science were pushed to their limits; the ship would have to withstand many tests, including the test of time. It is very likely that Fleet Command was told "this is it for the next twenty or thirty years," and so they, in effect, tried to build a ship that could fulfill every conceivable role.

To their credit, they succeeded admirably. The *Enterprise* and her sisters are capable of performing any action or function as well as any known starship, from scientific exploration to military patrol, from diplomatic courier to emergency transport. This versatility is shown time and time again when the *Enterprise*, with Scotty's help, manages to pull off some impossible feat. With three refits, she manages to serve almost forty years (possibly more), an incredible task that speaks for itself in terms of vessel integrity. Following her final refit after Kirk's five-year mission, she takes on one of the most powerful being/ constructs ever encountered in what may be, as far as we can tell, the crowning moment of her career.

Unfortunately, although the design succeeded better than could have been imagined, the design goals and parameters were faulty from the start. Stated in simple terms: Although it may save money to build one ship capable of both military and scientific duty rather than two ships, each capable of only either duty, it won't help if a military craft is needed at one end of the sector and a scientific vessel at the other. This is confirmed time after time when we learn that the *Enterprise* is the only ship capable of performing a given mission in an area, or worse yet, the only ship in the area at all. Starfleet did indeed have its jack-of-all-trades design, which met or exceeded all specifications, but the expense was simply too prohibitive to build enough of the ships to go around. Later, the Destroyer design was introduced, but it has serious shortcomings in size and power, and couldn't be considered a match for Klingon battlecruisers (and we can assume that the Empire operates these in far greater numbers than the number of operational Federation Heavy Cruisers, for they are routinely seen deployed in groups of three, even by the Romulans!). The Dreadnought design had been under study for quite a while, but, if anything, it was more expensive than the cruisers.

Thus it was probably during Kirk's mission that Fleet Command began to consider going back to a dichotomy in the design process. Signs of this appear even earlier, in the Scout, a modified Destroyer that is capable of performing exploration duties at the expense of almost all of its military capability, and the aforementioned Dreadnought, which would be much too expensive to operate on a regular basis and would likely be held in reserve until the outbreak of war.

Although a rethinking of the design process was in order, Starfleet had to deal with the question of the impracticality of its cruiser designs, especially because at least four (and possibly more) had been lost in the line of duty, bringing their strength dangerously low. A design which quickly came to the forefront would have been that of the *Reliant*-type vessels. The ship is obviously a war cruiser, small, powerful, and very well and prominently armed. This assumption is supported by the fact that Captain Terrell is at least a match in terms of military bearing for any of the other captains we see or hear during any episode or movie. Even during his earliest moments onscreen we hear him complaining about being assigned to Project Genesis. Where would he rather be? Out patrolling the front, of course.

The *Reliant* Class ships were based on the *Constitution* Class hull, engines, and mechanicals, making them very feasible economically, and almost immediately ready for production. Furthermore, a small amount of explorative duty could be performed by them, allowing them to take over from or supplement scouts and other such vessels in sensitive areas when the capital ships were required elsewhere.

The other side of the design dichotomy shows up in *The Search for Spock:* the USS *Grissom* of the *Gargarin* Class. These ships are purely for research; surely if the *Grissom* had any type of armament, Captain Esteban, a cautious man, would have had it ready and standing by in an area as potentially troublesome as the Genesis Planet. We are forced to wonder if Starfleet went too far in trying to split designs; these vessels are far too helpless for duty in deep space. Perhaps they are not meant to be operating a great distance from a port. It is possible that Esteban was promised a blockade by Admiral Morrow (who was too busy trying to track down the *Enterprise* to do much else), but he still should have had any available armament at the ready.

Interestingly enough, the apparent roles of the *Reliant* and the *Grissom* in the second and third movies are exactly the opposite of what they should be: The *Reliant* is performing the explorative duties and the *Grissom* is sent to Genesis when the Fleet should be expecting danger. Obviously, though, Starfleet was well aware of the possibility of armed conflict and had assigned *Reliant* to protect Project Genesis for the duration. When *Reliant* was destroyed, Morrow was forced to resort to one of the smaller research vessels at his disposal. As mentioned above, Esteban was probably expecting the area to be sealed off, leaving his ship to perform the mission for which it was commissioned.

These new vessels explain, in part, why the *Enterprise* is broken to a training vessel in *Star Trek II: The Wrath of Khan.* By training its cadets on ships using much of the same equipment and procedures as the front line ships, the Fleet can assure maximum efficiency from the training process.

Another part of the explanation, however, lies with the Organians, and in particular their much-alluded-to "Peace Treaty." Probably this treaty imposed strength limits upon each belligerent, including a maximum number of ships of each type, and a maximum amount of firepower per ship per fleet. Because the Klingons could be counted on to act aggressively at some time in the future, Fleet Command decided on a shipbuilding program that would enhance the Fleet's defensive and offensive capabilities, hence the war cruiser *Reliant* Class and the battle cruiser *Excelsior* Class. It is probable that Starfleet dropped plans for the more expensive and less powerful Dreadnoughts in favor of this latter class, which may even have been designed to take particular advantage of the new transwarp technology.

However, with the *Excelsior* ready to go on trial runs (and soon thereafter, no doubt, to enter service), Starfleet would soon be forced to lower its number of cruisers by one to comply with the treaty limits. This unfortunate one was to have been the *Enterprise*, probably stripped of her usable components for future building and then melted down to reuse her metal. (How grateful we are to Admiral Kirk for seeing to it that Our Lady of Adventure comes to a more fitting and glorious end.)

Morrow is therefore willing to do just about anything to convince Kirk to leave the *Enterprise* and take up residence Earthside once more and, if the truth be known, Fleet Command is probably worried that he'll abscond with the ship before he can be stopped (as he did at the end of *Star Trek: The Motion Picture*). The fact that she is damaged from the battle with Khan and "over twenty years old" are tools for Morrow to use; it seems as if Starfleet will never be through using James T. Kirk. Morrow's statements on the age of the *Enterprise* are probably a simple mistake; although it is admittedly difficult to imagine anyone in the Fleet not knowing even the approximate age of a Fleet capital ship, let alone the Commander of Starfleet. Is is possible that he received faulty information from a subordinate, or reviewed the wrong file? He has had a lot on his mind recently.

Sadly it seems that the *Constitution* Class vessels will be retired from active duty in the near future (if they have not already been pulled), although a handful may be put into reserve for use as replacements for destroyed line units, and we know that at least one has been used as a training vessel. An incredible career lies behind these ships, and who knows what might await them in the future? Perhaps some unforseen occurrence will result in a problem that will require the *Constitution* Class ships to be optimized.

This, then, is the Story of the Starship *Enterprise*, and her many five-year missions, her predecessors and her descendants, and finally of her end . . . painful though it may be, it has hit a harmonious note with us all.

MIND TREK

By M. H. Lewis

We must admit that we're continually surprised by the fact that the most basic themes of Star Trek have counterparts in classical literature, religion, history, science, philosophy, and so forth. Marie Lewis is a student of classical philosophy, and in the following article, tells us how the characters of Kirk, Spock, and McCoy reflect (and "live") three of the most basic and well-known of ancient philosophies. By the way . . . if you enjoy this article, Marie wants you to consider this: What do the seating arrangements in a Viking longship have to do with the relationships of the personnel of the Enterprise? *What do European tribal laws on bloodprices have to do with Number One, Uhura, Ilia, and Saavik? And what does a horse-god have to do with "Arena"?*

Thoughtful Captain Kirk, logical Mr. Spock, emotional Leonard McCoy—all have secrets Gene Roddenberry either doesn't know or doesn't admit to knowing. William Shatner, Leonard Nimoy, and DeForest Kelley perform their roles in accordance with these factors without reference to them. The many writers who have assisted in creating the episodes of their biographies also seem to be working in the dark.

Each of these characters is not only himself. Their creators, the writers and the actors, have made each of them consistently act and react according to the principles of three Western classical philosophies: Platonism (Kirk), Stoicism (Spock), and Epicureanism (McCoy).

The principles of these philosophies, unknown to most of us

as such, have shaped our culture so pervasively that those gifted people have unwittingly embodied them for us in these characters. We in turn found these principles so naturally admirable and attractive that we reacted with acceptance and affection to characters living by them. Fascinating!

Captain James T. Kirk is a Platonist. He is a man of high abilities who accepts the responsibilities of leadership because others need the leadership of a man of his capabilities, and not because he enjoys the prerogatives of power.

That is the definition of the Platonic "philosopher-king" —one who rules for others' benefit, not his own satisfactions. That is also the definition by which personnel of the *Enterprise* have often times recognized the real Jim Kirk from impostors.

Spock knew the real James Kirk from the "identical" madman in "Whom Gods Destroy" when the real Kirk suggested securing the *Enterprise's* safety by destroying them both. Kirk-2 in "Mirror, Mirror," who ruthlessly enjoyed absolute power and the prerogatives of power on his own Imperial Starship *Enterprise*, was detected immediately as not being "our" Jim Kirk. The "other side" of Kirk revealed his identity on the Bridge by unconcern for others in "The Enemy Within." "Kirk/J" in "Turnabout Intruder" revealed her own spuriousness by displaying fury when questioned or disobeyed.

A person's "Last Statement" is supposed to contain his deepest beliefs. In "The Tholian Web," James Kirk's "last statement" was heard when he was believed lost. It told Spock to "trust intuition" when logic fails.

Plato attributed to his teacher Socrates statements that a human could reach true knowledge by two methods: logic and intuition.

Logic, the lesser method, was a mental skill. It could be developed and exercised by studying math, geometry, and astronomy, and by engaging in logical dialogues with opponents.

For some kind of judgments, the kind we now call "value judgments," logic is inadequate. Logic will never give us adequate definitions of beauty, truth, justice, God. These are perceived by intuition, a function of the soul, not the mind. We "know them when we see them."

We have these choices: to develop our mind's capacity for logic by choosing to exercise it; to neglect the capacity and let it atrophy; or to deliberately destroy it either temporarily or permanently with drugs, alcohol, or indulgence in extreme emotions, such as anger to the point of "seeing red" or total panic. In the latter cases we know the emotions cause the flooding of the brain with self-generated chemicals, creating a case of auto-drug-intoxication. That we can deliberately choose to induce these states is reflected in such common expressions as "working himself up a temper" or "getting himself into a state."

We also have these choices: to develop our soul's capacity for intuition by always acting in the way that seems good and right to us, by seeking out the beautiful in nature, art, or music to increase our sensitivity, and by directing our attention to good and noble persons or actions in life, history, or fiction, rather than cause our soul's capabilities to atrophy by constant attention only to what will pay, by exposing ourselves deliberately to the evil and the ugly, and by failing to do a good act or deliberately doing a bad one.

As for alcohol, Plato was not a teetotaler, nor is James Kirk. But Plato totally rejected drinking to the point of unconsciousness as a way to "have fun," nor have we ever seen James Kirk choose that form of recreation. Even at the wake for Spock (in the novelization of *The Search for Spock*), James Kirk did not set out to drink to the point of numbing grief.

The quickest way to develop the soul's intuitive capabilities is through love; either by intense emotional attachment *with no content of physical desire* for persons of either sex, or by intense emotional attachment, including sexual desire to a single good or noble person. We call the first type of relation friendship. It was once known as "Platonic love." We call the second type of relationship "romantic love."

In almost every episode of Star Trek the friendship between those good and worthy persons Spock, Kirk, and McCoy is perfectly clear, and so are the many ways in which each of them is a slightly different and better person because that friendship exists.

The Platonic teaching about "romantic love" as an aid to the development of the soul's capacities has supplied the plots for at least three episodes of Star Trek.

In "The Cloud Minders," Droxine would not have changed her ideas about the "just" way to live and the "right" way to treat the Troglytes nearly as quickly if she had not felt so strong a physical and emotional attachment to Spock. Her "noble" decision to "go to the mines" was clearly made in order to be the kind of person Spock, who perceived the possibility of such nobility in her, hoped she would be. This is what Plato meant when he said that the desire to appear good and noble to the beloved would cause the lover to become good and noble.

The "role of love" in developing the soul and the intuition is even clearer in the case of Reena the android. Her creator, Flint, introduces her to Kirk specifically because her capacity for feelings cannot become operative unless she "loves." Love for Kirk indeed produces in Reena an intuitive understanding of right and wrong all her logic circuits could not arrive at, causing her to tell Flint she will hate him forever if he harms the *Enterprise* and its crew. If an intuitive capacity to perceive right and wrong and react strongly against the wrong is a "soul," love for Kirk created a soul in Reena—and possession of a soul means the possibility of "death" in a sense not otherwise possible for an android.

Kirk, however, can only feel an intense physical desire for Reena in response to her physical attractiveness. This only damages his soul to such a point that Flint's rights and needs elicit no response of justice or compassion in Kirk, only a younger, stronger male animal's violent rage against the attempt of an older, weaker male to keep and mate with a physically desirable female.

In "City On the Edge of Forever," Kirk does love a noble person, Edith Keeler, a woman whose abilities and ethics are such she may well be his Platonic "soul mate"—the only soul ever created in all the universe to be his "other half," the perfect completion for his soul.

Spock trusts James Kirk to do the right thing because of Jim's very love for Edith. Loving Edith, Jim will not let her live to see that she has delivered her world and her generation to the hideous evil and cruelty of the Nazi dictatorship. Nor can Kirk be the person Edith's love expects him to be, and permit her continued life to destroy the entire good development of the universe, as he knows it can be and will be if she dies.

So love enables Jim Kirk to destroy the physical life that could have saved him from perpetual unfulfillment.

The feelings in general, other than love, are referred to by Plato as the "horses of the chariot of the soul," whose charioteer is Reason. Under the control of Reason, their strength and power are to be used, not rejected as evil. This is the relationship Kirk reached with his "other side" at the conclusion of "The Enemy Within."

Plato strongly rejected myths of the gods as representing unworthy ideas of the divine. The ultimate aim of Platonism was an intuitive vision of God as the Ultimate Beauty and Goodness. In essence, Kirk's statement to Apollo in "Who Mourns For Adonais?" that for men *one god* is now sufficient implies that the ability Apollo has just demonstrated, to take and restore life, is no longer sufficient qualification for worship. Mere power beyond human comprehension is only superior force, if unaccompanied by morality.

The ultimate test of morality for Plato is this: Given such power that any act can go unpunished, will the powerholder finally choose to do nothing wrong? Apollo fails this test. So do "Plato's Stepchildren." James Kirk, Mr. Spock, and Leonard McCoy, given double-ESP powers, pass the test. They subdue their tormentors but do not engage in counter-torture. They do not even wish to continue to possess the power and ability to control others against their will.

The final form of Platonism, in Plotinus, declared that God is One and the proper fulfillment of the human soul is mystic union with the One. The ultimate tragedy, then, is to commit an act so evil or omit a good act so essential that the soul be so permanently damaged that it must be forever incapable of such fulfillment. This is the meaning of Kirk's final statement to Spock's father, Sarek, at the end of *Star Trek III: The Search for Spock*. If Kirk had failed to do everything possible for Spock's restoration, at all costs to himself, he would have "lost his soul," which would have suffered that kind of permanent damage.

Strangely, what Plato declared to be the only possible complete satisfaction for a human soul, an intuitive union with its Creator, is achieved by a machine in *Star Trek: The Motion Picture*. V'Ger has found the perpetual collection of knowledge and the attainment of immense power unsatisfying. There is "something more" it has to have, and this "something more" can only be had by "merging" with its Creator, Man; a satisfaction it is granted after long, blind groping after a creator it does not understand and cannot recognize upon meeting.

Mr. Spock's intense reliance on Logic is in complete accord with the human philosophy of Stoicism, which arose after

Platonism and in opposition to it. There are for Stoics three good states of mind: joy, a rational elation; caution, a rational avoidance; and will, a rational wish. These include the limited list of permitted feelings: benevolence, placidity, affection, reverence, modesty, delight, mirth, and good spirits. Mr. Spock rarely exhibits an emotion outside this list, and is little given to the last three.

"Delight" for Mr. Spock chiefly exists in fulfilling what Stoicism taught was the logical role of a rational organism in a universe: to be the spectator-who-understands and applauds the wonders of the Creator's creation. The word *fascinating*, applied to many different phenomena, is Mr. Spock's form of applause.

Benevolence, goodwill, is listed first among right feelings. The Stoics insisted it is also logically part of a rational organism's role in the universe to recognize all other rational beings as his kin by that rationality. In a time when human loyalties were restricted to genetic kin, tribe-of-common-descent, and the city-state, Stoicism said, "Call the universe your city and every reasoning being your fellow citizen."

The Vulcan Seventh-Sense, described in a footnote to the novelization of *Star Trek: The Motion Picture* as a direct sense of the Oneness of the Part with the All, is in accordance with the Stoic view of the universe as a living being, in which each rational being, as a self-conscious part, may choose to accept willingly and cooperate with whatever happens to that part as being in some way for the good of the whole. A Stoic who has a fever knows his sickness is "natural," and therefore in some way the existence of fevers must be for the good of the whole. He will cooperate with any effective treatment because to seek to be cured is also "natural," and therefore also for the good of the whole. He will not complain because he happens to be the "part of the whole" this fever happened to, nor be any more trouble or distress than he can help to others on account of his sickness.

In his memo to himself, the Stoic Emperor Marcus Aurelius reminded himself in each act to do his duty as a Roman—a member of his particular nation and culture—and as a man—a rational being akin to all other rational beings. In our time we have seen the difference between humans who only did their duty as Germans in facilitating the murder of more than six million human beings, and those Germans and others who knew they had a duty as human beings and did what they could to help save three million.

In almost every episode of Star Trek, we see Mr. Spock logically calculating his duty as a Vulcan, as an officer of the *Enterprise*, as a friend, as a rational being. In "Errand of Mercy" and in "Day of the Dove," it is predicted that even the deadly enemy, the Klingon Empire, will one day unite with the Federation in peaceful cooperation and development. The question follows: Then why not now? Why not avoid the slaughter in between? Kirk puts this question to the "other Spock" in "Mirror, Mirror": Can't the evolution of peacefulness be speeded up? Now the real survival of our real species on this real planet depends on a real answer to this fictional question!

One of the "good examples" of proper rational Stoic actions recommended to his students by the Stoic teacher Epictetus, himself an ex-slave permanently crippled by torture inflicted on a whim by his former master, was the death of a female slave who contrived to kill herself in the Imperial torture chambers rather than risk betraying the master she loved. As she decided it was more reasonable to die herself for the good of her master and his fellow rebels, so Spock, in *Wrath of Khan*, decided it was reasonable the one should die for the many, and acted on his logic.

Leonard McCoy shows himself to be an Epicurean by insisting on validity of all feelings as necessary guides to understanding and action. Although bitterly attacked as immoral and antirational, Epicureanism was based on more "scientific" teachings than either Platonism or Stoicism. Its arguments for the feelings were based on a protoevolutionary atomic theory.

Forces for destruction, creation, and preservation are continually creating all things by combining atoms and then destroying them by breaking up those combinations. What survives must be so combined as to effectively resist the forces of destruction. The inborn human feelings must then be such as will effectively aid the combination of atoms of a human being to maintain that combination.

Pain therefore indicates what is bad for a human being and should be avoided. Pleasure indicates what is good for a human being and is to be sought. Reason should not ignore or override these reactions, but select from among them, so that the greatest amount of pleasure can be secured to each of these unstable combinations of atoms into a human being during its inevitably limited lifespan.

The "soul" is constructed of finer atoms and can only survive while protected in the container of the body, made of coarser atoms. Separated from the body when the body is destroyed, the soul is necessarily destroyed also. Although Platonist and Stoic believed the soul to be immortal and the body a comparatively unimportant hindrance to right understanding and a temporary barrier to union of the soul with God the Ultimate Goodness (Plato) and the Divine All (Stoic), Epicurus taught that the unstable soul-body combination and the earthly life was all there was.

McCoy's continual violent dislike of transporter travel is squarely based on this dislike of dispersal of the body and anxiety about the soul. The first Star Trek novel, *Spock Must Die!*, begins with McCoy stating his fear that the disembodied soul must die at a man's first transport, that every reassembled body is simply a soulless automaton, and therefore transport is really murder. Scott's complete unconcern is based on his assumption, contrary to McCoy's, that souls are indeed immortal. Kirk's answer, that the question itself proves McCoy has a soul present, is based on the Platonic division of factual questions to logic and the mind, and moral questions and concerns to the capacity of the soul.

Many Star Trek episodes seem to refer to souls requiring a "body-container" for survival. McCoy reacts violently against the loan of human bodies to the globe-contained souls in "Return to Tomorrow." He reacts most violently against Thlassa's wish to trade Anne Mulhall's body for Kirk's life, thereby making it impossible for Anne to live out her life.

In *Star Trek III: The Search for Spock*, McCoy himself becomes the "container" of Spock's soul until it can be united with some other form of "container" in the Hall of Ancient Thought. Without such a container, Sarek makes clear, the soul must be eternally lost. When the extraordinary processes of the Genesis world create a "new body" for Spock, then a resurrection-life in that body becomes possible if the soul can be transferred. Without the soul, the body must remain a living blank.

Naturally, the importance of obtaining the maximum fulfillment in the limited lifetime is a constant theme of McCoy's. In "Metamorphosis," the Companion, who was otherwise potentially immortal and has been maintaining a human in practical immortality, takes a human form so that both may love at the price of mortality for both of them. Kirk states, and McCoy affirms, that love, not for an eternity, but for a lifetime, is enough for humans.

In "Tomorrow Is Yesterday," McCoy tells the jet pilot that he has a sixty-year lifetime left before ceasing to be. Sharing mutual love with his family rather than being a spectator of the advanced knowledge of the future is McCoy's prescription for the most satisfying way for Christopher to spend that lifetime.

In "For the World Is Hollow and I Have Touched the Sky," McCoy believes he has one year left to live and chooses to spend it in a loving relationship rather than in continued duty on the *Enterprise*. Valuing affectionate relationships over knowledge, achievement, or power is a constant Epicurean principle.

The great value placed on affectionate relationships means that for Epicureans it is not "worth" avoiding any amount of pain or even death itself if a friend must be lost as a result. For that reason, McCoy gave himself to torture and death to save Kirk and Spock in "The Empath." The purpose of the Vians was to discover in the humans the emotions necessary to make survival of Gem's race rational: the will to survive, compassionate love, the will to save others at the risk of self. When they are denounced for lacking compassion themselves, they state they are still capable of one emotion: gratitude. This was one of the Epicurean's most highly valued feelings; counting up all the "unexpected and undeserved good things" of a lifetime was a recommended Epicurean activity. "The Empath" ends with both Kirk and McCoy urging Spock to take note of the very high value the Vians place on a race feeling the necessary emotions to make its survival a good risk.

One of the chief duties of friendship among Epicureans was to be the "best friend who would tell" another friend he was making a mistake in life. This is as consistent a part of McCoy's behavior to Spock and Kirk as Mr. Spock's logic is consistent with his behavior.

Finally, *The Search for Spock* has an almost totally Epicurean plot. In it all the *Enterprise* personnel set a fully Epicurean value on friendship: it is more important than country (the Federation), profession (Starfleet discipline), personal success, or personal safety. At the end of *The Search for Spock*, thanks to the temporary union of McCoy and Spock, Spock has come to comfortably accept his feelings toward his friends. He has personally achieved the compromise between Stoic teachings on reason and Epicurean teachings on feelings that Marcus Aurelius reflected by writing down both Stoic and Epicurean "words to live by" in his personal notebook. *Star Trek II: The Wrath of Khan* ended with the Stoic teaching that it is reasonable that one should die for the many. *Star Trek III: The Search for Spock* ended with the Epicurean statement that sometimes the many must spend themselves for the welfare of the one.

As we have seen, the philosophical principles of Platonism, Stoicism, and Epicureanism have not only been embodied in (respectively) Kirk, Spock, and McCoy, but have been shared between them as well. Taking the best of each of us and using it to make all of us stronger is indeed one of the basic principles of Star Trek.

STAR TREK: ODYSSEY OF SALVATION

By Sister Mary William David, S.N.D.

We receive a surprising number of articles and letters which have a religious orientation; apparently a great many fans find an appealing similarity in the pro-humanistic viewpoints of Star Trek and their chosen religion. Below, Sister Mary William David takes a look at how the events in the first two Star Trek films (this article was written before the release of The Search for Spock) *can be interpreted in relation to events in the life of Christ . . . with special emphasis, of course, on Mr. Spock.*

"Trekkie" is the term affectionately applied to a person suffering from video addiction to Star Trek. I have just lately become a "Trekkie." Why? Adventure and Imagination, yes, but there's something more. When I first began watching the science fiction program, the characters touched a responsive chord in my own life, in my own thoughts, desires, and struggles. So, I looked forward to seeing the two feature-length films. What I found there was a more universal message, a parable of redemption echoing the life and mission of Jesus.

The crewmembers of the Starship *Enterprise* represent all persons confronted with the mystery of being, of good, and of evil; persons in search of their meaning. Captain James Kirk, authority figure, represents the official in each of us, tied to duty and responsibility, patriotic, aware of the rules of the game of life—sometimes challenged to break the letter in order to fulfill the spirit. Doctor Leonard McCoy, the healer, concerned to alleviate human pain, angered at the waste of human life, is the most often argumentative and emotional. "Bones" is that side of us that would do away with all suffering, that becomes enraged at the lack of feeling in others, that longs to return to the soil, the life of nature, that believes in the innate goodness of unspoiled creation. Mr. Spock, First Science Officer with the unpronounceable and unpronounced first name, the head, the brain, the computer of the Starship *Enterprise*, cannot understand let alone enjoy a good laugh, or love, or any of the emotions because they are illogical. Yet a single raised eyebrow reveals a depth of emotion held in check only by a stronger Vulcan pride. Spock represents the thinking and reasoning side of human nature; the calculating logical side which, although invaluable in times of crisis and dilemma, is by itself a terrible emptiness and loneliness.

The interrelation of these characters in the episodes is a human parable. The characters are part of us all. Their challenges are ours as we move within the microgalaxy of our daily lives. Therefore when the characters are transported from the everyday planet of video into the galaxy of the theater for two full-length motion pictures, it is not surprising that they also take on a more cosmic meaning. Because of my background as an English teacher and a religious sister I found myself paralleling both films to the whole drama of salvation. This is not to say that the screenwriters and directors hoped to produce a Gospel According to Spock; only that beauty is sometimes in the eye of the beholder even if it may not have been in the camera of the creator. Each movie taken separately has a death/resurrection theme. However, if the character of Spock is traced through both films, the Christ-figure is more clearly detailed. The following is not meant to be a technological exposition; simply one person's thoughts and responses after seeing both films.

The Direct Experience: In the beginning of *Star Trek: The Motion Picture* Spock enters the Vulcan desert to discipline himself, shed all emotion, and complete and secure his Vulcan heritage. He goes in search of his meaning—"who is he and is this all there is to life"—as he later verbalizes it. At the end of his desert trial he is called out of the wilderness to accept the symbol of his successful completion of this Vulcan discipline. He refuses the Vulcan insignia because he already knows what the Matriarch will speak after reading his thoughts: "He will not find his answers with us." He must follow the call which he senses vaguely (even if illogically) from outer space.

Jesus, after his forty days in the desert, refused the easy salvation offered him by the devil: "Man does not live by bread alone." He will not find his answers here, but only by going out into the desert in response to the call and mission of his Father.

Spock is drawn to the mission on which the *Enterprise* has already embarked in order to answer his own questions about life's meaning, as well as to save both the alien creature and the human race. We may also believe that Jesus' understanding of the meaning of his life grew gradually as he fulfilled his mission of salvation.

Mind Meld with V'Ger: At a vital point in the conflict with V'Ger, Spock decides he must go alone to study the alien. He joins in a Vulcan mind meld with its transmitter in order to gain information about this creature of perfect logic. Recovering in Sickbay from the damage to his central nervous system caused by the powerful energy of the machine-creature, he comes to a realization that changes his life. In uniting with the alien, Spock experiences the emptiness of its pure logic. He comes to an appreciation and acceptance of his human companions and, more important, his own human capabilities to experience that which is not "illogical" but "beyond logic": beauty, love, mystery, the simple feeling of a friend's handclasp of support. He discovers the meaning in his own life and at the same time, recognized that this meaning will grow as he continues on his journey; the answer are not "found" but "lived." He is no longer surrounded only with the cold, unfeeling questions, but with living and caring companions on a similar quest into the mysteries of life.

This could parallel Jesus' baptism in the Jordan where he accepts and comes to understand his identity as Son of the Father, where he is given a glimpse into the true meaning and power of his existence. It could also be seen as the experience of Christ's Transfiguration, a step into the fuller than human existence which was Jesus'. It takes place before his passion and death. It is not the end of the struggle but an experience that can give meaning to that suffering.

Tears Over V'Ger: Possibly the most unexpected moment of the film comes shortly after the Captain has given the standby order for self-destruction, a measure both to prevent the alien from collecting their data and to destroy it along with the Starship *Enterprise*. (Note: I personally cannot understand why this scene was cut from the movie and only shown in the TV version because it is so important to understanding the growth in Spock's character.) Kirk's surprised response to the unlikely (and most illogical) Vulcan tears—"Not for us, Spock?"—is as much an admonition as a question. However, Spock's reply is that he weeps for V'Ger as one would weep for a brother, for it was as such a brother that he first joined this mission. He weeps that V'Ger will never find the answers to its questions; will never experience, as Spock has just experienced, the value of the supra-logical; will be condemned to death having never experienced true life.

Jesus' words as he wept over Jerusalem come to mind easily. "Would that you understood the time of your visitation. How I longed to gather you as a mother hen does her chicks, but you would not."

Life From Death: At the end of *Star Trek: The Motion Picture*, it seems that Decker takes over the Christ-character that up to this point was Spock's role. Still, death-resurrection is accomplished in the union of V'Ger with its creator, man. That death has not been triumphant is borne out in two ways: Doctor McCoy's reference to the birth of a new life form, and Kirk's final lines listing the two crew members as "missing" instead of dead.

However, this need not be the redemption yet; rather let it be a foreshadowing of the new life to be given to man. The Raising of Lazarus to life was such an event in the life of Christ. Preceding the passion and death of Christ as a sign of hope, this miracle restored Lazarus to earthly life, not the eternal life that Jesus would give by his death. Interpreting the end of *Star Trek: The Motion Picture* in this way allows Spock to keep the role that he will fulfill in *Star Trek II: The Wrath of Khan*.

The Teacher: Spock's role at the beginning of *Wrath of Khan* is that of a teacher—in charge of passing on the command of the *Enterprise* to the younger generation. So was Jesus in his public life, the teacher, the Rabbi, eager to pass on life and leadership to his apostles and disciples. Albeit that makes Lt. Saavik a feminine St. Peter, but all analogies hang loose at some point.

Actually, Spock's training of the half-Vulcan, half-Romulan orphan girl—now the young commander trainee—reminds me more of Jesus' redemption of Mary Magdalen. Here the novel based on the movie is helpful in filling out the details of their relationship and explaining how Spock has saved Saavik from a life of total barbarism. And by the end of the story she begins to understand and accept the mystery of love and death along with a future of hope for herself.

I have called you friends: During a birthday visit when Dr. McCoy tries to convince his friend and patient, Admiral Kirk, of the importance of returning to command the Starship *Enterprise*, he only succeeds in angering him. Spock, on the other hand, shows genuine sensitivity to Kirk when he presents the Admiral with an antique copy of *A Tale of Two Cities* for his collection. Later, when Spock tries to explain that the good of the many outweighs the good of the few "or the one," he turns to Kirk and states simply that no matter what his decision, "I will always be your friend." Jesus, at the Last Supper, on the night before he was to die for the good of the many, said, "I call you friends."

Passion, Death, and Resurrection: Spock's death must be seen as an act of redemption. It is obvious that he weighs the consequences before leaving the Bridge; he makes a decision to give his life for the life of the *Enterprise* as Jesus made his surrender in the garden. Jesus forgave his enemies before he died. Spock finds the way barred at the door of the reactor chamber by Dr. McCoy. After overpowering his constant antagonist with the Vulcan nerve pinch, Spock touches the Doctor's head and speaks softly, "Remember," paralleling Christ's words at the Last Supper: "Do this in remembrance of me."

Once locked in the radiation chamber, Spock knows there is no turning back, although death will not come until after the reactors are back on line and the *Enterprise* well out of danger. Visually the scene is one of beauty and transfiguration before death. A halo of radiant energy envelops and fans out from Spock's body as he struggles with all the strength that only he as a Vulcan can call forth to pull the off-line cables back into place.

Just so, Jesus was the only one who could save the human race. Although his death was one of unspeakable horror, Christian art often represents it as a scene of triumph: Jesus reigning from his cross. A true picturing needs to include the resurrection glory even amid his agony. He himself said that no one took his life from him, but he laid it down willingly only to take it up again on the third day.

Beneath the cross of Jesus stood his friends, who listened to his final words of love. At the end there is a trio of the Vulcan's friends present: Kirk, McCoy, and via the intercom, Saavik. Spock uses his last strength to pull himself up to full stature and speak words of friendship and consolation to the companions who look on helplessly from the other side of the sealed door. "Do not mourn . . . The good of the many outweighs the good of the few . . . I will always be your friend." His burned and withered hand forms the sign of Vulcan blessing on the glass. "Live long and prosper."

Before he dies, Spock experiences the resurrection through the words of Lt. Saavik, who calls over the intercom the beauty of the newly formed Genesis World. In the novelization of the movie, it is clear that Saavik realized where Spock was heading when he left the Bridge and what the consequences would be for him and for her. She accepts his sacrifice and only wants him to know that it does have great meaning and consequence. Pardon me for seeing in this Mary, his Mother's acceptance and participation in her son's death on the cross and her faith in God's ultimate triumph.

Before Spock's body is launched from the *Enterprise*, Kirk says of the Vulcan: "Of all the souls I have met . . . his was the most human." This serves at least as a faint reminder of the Centurion's words of Jesus: "Truly this was the son of God."

Finally, both McCoy and Kirk make references to resurrection as they watch the torpedo casing with Spock's body orbit around the new planet. The doctor states that "he isn't really dead as long as we remember him"—an echo and perhaps an effect of Spock's parting words to the unconscious McCoy—"Remember." And the admiral? When asked by his concerned physician, "Jim? Are you all right? How are you feeling?", he responds, "Young. I feel young."

Perhaps it seems a bit much to put a pointy-eared half-breed side by side with the Lord, no matter how many comparisons can be drawn. The Gospels, however, so lead me to believe that

Jesus wouldn't have objections. He who was friend of sinners and outcasts, and who promised that these followers should expect their lives patterned after his, might feel right at home. Star Trek appeals to me because if Spock is Jesus, so are we all called to be. The human personality parabled in the TV series, through the two motion pictures, led to its Christian fulfillment: sacrificial death leading to new life. Popularity ratings notwithstanding, here is certainly worthy material for eternal reruns.

IN DEFENSE OF *PON FARR*

By Katherine D. Wolterink

Katherine Wolterink, who in past volumes has proffered her views on the Vulcan language, now takes on "the Vulcan heart, the Vulcan soul"— Pon farr, *the time of mating. Looking at things objectively (something most fans who write about this subject seem to have difficulty doing), Kathy integrates information from the series with scientific observation into a logical conclusion.*

In his article, "Why Spock Ran Amok," in *Best of Trek #7*, Kyle Holland makes a startling suggestion: that Vulcan females can and do control the onset of *pon farr* in males with whom they are bonded. If he is correct, this discovery would have profound implications for our understanding of Vulcan culture. Three steps lead him to this conclusion. The first is the claim that the phenomenon of cyclic male sex drive or rut in carbon-based life forms occurs only as a response to female estrus. Having identified this as the basis of *pon farr*, Holland goes on to suggest that the Vulcan female is able to induce the necessary hormonal changes in the male at the desired time through her telepathic link with him. Finally, if *pon farr* is a result of intentional manipulation by the female, her mind link with the male must be a voluntary one. Thus the woman could sever her link with her bond-mate at any time and could initiate a link with another male. Pretty radical stuff!

If Vulcan women had such abilities, it would give them almost unlimited power over the men with whom they were bonded. Such a woman would be able to induce in her husband—at will—a state in which he is reduced to irrational, violent sexual lust. The Vulcan male becomes the victim of a state he is powerless to control, one that has been deliberately induced by the woman who has the power both to free him from *pon farr* and save his life by mating with him. A society in which women can exercise such power over men—virtually the power of life and death—whenever they wish suggests a matriarchy, rather than the characteristic patriarchy we see in "Amok Time" and "Journey to Babel," and which Rebecca Hoffman has so convincingly described in "Vulcan as a Patriarchy" (*Best of Trek #3*).

Let's take a closer look at these points. The first concerns the cause of rutting activity. Animal behaviorists are agreed that the breeding rhythm of life forms which experience rut is based on an internal pattern. E. Bunning, in a report published in 1964, states that cyclical breeding activity is dependent on an inherent "psychological clock" which may be triggered by environmental factors, the most significant of which is photoperiodicity—the number of hours of daylight. It is a genetically inherited rhythm rather than one that is learned. Periods of heightened sexual activity—rut—in males are environmentally triggered to *coincide with* the period when the majority of females available is in estrus. However, rut does not occur *because of* the presence of one or more females in estrum. In fact, in all the species we know of in which males experience rut annually, the females have a reproductive cycle ranging from sixteen and a half to twenty-one days. Breeding takes place only during the short annual breeding season when female estrus and male rut coincide.

It is always dangerous to base speculation about the nature of one species on what we know about another, especially when comparing life forms from different planets. As Spock has often pointed out, however, the operation of natural law and certain natural processes, including evolution, is the same everywhere. In explaining *pon farr* to Kirk, Spock compares the drive to return to their ancient breeding grounds in Vulcans with the homing instinct of the giant eel-birds of Regulus V and the salmon of Earth. Consequently, the idea that our knowledge about cyclical rut in species we are familiar with might shed light on the nature of *pon farr* does not seem too far-fetched.

Is it possible that Vulcan females are able to stimulate the release of hormones which brings about the onset of *pon farr* at will? On the face of it, if a Vulcan woman had a choice in the matter, it seems unlikely that she would induce *pon farr* in her mate because her sure reward would be a violent sexual attack by a powerful male who has been reduced to an irrational animalistic state. Who in her right mind would choose such a fate, either for herself or for her mate? I must agree with G. B. Love, who states in his article, "How And Why Vulcans Choose Their Mates" (*Best of Trek #5*), that *pon farr* must be binding on the female as well as the male. Certainly that is the implication of Spock's remark during his explanation of his bonding with T'Pring: a telepathic link was established between them, ". . . so that at the proper time we would both be drawn to *Koon-ut-kal-if-fee*." The woman does not draw the man to her; *both* are drawn to the appropriate place at the appropriate time.

I am not prepared to agree that Vulcan females also face death if they do not mate, because a reproductive cycle that exhibits a much shorter period—like the female reproductive cycles of other species in which males experience rut—is more likely to ensure fertility at the appropriate time and survival of the race. If this is the case, the female cannot be in danger of death if she does not mate every time she is in estrus, because her fertile period and her mate's *pon farr* will coincide only once every seven years. The reason T'Pring did not simply leave Vulcan during the period of Spock's *pon farr*, thus condemning him to die in agony, is not the fact that she herself would die if she did not mate. It was psychological, but it was also cultural. Although she was irresistibly drawn to *Koon-ut-kal-if-fee*, she was also intent on using it as the only legal and socially acceptable solution to her problem with Spock. In her explanation to him, she states her intention specifically: ". . . I came to know I did not want to be the consort of a legend. But by the laws of our people I could only divorce you by the *Kal-if-fee*." For T'Pring, *pon farr* is a two-edged sword. She cannot escape its summons to join Spock at the appointed time and place, but through the *Kal-if-fee* there is at least the possibility that she may free herself of him.

What of T'Pring's telepathic bond with Spock? Is it, for her, a voluntary link that she can sever at will, as Holland suggests? Has she established such a link with Stonn in Spock's absence? Spock's description of the ritual bonding of Vulcan children suggests that the link between them is exclusive. He tells Kirk and McCoy, "One touches the other to feel the other's thoughts. In this way, our minds were locked together . . . ." If the bond is an exclusive one, has T'Pring broken her tie with Spock in order to bond with Stonn? From our first look at her, when she appears on the main viewscreen on the *Enterprise* Bridge, it would seem that this is not the case, for she greets Spock with the words, "Spock, parted from me and never parted; never and always touching and touched; I await you." Clearly, their bond is intact. Much as she might wish to sever her link with Spock, T'Pring cannot do so by herself. His death in the combat provided by the *Kal-if-fee* would do it, but it must also be possible to dissolve the tie by mutual consent, for T'Pring believes that even if Spock is the victor he might be willing to divorce her.

Kyle Holland suggests, as have many others, that what Spock experienced was a false *pon farr*. We are given to understand that a Vulcan male in *pon farr* who does not mate will die. This understanding is based on Spock's statement to Kirk that although he had hoped to be spared, "The ancient drive is too strong. Eventually, it catches up with us and we are driven by forces we cannot control to return home and take a wife. Or die." But, fans are quick to point out, look what happened to Spock. Although he did not consummate his relationship with T'Pring, he didn't die. Not only that, when he thought he had killed Captain Kirk, he lost interest in her (not a survival-enhancing characteristic). It can't be the real thing.

This view seems to me to overlook one crucial fact: the effect of the challenge on the *pon farr* male. *Pon farr* is a state of intense sexual lust brought about when the genetically determined physiological rhythm in the male triggers the release of gonadatropic hormones. In the majority of cases, the male and his bond-mate meet at *Koon-ut-Kal-if-fee*, they retire to a place of privacy, and his lust is sated. All is well.

In those few instances in which the woman chooses the challenge, things happen very differently. There is a significant change in the physiology of the *pon farr* male after the declaration of *Kal-if-fee*. His temperature rises, his rate of respiration increases rapidly, and his pulse speeds up. He enters a state of intense single-mindedness, and is usually unable to speak. The stage that is characterized by this dramatic change in the male's physical and psychological condition is called *plak tow*—the blood fever. Sexual lust has been replaced by blood lust, and the male is consumed by one overriding need, the need to kill. Spock understood. When he told Kirk and McCoy that he had lost interest in T'Pring, he said, "It must have been the combat." The satiation of blood lust—the act of killing—as well as the consummation of sexual desire, has the power to alleviate the symptoms of *pon farr* and consequently save the life of the threatened male. This is an idea which, no doubt, many will find offensive. However, the identification of sex with death has been recognized as an archetypal image by psychologists, and by authors of great literature for thousands of years.

The reactions of the other Vulcans at Spock's *Koon-ut-Kal-if-fee*, all of whom believed that Kirk was dead, is further proof that this conclusion is the correct one. T'Pring, when called upon to explain her actions, tells Spock, "If you were the victor, you would free me because I dared to challenge. . ." Clearly, she does not expect him to die, although this arrangement would preclude the consummation of their relationship. She has obviously thought it all out very carefully, and her decision is based on the assumption that, if Spock is the victor in the combat, the fact of his having killed his opponent will have dissipated the effects of *pon farr*. I suspect that, although the male will no longer die if he does not experience coitus, he is still capable of sexual intercourse, for T'Pring goes on to say that she is prepared to mate with Spock if he will not release her. However, it no longer appears to be imperative. It is unlikely that a victorious male in *pon farr* would release his bond-mate if it meant he would die. Spock's *pon farr* was the real thing, all right. He escaped death, in spite of his failure to consummate his union with T'Pring, because he believed that he had killed Kirk. The satisfaction of his blood lust released him from *plak tow* and the effects of *pon farr*.

For good or for ill, *pon farr* is one of the immutable facts of Vulcan experience. Its purpose is to assure procreation and thus the continuation of the species. The cyclic nature of *pon farr* is a result of an inherent genetic pattern which has evolved over a period of thousands of years. It is not biologically possible that such a pattern could evolve in the short period (in evolutionary terms) since the Great Awakening on Vulcan and the Reforms of Surak. Just as *pon farr* is at the foundation of Vulcan experience, the social institution of *Koon-ut-Kal-if-fee* is at the heart of Vulcan culture. T'Pau tells Kirk and McCoy, "What thee are about to see comes down from the time of the beginning, without change. This is the Vulcan heart. This is the Vulcan soul. This is our way." In issuing her challenge to Spock, T'Pring uses the phrase, "As it was in the dawn of our days . . ." Like the *pon farr* cycle, the ritual of "marriage or challenge" has its origins in Vulcan's ancient past.

Although they have overcome their violent, emotional behavior, and embraced the philosophy of logic, Vulcans have been forced to accept the inescapable biological imperative of *pon farr*. Once every seven years the male is plunged into a state of violent lust which must be satisfied or he will die. All the species we are familiar with in which males experience rut have a limited breeding season; that is, they mate only during the rutting periods. During the remainder of the cycle, the libido in both sexes is extremely reduced or nonexistent. Does this mean that Vulcans experience sex only during *pon farr*?

Vulcan social mores seem to support this conclusion. The Vulcan attitude toward love and sex, with its potential for creating violent emotions, forbids any overt expression of them. Love and sexual desire, like all other emotions, are to be thoroughly controlled. However, the Vulcan's first experience of coitus takes place in the context of *pon farr*, under frightening and humiliating conditions over which neither partner has any control. Consequently, there are strong cultural and psychological reasons for the Vulcan libido to remain nonfunctional outside *pon farr*.

During a conversation in "The Cloud Minders," the lovely Droxine asks Spock if it is true that Vulcans take a mate only once every seven years. Observant fans will have noticed that Spock never gives her a direct answer; he tells her that the seven-year cycle is biological. However, his remark implies that in Vulcans, mating is limited to a specific breeding period.

I have noticed a tremendous resistance to this idea among Star Trek fans, especially as it applies to Spock. The idea that any humanoid could experience sex only once every seven years and yet live a normal, healthy life is so foreign that we cannot accept it. It is perhaps over this issue more than any other that we exhibit what Joyce Tullock calls a "split personality" in our attitude toward aliens ("The Alien Question," *Best of Trek #6*). Even if we can bring ourselves to recognize this difference it is not one we are prepared to celebrate. Quite the opposite: Immense creative effort on the part of fans has been devoted to reducing this difference between humans and Vulcans, to explaining it away.

At this point, inevitably, a familiar figure arises. Even if it were possible for Vulcans to be healthy and happy (?) under these conditions, what about Amanda? How is it possible that she and Sarek can enjoy the warm, close relationship they obviously share if they do not have regular, "normal" sexual relations? We must remember that when we speak of "normal" sexual relations, we speak not only from a human point of view, but from an extremely narrow, ethnocentric point of view which is largely dictated by the dominant values of our society: white, middle-class, American (not even Western) values. The range of human sexual activity is so broad in every aspect, from sexual preference to position to frequency, that it defies any attempt to define what is "normal" except within a very limited, localized cultural context.

In terms of frequency of intercourse alone, humans exhibit the entire spectrum of possibilities. Many perfectly healthy and well-balanced adults practice complete celibacy for religious or personal reasons. When he was conducting research into the sexual practices of the Serbians in 1967 the anthropologist, Hammel, asked villagers about the monthly frequency of intercourse and was told that questions about the yearly frequency would be more appropriate. Alfred L. Kroeber, in his research among the Yurok Indians of California, found that couples engaged in coitus only during the hottest months of the summer, when they moved from their homes into separate "sweat houses." In his *Sexual Life in Ancient China*, R. H. Van Gulik states that during the Chou Dynasty the Emperor and Queen engaged in sexual intercourse only once a month, on what was presumed to be her most fertile day. By contrast, Edgar Gregerson reports present-day natives of the Marquesas Islands in the South Pacific are said to have intercourse as often as five times a night, on a regular basis. Among these divergent practices, who can say what is "normal" and what is not? If there is such diversity among members of the human species, how can we expect that there will not be even more among races from different planets?

Amanda Grayson is a remarkable woman, not only in her quick intelligence and native grace, but perhaps most significantly in her ability to adapt to an alien culture radically different from her own. Even if Amanda and Sarek engage in intercourse only during *pon farr*, it does not seem impossible, given the wide range of human sexual practice, that they would be able to develop and sustain a deep rapport or that Amanda should find her life with Sarek satisfying.

So, do Vulcans have sex outside of *pon farr*? I lean toward the view that they don't. However, I confess to playing devil's advocate for an unpopular opinion. I don't know, and it doesn't seem to me that there is enough information in the canon universe (the original television episodes and the three movies) to provide absolutely convincing evidence to either side. Compared to humans, Vulcans exercise a remarkable amount of voluntary control over the autonomic nervous system. Perhaps they are also able to consciously trigger the release of hormones which brings about sexual arousal. If they don't engage in sex except during *pon farr*, perhaps it is a cultural or psychological prohibition, rather than physical inability—one which certain Vulcans are able to overcome. I continue to harbor a deep suspicion about our tendency to try to reduce differences, though—our need to make "them" more like "us" and consequently less alien, less threatening. We would do well to take to heart the anguished assertion Spock once made to Kirk. When the Captain tried to reassure Spock by saying he was not a bird or a fish, Spock replied, "Nor am I a man. I am a Vulcan."

[I wish to acknowledge the following books for background material for this article: Andrew Fraser, *Reproductive Behavior in Ungulates* (1968) and Edgar Gregerson, *Sexual Practices: The Story of Human Sexuality* (1983).]

ABOUT THE EDITORS

Although largely unknown to readers not involved in Star Trek fandom before the publication of *The Best of Trek #1*, WALTER IRWIN and G. B. LOVE have been actively editing and publishing magazines for many years. Before they teamed up to create TREK® in 1975, Irwin worked in newspapers, advertising, and free-lance writing, while Love published *The Rocket's Blast—Comiccollector* from 1960 to 1974, as well as hundreds of other magazines, books, and collectables. Both together and separately, they are currently planning several new books and magazines, as well as continuing to publish TREK.

⓪ SIGNET SCIENCE FICTION (0451)

THE UNIVERSE OF TREK...

- ☐ THE BEST OF TREK #2 edited by Walter Irwin & G.B. Love.
  (134664—$2.95)*
- ☐ THE BEST OF TREK #3 edited by Walter Irwin & G.B. Love.
  (130928—$2.95)*
- ☐ THE BEST OF TREK #4 edited by Walter Irwin & G.B. Love.
  (134656—$2.95)*
- ☐ THE BEST OF TREK #5 edited by Walter Irwin & G.B. Love.
  (129474—$2.95)*
- ☐ THE BEST OF TREK #6 edited by Walter Irwin & G.B. Love.
  (124936—$2.25)*
- ☐ THE BEST OF TREK #7 edited by Walter Irwin & G.B. Love.
  (142047—$2.95)*
- ☐ THE BEST OF TREK #8 edited by Walter Irwin & G.B. Love.
  (134885—$2.95)*
- ☐ THE BEST OF TREK #9 edited by Walter Irwin & G.B. Love.
  (138163—$2.95)

*Prices slightly higher in Canada

**Buy them at your local
bookstore or use coupon
on next page for ordering.**

⓪ SIGNET SCIENCE FICTION

WHERE NO MAN HAS GONE BEFORE...

(0451)

- [ ] **GOLDEN WITCHBREED by Mary Gentle.** Earth envoy Lynne Christie has been sent to Orthe to establish contact and determine whether this is a world worth developing. But suddenly Christie finds herself a hunted fugitive on an alien world and her only chance of survival lies in saving Orthe itself from a menace older than time. (136063—$3.95)†

- [ ] **DRIFTGLASS by Samuel R. Delany.** From Ganymede to Gomorrah, a bizarre breed of planet-hopping humans sell their sexless, neutered bodies... so that others may explore the outer limits of sexual perversion. Delany's universe is rooted in the present, projected into the future. It is an existence where anything can happen—and does! (144244—$2.95)*

- [ ] **THE WIND FROM THE SUN by Arthur C. Clarke.** Can anyone journey farther than Arthur C. Clarke, through the universe? Board the Clarke starship to the future and experience his eighteen wonders of the imagination for yourself! "Highly recommended."—*Library Journal*
(114752—$1.95)*

- [ ] **THE BRANCH by Mike Resnick.** On the planet Earth the day after tomorrow, Solomon Moody Moore had built himself an empire by finding even more innovative ways to excite Earth's bored masses. All Jeremiah wanted was everything Moore already had. Jeremiah had a secret weapon that Moore hadn't counted on—a power older than time and just as unstoppable. (127781—$2.50)*

*Prices slightly higher in Canada
†Not available in Canada

Buy them at your local bookstore or use this convenient coupon for ordering.

NEW AMERICAN LIBRARY,
P.O. Box 999, Bergenfield, New Jersey 07621

Please send me the books I have checked above. I am enclosing $_____
(please add $1.00 to this order to cover postage and handling). Send check or money order—no cash or C.O.D.'s. Prices and numbers are subject to change without notice.

Name_____
Address_____
City_____Zip Code_____

Allow 4-6 weeks for delivery.
This offer is subject to withdrawal without notice.

⊘ SIGNET (0451)

Travels in Time and Space

- ☐ **CASTAWAYS IN TIME.** It was a storm to end all storms, but when the clouds finally cleared, Bass Foster and his five unexpected house guests find they are no longer in twentieth-century America. Instead, they are thrust into a bloody English past never written about in any history books.... (140990—$2.95)

- ☐ **CASTAWAYS IN TIME #2: THE SEVEN MAGICAL JEWELS OF IRELAND.** Drawn through a hole in time, twentieth-century American Bass Foster finds himself hailed as a noble warrior and chosen to command King Arthur's army. Now Bass must face the menace of an unknown enemy that seeks, not only overthrow Arthur's kingdom, but to conquer and enslave their whole world.... (133404—$2.95)

- ☐ **CASTAWAYS IN TIME #3 OF QUESTS AND KINGS.** Bass Foster, one of King Arthur's most valued commanders, is given a seemingly impossible mission—to unite the warring kingdoms of Ireland under Arthur's loyal allies. But in Ireland waits both treacherous friends—and foes who could destroy them all.... (145747—$2.95)

- ☐ **GLIDE PATH by Arthur C. Clarke.** From the starfields of *2001* Clarke voyages back to the glide paths of Earth. From JCD headquarters to Moonbase and the stars is the journey of mankind, and Clarke remains the expert in evoking the excitement of discoveries past or those yet undreamed of in the mind of man. (127604—$2.75)

Prices slightly higher in Canada.

Buy them at your local bookstore or use this convenient coupon for ordering.

NEW AMERICAN LIBRARY,
P.O. Box 999, Bergenfield, New Jersey 07621

Please send me the books I have checked above. I am enclosing $_____
(please add $1.00 to this order to cover postage and handling). Send check
or money order—no cash or C.O.D.'s. Prices and numbers are subject to change
without notice.

Name_____

Address_____

City_____State_____Zip Code_____
Allow 4-6 weeks for delivery.
This offer is subject to withdrawal without notice.